The TREE
STUMP

ARABIC LITERATURE & LANGUAGE SERIES

The Arabic Literature and Language series serves to make available Arabic literature and educational material to the general public as well as academic faculty, students, and institutions in collaboration with local Arab writers from the region. The series will focus on publishing Arabic literature translated into English from less commonly translated regions of the Arab world and from genres representing vibrant social issues in Arabic literature. The series will make available poetry books in dual languages (Arabic/English), novels, short stories, and anthologies. It will also publish textbooks for teaching Arabic language, literature, and culture, and scholarly works about the region.

SERIES EDITOR

Nesreen Akhtarkhavari, *DePaul University*

The TREE STUMP

AN ARABIC HISTORICAL NOVEL

Samiha Khrais

Translated by Nesreen Akhtarkhavari

⊖ The paper used in this publication meets the minimum requirements
of ANSI/NISO Z39.48-1992 (R 1997) (Permanence of Paper).

Michigan State University Press
East Lansing, Michigan 48823-5245

The publication of this book was partially funded
by a grant from the Jordanian Ministry of Culture.

Printed and bound in the United States of America.

28 27 26 25 24 23 22 21 20 19   1 2 3 4 5 6 7 8 9 10

LIBRARY OF CONGRESS CATALOGING-IN-PUBLICATION DATA
Names: Kharis, Samiha, author. | Akhtarkhavari, Nesreen, translator.
Title: The tree stump / Samiha Khrais ; translated by Nesreen Akhtarkhavari.
Other titles: Qurmeiyah. English
Description: East Lansing : Michigan State University Press, 2019.
| Series: Arabic literature and language series
Identifiers: LCCN 2019004347| ISBN 9781611862782 (pbk. : alk. paper) | ISBN
9781609175580 (pdf) | ISBN 9781628953268 (epub) | ISBN 9781628963267 (kindle)
Subjects: LCSH: Middle East—History—1914-1923—Fiction. | World War, 1914–1918—
Campaigns—Middle East—Fiction. | Turkey—History—Ottoman Empire, 1288–1918—
Fiction. | Bedouin—Jordan—Fiction. | GSAFD: Historical fiction
Classification: LCC PJ7842.H326 Q3813 2019 | DDC 808.83/81—dc23
LC record available at https://lccn.loc.gov/2019004347

Book design by Charlie Sharp, Sharp Designs, East Lansing, MI
Cover design by Shaun Allshouse, www.shaunallshouse.com

Michigan State University Press is a member of the Green Press Initiative and is
committed to developing and encouraging ecologically responsible publishing
practices. For more information about the Green Press Initiative and the use of
recycled paper in book publishing, please visit *www.greenpressinitiative.org*.

Visit Michigan State University Press at *www.msupress.org*

Introduction

About the Author

Samiha Khrais is an award-winning novelist and one of Jordan's most prolific and highly celebrated writers. She has written twelve novels and three short-story collections. Several of her works have been adapted for television, radio, and theater. A few of her novels have also been translated into foreign languages, such as *The Plate,* translated into German, and *Memoirs of the Flood,* translated into Spanish and German. *The Tree Stump* is Khrais's second novel translated into English; her first one was *Slaves' Peanut,* which won her the Katara Prize for Arabic Literature in 2017. In addition to the Katara Prize, she received the Abu al-Gasim al-Shabi Prize for her novel *Memoirs of the Flood* (2004), the Literary Creativity Prize from the Center of Arab Thought (2008), and the Al-Hussein Medal for Distinguished Creativity from the Jordanian Ministry of Culture (2015). Much of her work focuses on social, political, and religious issues in the past and present-day Arab world.

In addition to her literary work, Khrais is an accomplished journalist. She worked as the managing editor of the culture section of *Al Ra'i,* a prominent Jordanian newspaper, and as the chief editor of *Hatem* magazine, a Jordanian children's publication. Her journalism career includes working for the daily Jordanian newspaper *Addustour* as well as the Abu Dhabi–based newspaper *Al Ittihad.* She has also written for Arab newspapers in Cairo, Beirut, and London and developed scenarios for notable children's publications including *Majid* magazine. Further, she trains and mentors young Jordanian writers through an organization she created for this purpose. She is also a member of the Jordanian Journalists Union, the Jordanian Writers Society, the Arab Writers League, and Pen International Association–Jordan Branch.

Samiha Khrais was born in Amman on August 16, 1956. She grew up in a household that valued education and literature. Her paternal grandfather was a farmer, but despite his limited education, he was keen on ensuring that his many children received the highest education and professional training. Khrais's father studied at the American University of Beirut and held important positions in Jordan, including minister of labor and public affairs, president of the national phosphate industry, and ambassador to Sudan, the Emirates, and Syria. Her mother was the daughter of an aristo-cratic land baron, and her maternal uncles were politicians, professionals, intellectuals, and poets. Khrais's mother who had only a middle-school education (because schools where she lived at the time did not offer education beyond middle school), was an avid reader and a skilled oud[1] player. This helped her socialize within the diplomatic and literary circles of her husband. She was a great hostess who enchanted her audiences with stories and vivid descriptions of people and places where she visited and lived. Like her mother, Khrais was surrounded by books, literature, and politics, and nurtured by an extended family grounded in Jordan, its culture and history, and the real life of its people. Further, Khrais's extensive travel exposed her to a wide range of cultures and lifestyles. She finished her primary education in Qatar and completed her high school and college in Sudan where she received a degree in social science from the American University of Cairo in Sudan.

Her immediate family is relatively small, but her extended family is made of twenty paternal uncles and aunts and three maternal uncles, not counting the cousins who are as diverse in their educations, professions,

---

1. A traditional musical string instrument similar to the lute.

and personalities as Jordan itself. The women in her life ranged from so-phisticated aristocrats like her mother to strong and influential matriarchs like her paternal grandmother, who ran the household, set the rules, and commanded respect from all. These women helped form Khrais's perception of self and others and greatly influenced her writing. About this, she said,

> I write about women I know. They come out of the sleeves of the peasant dress my paternal grandmother wore, the kohl in my other beautiful grandmother's eyes, and from the vivid dreams of my mother and her love for life. All the women that appear in my work are images of women from the heart of Jordan; I selected them from among others because of their strength, commanding presence, influence, and ability to lead and create change. I will never forget my paternal grandmother who ran the tribe with its men and women. She managed the extended family's budget and made the rules and enforced them. This never stopped her from being soft and compassionate with the weak, a tyrant with wrongdoers, and decisive with the confounded. She managed the world around her as if it were made of puppets—its strings held between her fingertips. This exceptional grand-mother appears in all my novels, with her full commanding personality at times and in fragments at others. She is always present—lending her voice to the weak and empowering women to live free with dignity.[2]

Despite addressing serious social issues and advocating for human rights and gender equality in her work, Khrais does not see herself as a feminist writer. She is not engaged in literary gender debates or the effort to define and set the boundaries of feminist work or to answer the question of whether men can effectively address women's issues in their work. She is keenly aware of gender inequality and the injustices women are subjected

---

2. From an unpublished interview with the author by Nesreen Akhtarkhavari on April 15, 2017. Most of the information in the introduction is based on this interview, unless otherwise specified.

to in her Arab world, but she is optimistic that the culture itself carries within it, if correctly invoked, the potential roots of greater morality and traditions capable of addressing its current transgressions against women. She sees literature as a tool to reflect intricate social realities, positioning female protagonists as agents of change capable of improving social conditions.

Khrais observes that many female Arab writers who strongly advocate for women's rights often depict women as weak, defeated, and yielding, their personalities wiped out by love or rendered submissive by the burden of motherhood. These depictions cause her to reflect on the nature of women in her own work, and she is pleased to realize that, despite being in male-dominant societies, her female protagonists are traditional, strong, determined, and active players in life, without compromising their dignity in love. She admits that her female protagonists' authority is derived from the women she knew at the core of the Jordanian cultures and traditions. She does not shy from addressing cultural taboos, injustice, and the oppression of women in her society and the Arab world at large.

Khrais's upbringing, education, and professional experiences enabled her to create female protagonists freed from perceived cultural restrictions and taboos and allowed her to offer us a more realistic view of a wide spectrum of Arab women, including women that made a difference in their own world, carrying the same social burdens as men, if not heavier. Khrais admits that, in her own creative experience in Jordan and the Arab world, she was not subjected to discrimination and was not marginalized by her counterpart male writers. Her work was judged on its merits. The men in her life have been supportive and encouraging. About that, she says,

> There is nothing in my life that makes me perceive men as enemies. They were the loving, kind, and enlightened father and all that this implies, the understanding husband that allowed me the space and freedom I needed to be myself, the friend that provided a relationship in which I was able to practice my humanity, the lover in a mutual relationship where no one

owns the other. This good fortune made me different from many other Jordanian and Arab female writers who had to struggle to gain the space they needed to write and assert themselves.[3]

Khrais believes that she belongs to a generation of writers between the past and the present. In her opinion, the younger generation do not carry in their memories grandmothers like hers. Many are subjected to a society that allows them to be educated and work but does not give them access to any of the privileges their male counterparts enjoy. This leaves behind a bitterness that is reflected in much of their writings. Further, she believes that many of the writers of the generation before hers followed trends and patterns established by men, with very few breaking away from these patterns. Khrais believes that many Arab women writers are occupied with their personal and social struggles and search for identity, and only a few engage in addressing historical and global concerns, but she sees this gradually changing.

Khrais tackles social and global issues early in her writing, depicting social norms, intricate interactions, and social ties that govern people's lives and form the mechanism by which society operates, moving between different contexts and spaces within Jordanian cultures, from countryside to the desert to the city, with ease and fluidity. In all her work, women are strongly present, drawn from the images conjured in her memory of the women she knew, equipped with her own wisdom and global perspectives. Khrais is able to create a well-constructed, elaborate, and meaningful story using older, wiser, and more powerful female protagonists; these characters are able to help other women who are intellectually, socially, or psychologically challenged. These women resemble, to a large degree, Jordanian grandmothers and maternal and paternal great-aunts that the society knew once but is not talking about anymore, with few exceptions. They are definitely different from what

---

3. Ibid.

the West imagined and came to believe about Arab women in general and Bedouin women in particular.

After writing social and ethnographic novels, notably her duology *The Tree of Leopards,* Khrais moved to writing historical novels, extensively researching the Middle East's history and projecting an alternative reading of it from the Arab perspective—not elitist Arabs but common people that make up the core of Arab society. Her work went beyond describing events to actually examining the perspectives that governed the development of these events. *The Tree Stump* was her first novel in that genre. The focal point of the novel was the role of the Jordanian tribes in the Arab Revolt and their encounters with the other players in the conflict, the forces of the Sharif from Mecca, the British, the Ottomans, and other Arab nationals.

After *The Tree Stump,* Khrais wrote *Yahya,* which traces the root causes of fanaticism—the intermingling of politics and religion—in the Levant and beyond. Khrais then ventured into other nations and topics in her novel *The Ebony,* which beautifully tracks issues of race, tribal conflict, war, and human trafficking in Sudan, a country she loves and knows well. Aware of the boundaries and sanctity of place and its gatekeepers, Khrais started her novel by symbolically asking for permission to depict Sudanese history in the novel's dedication from al-Taib Saleh, the father of the Sudanese novel and the author of the masterpiece, *Season of Migration to the North.* Following this, she continued to write in the familiar space, Sudan, addressing an even more historically and socially complicated issue—slavery—in *Slaves' Peanut,* and for this, she won the Katara Prize in 2017 for best novel, one of Arabic literature's most prestigious awards, distinguishing herself among her peers of Arab novelists, both male and female.

About the Novel

The Tree Stump is a historical novel that provides an alternative reading to the narrative provided by the acclaimed autobiographical account of T. E.

Lawrence in the *Seven Pillars of Wisdom,* which he wrote when serving as a British liaison officer to the Arabs during the Arab Revolt against the Ottoman Turks from 1916 to 1918.[4] The novel highlights the role of the Jordanian tribes and Arab forces in freeing much of Transjordan territory and their contributions to the allies' victory in World War I.

Khrais embarked on writing *The Tree Stump* motivated by telling the story of her people from their point of view after being told for decades by the pens of others. It all started one day when she watched the movie *The Lion of the Desert*[5] featuring the story of Omar al-Mukhtar,[6] and a Yemeni colleague told her, "Jordan has its own hero, but no one is writing about him." When she asked, he told her, "'Auda Abu Tayeh." This caused her to learn more about Abu Tayeh. She found plenty of references about the period written by Western writers, but what she read did not reflect what she knew well about the Arab tribes, especially in the region, and their lives, values, and practices.

Reading T. E. Lawrence's accounts of that period and his depiction of 'Auda and the Arab tribes' involvement, further dramatized by the movie that carries Lawrence's name, annoyed her. Khrais agreed with Charles Hill's position that Lawrence's accounts of the period were a "novel traveling under the cover of autobiography, capturing Lawrence's highly personal version of the historical events described in the book."[7] She felt that the accounts by Lawrence reflected his perspective, making him the focal point of the story and its orbit. Khrais wanted to be the voice of her people and offer an alternative narrative because she

---

4. T. E. Lawrence, *Seven Pillars of Wisdom,* unabridged Oxford ed. (1922; repr., P. N. Publishing, 2008).

5. *Lion of the Desert* is a 1981 Libyan historical action film starring Anthony Quinn as Libyan tribal leader Omar al-Mukhtar fighting the Italian Royal Army in the years leading up to World War II.

6. 'Omar al-Mukhtār (1858–1931) is Muḥammad bin Farḥāt al-Manifī, the leader of the native resistance in Cyrenaica—currently Eastern Libya—under the Senussids, against the Italian colonization of Libya.

7. Charles Hill, *Grand Strategies, Literature, Statecraft, and World Order* (New Haven, CT: Yale University Press, 2010), 8.

believed that the events that took place at that time continue to affect the politics and the destiny of the region.

Khrais read everything that she could get her hands on about the Arab Revolt written by both Arab and Western writers, politicians, contemporaries, historians, tribesman, and political analysts, in an attempt to establish a comprehensive narrative of the events that took place, the perceptions that accompanied them, the people involved, and their context. To her dismay, in general, the Arabic sources were scarce and fragmented.

She needed more details to create an authentic narrative. To do so, she traveled extensively throughout the region and used her skills as a social scientist to systematically and meticulously collect the oral history of that period preserved by the tribes that were involved in the fighting. She credits much of the information she gathered to her meetings with the tribal elders in south Jordan. As she expected, the information they provided and their recall of the revolt challenged the narrative that Lawrence and most Western historians provided. The new information was the foundation on which she built her novel.

Retelling the story from the Arabs' perspective was a challenging task. The Jordanian Bedouins' view of Lawrence was complex and reflected to a large degree the uniqueness of the intercultural encounter of the tribesmen, and Arabs in general, with Lawrence and his constant effort to cross boundaries and engage them, not only politically and militarily but also on a personal level. Even though most Arabs believed that Lawrence was a spy, many admired and sympathized with him, and some loved him and went as far as naming their offspring after him. Khrais's data did not challenge many of the events that T. E. Lawrence and other Westerners provided. The differences were in the detail, in the perceptions, and in who owned the cause. Khrais suggests that, while T. E. Lawrence closely worked with the Arabs and helped them at times, he was looking for personal fame, glory, and grandeur. Meanwhile, the Arabs had a cause; they were on a quest for freedom, the preservation of their way of life, and a dream of unity and self-preservation that still glares in the minds and hearts of many Arabs today.

Relying on her talent and skill as a storyteller, Khrais wove a narrative around the facts she meticulously gathered, filling in the blanks with fragments of characters and events she pulled from the memories, mythological tales, and mystical stories that the desert people recalled through the ages. In her novel, Khrais realistically portrays the tribes and other Arabs and shares their customs, beliefs, and traditions, providing her readers with the rules, morality, and convictions that governed the way these people thought and behaved. She was keen to depict accurately the locations where the events took place. To do so, she traveled to all the places she wrote about in the novel, weaving the details she gathered around them, and pulling the strings of the novel together in a tale grounded in the divine relationship the Arabs believe exists between man and his land. This made the novel not only historical but also authentic. She recalls describing a scene of a horse galloping through the desert leaving a storm of dust behind her, but when visiting the area afterwards, she noticed that the desert ground in that location was full of small volcanic rocks that covered the sand. She realized that the rocks created sparks under the hooves of a galloping horse, not dust storms. Thus, Khrais went back and rewrote the scene to reflect more accurately the reality of the terrain.

With skill and imagination, Khrais placed in her novel the information she gathered, projecting the characters that participated in the struggle like Faisal, 'Auda, and others within their historical and cultural context. She further, created a man and a woman, 'Oqab and Mizna, orphans with no ties to a specific tribe or clan, representing the body, heart, and soul of the desert and its people. Then, she dug deep into the imagination of the desert people and borrowed from the core of their myths and tales—a wise man, a falcon, and a horse—and with the skill of an artist, she painted the rest of the details.

The novel is made of nineteen chapters. On the first page, Khrais provides definitions of the novel's title, *The Tree Stump*. Many of her fellow writers who read the draft of the novel before publication objected to the name. They told her that it was a dead and antiquated expression, rarely used in modern times. She was surprised; her experience with the expression was different. She explained,

> This contradicted the fact that I have frequently encountered the word used by people in traditional communities fully aware of its meaning and implications. They used the word or its derivative to describe the roots of the olive tree, old grandmothers, and a genuine man. These uses were common among the people in Jordan. Perhaps it was no longer common among the educated elite, but it was well and alive among the masses. I looked it up in the dictionary, and to my pleasant surprise, I found out that people's use of the word matched the definitions listed in the dictionary. There was even more; it was used to refer to a thoroughbred horse saved for battles, a person who was emotionally mature, and the dough that sticks to the inside of the tandoor and cannot be removed. Suddenly, I realized that all these meanings are exactly what I wanted to say in this novel about its men, women, horses, connections, victories, disappointments, and the historical events tied to our souls' dreams, which continue to chart our future.[8]

In addition to its literary, political, and social dimensions, Khrais had a personal reason to insist on the title of the novel despite her friends and advisors' recommendation to abandon it. She admitted that,

> The title was also associated with something else that had nothing to do with the content—a child's memory of my uncle planting an old olive tree with great roots in our yard. It was the first time I saw a tree stump; I watched my uncle widen the hole in the ground for the enormous strong

---

8. Hassan Fahed Hussein, *Amam al-Gandeel: Hewarat fee Kitabat al-Rewaya* [*In front of the Lantern: Discussions on Writing the Novel*]. The Arab Institute for Research and Publishing, Amman, Jordan. 2008. pgs. 103–104.

root. The event and the meaning of the word stayed dormant in my subconscious mind until it was recalled when I wrote this novel.

Khrais wanted this novel to be the resurrection of the story of her people that would grow from its rightful place where its roots belonged, the retelling of history in its appropriate context, a witness to her people's struggle, pride, and sacrifice. She saw herself as the farmer tending the tree, widening the hole where it will be replanted, as someone in charge of ensuring its survival. Khrais must have felt that by doing so, she would not only reclaim the past but also contribute to writing the future.

Khrais was confident that her readers would find the connection between the title of the novel and its content. She ensures this through her protagonist's voice, choosing a glorious time to present it, at the culmination of Arabs' victories and dreams, right after entering Damascus.

'Oqab affectionately contemplated the nature of his beloved city and concluded that Damascus had the scent of the south, the braids of Mizna, and the eyes of al-Kahilah. He also concluded that the waves of Barada crash just like the waves in the sea of 'Aqaba. He discovered with astonishment that love could not be divided; as if it was a huge tree stump with roots spread through the plateaus—like the springs beneath the desert sand—and above the soil of the orchards, it interlocked, intensified, and spread life over the land. It is the tree of life, the tree of wisdom, which cannot be reached, but can be felt. Its sap travels through our blood and mixes with the fibers of our flesh, nourishing our bones, and holding us close to it with an eternal bond.

The symbols used in the novel reflect common references in Arabic literature in general, and Khrais's work in particular. The "south" refers to southern Jordan, which symbolizes resistance and freedom in Khrais's work. 'Oqab's recollection of the "braids" of his wife Mizna indicates his yearning for her as the object of his love and the connection of man to his people, to the land, to the sky, and to the dreams that stretch throughout his soul. Additionally, the "eyes of al-Kahilah," the loyal horse, represent man's companion and are a sign of freedom, determination, bravery, loyalty, and pride.

Khrais recalls in the novel the transgressions committed by some who participated in the revolt but remains optimistic that these mistakes will not destroy her people whose roots are solidly grounded in the heart of their land and its traditions. Referring to looting by Bedouin volunteers that took place after entering Damascus, she clarifies,

> Because 'Oqab was aware and enchanted with the charm of the tree and a thirst to know more, when serious events took place in front of his eyes, he ignored them, not because he did not understand, but for his certitude that his holy stump was deeply rooted.

She explains that the transgression took place in Damascus because the people who carried them out, "had never touched the oil of the blessed tree stump." Thus, Khrais turns the stump into a vessel of the culture, history, and morality of the desert and its people. The roots of the blessed life-giving tree became the source of wisdom and the eternal connection of humans to their land and its sky. Lawrence's dismissal and trivialization of this bond in his account of 'Auda Abu Tayeh and the Arab tribes' role in the revolt led Khrais to retell the story.

Each of the novel's nineteen chapters start with one or more quotations. These vary in content, source, and format. Some are from religious holy texts including the Old Testament, the New Testament, and the Quran, or they are by philosophers and Sufi thinkers, such as Rumi. Others are social and political: a pledge, excerpts from literary works, or verses of poetry, both old and new. The quotations were carefully selected and appropriately positioned to help frame the section and focus the attention of the reader on the main themes of the chapter.

Khrais starts the first chapter of the novel with the Biblical quotation that inspired the title of Lawrence's book *Seven Pillars of Wisdom:* "Wisdom has built her house; she has hewn out her seven pillars." To that, Khrais adds another verse from Proverbs,

> Happy is the man who finds wisdom,
> And the man who gains understanding; . . .
> She is more precious than rubies,
> And all the things you may desire cannot compare with her . . .
> Her ways are ways of pleasantness,
> And all her paths are peace.
> She is a tree of life . . .

In using these two quotes at the beginning of the novel, Khrais acknowledges that for both her and T. E. Lawrence, "wisdom" is the "tree of life"; the difference she implies is that her protagonists are connected to this tree of wisdom, while Lawrence and his people are not. Thus, she starts the first chapter of her novel by telling the story of her people's resistance, and the wise man, the sage who sanctioned it. An attempt to replace the self-proclaimed English savior, T. E. Lawrence and his narrative, with the narrative of her people that was kept from generation to generation through oral history.

To establish further historical relevance, the events of the first chapter begin with reference to the historical resistance of the southern Jordanian tribes against the Ottoman occupation that preceded the Arab Revolt initiated by the Sharif of Mecca and long before the West became engaged in the fight against the Ottoman Empire. The resistance was begun by Jordanian tribal women refusing to obey the Turkish soldiers' orders to carry water to the Turkish garrisons. This started the fight between the tribesmen and the soldiers and led to the tribal men's arrest. With this, Khrais clearly claims a place for women in the story from the start. Khrais draws her mythology and fiction from concepts and beliefs embedded in the core of tribal culture. A sage appears at the beginning of the first chapter and ends his seclusion with the arrival of a miracle-child hatched from an egg tended by a falcon and protected by a tiercel, carried in a saddle of a thoroughbred horse, shielded by a cloud that brought rain, a sign of hope and a new beginning. With this, Khrais announces the start of her story, a new chapter in history.

Throughout the novel, Khrais traces and reasserts Jordanian tribal ties to their historical roots and intimate connections to the ancient places in their homeland. She mentions Petra, founded by the Nabataeans, a nomadic Arab tribe, several centuries before Christ was born, and throughout the novel, she references places in Jordan of historical significance not only to Muslims but also to Christians, Jews, the Pharaohs, and other ancient traditions. She weaves religious and mythical references to Biblical and Quranic characters such as Job, Moses, John the Baptist, and others into her novel. By doing so, she reminds the readers of the history of the place and illustrates that diversity, tolerance, and inclusion are part of the social structure and values of Arab tribes in Jordan where Bedouins, peasants, slaves, and free men lived in organic harmony since ancient time. The novel is riddled with religious symbolism, ancient and modern; a mix of pre-Islamic and Abrahamic traditions and local desert myths and customs rooted in the psyche of the Arab Jordanian tribes. These myths and traditions of many nations and races who lived in the land, prehistoric, Biblical, Islamic, modern, and otherwise, connect the fictional with the real and expose human vulnerabilities and struggles, intersecting with other traditions and establishing a common ground between the protagonists in Khrais's novel and all that took and still takes place in the region, and beyond.

Khrais wanted her readers to be aware that the dreams and aspirations of her people are like all other oppressed and marginalized people in their quest for justice and freedom. A freedom that is essential to the Bedouins who grew up enjoying the wide-open desert under a wide-open sky. A freedom to live and believe with a vision of the universe—simple, spontaneous, open—constructed from what people saw, heard, and sensed around them. A peaceful co-existence between humans and their surroundings. Khrais wanted her readers to know the Arab tribesmen of southern Jordan as she saw them and dispel the many misconceptions that portray them as nomadic barbarians, just like the native American's were portrayed in many early American narratives and films.

In *The Tree Stump,* like all other works by Samiha Khrais, the women protagonists are smart, strong, loyal, resourceful, and at times, can be seen overshadowing the male protagonists. Khrais explained that her intention in portraying these strong women was not to marginalize men but to highlight women's contribution to their families and communities at times of peace and war. Khrais further explained that she wanted to provide a realistic portrayal of gender roles in the tribes of the region that celebrate strong women, where the strength of the female is perceived as a source of honor and pride for the men of her tribe. This is best illustrated in the novel through 'Alia's bravery and her loyalty to her brother 'Auda and her willingness to place the affairs of the tribe above her personal love for her husband, a true portrayal of "the proud daughter of the desert."

> The drumming of war echoed in her heart, and she heard the men invoke her name in pride. "'Alia's brothers!" What could 'Alia do when the clear sky turns gloomy? A hot tear fell down her face; she quickly wiped it with the goat fur she laid on. 'Abtan embraced her, and the lover in her obliged; she generously made love with a trembling soul. As he calmly fell asleep, she quickly buried her heart in her fears and turned back to being who she truly was, the proud daughter of the desert.

Despite her love for her husband, 'Alia takes the side of her brother and his men in their raid on her husband's tribe. She wakes up early and unties the horses and rides to aid her brother and his men in their raid. To that the men reacted,

> Seeing her, with her long dark hair untied, risking her life to support them, filled them with pride and determination. . . . She called out, so

her brother's men could hear, "Abu 'Inad, my pride, when people see you, they stand."

'Auda replied proudly, "I am 'Alia's brother!"

The Jordanian tribes remain, to this day, loyal to the women whose names were emblazoned in the annals of the desert and its unfailing memory. They continue to be a source of pride and inspiration to the men who belong to these tribes. For example, in a response to an attack supported by ISIS in the south of Jordan, I observed numerous posts on Facebook, where the men from these tribes who helped defeat the attack invoked the names of their tribal heroines including 'Alia, to boast of their own bravery and pride. They actually used the exact expressions that 'Auda and his men used in the novel during their raids and battles.

Khrais never fails to place women in the center of her narrative. They are the mothers, the wives, the sisters, and the lovers that made them into the strong and noble men they were. This is clearly illustrated through the role 'Auda's mother 'Amsah, plays early in his life.

She stepped on her heart when he was a mere child, put on his goatskin coat, tied it around his slim body with a wide belt, and sent him out to bring back the tribe's herds that had been stolen during a raid. She had to do that to save the tribe, prevent a famine, and make him a man. She had no choice. His father, the shaikh, lay sick in his bed, crying over the death of his other sons, with no hope to be there for his remaining young son, 'Auda. She ignored her maternal instincts and told him, "If you come back without the herd, I will kill you with my own hands and cut off the breast that fed you."

That night, 'Auda came back with the herd, his coat soaked with blood. He became a man, a brave man, a shaikh in his own right.

Khrais's women are constantly present in the novel. They are there in peace and in war—mothers, sisters, wives, and lovers. They give birth, raise heroes, dance for rain, inspire men during races, support them in their raids, stand by them when they go to war, nurse them when they come back sick, and always wait for them to return.

The relationship between men and women in the novel, like in the work of many other progressive Jordanian writers, is balanced, equal, and compassionate. Their world is a witness and extension of their passion; it is present when they are alone and longing for each other, or together passionately making love with intention. Khrais is not shy in expressing love, like the people of the desert who are not shy in speaking and writing poetry about it. Describing the relationship of Mizna's parents, she writes,

> She waited for her man every evening, with her feet adorned with henna, in their small cave at the bottom of Petra, washed, her bed woven from the palm fronds ready, waiting for him. She offered her body, pure, eager, and fresh; he approached her with much love, longing, and desire.

Many years later, their daughter Mizna, unknowingly, chose to consummate her love with the same intensity, at the same place, with her husband 'Oqab.

> She basked in his scent like a doe sensing her partner and touched with the tip of her fingers the hair on his chest. His soul soared when he slid over her silky body; . . . Their breath intertwined, two in one. The place tenderly carried the echo of their whispers and witnessed their passionate love, sweet like honey, tender at times, and wild at others, pulsing with desire, burning with longing. They drank its wine and melted in each other. . . . The land burst with colorful flowers and became their soft bedding; they held each other in a long embrace in their private space, beyond all that surrounded them. . . . The early signs of dawn wrapped them in a sweet calmness lulled by a pure tenderness as if they were two leaves floating over a shimmering body of water. They wove their passion into a song and turned the rays of the morn into crowns that adorned their bare

heads. They hummed the sad melodies that they learned in their homeland with joy flooding through their trembling voices, occupying the distance of this stretched land.

In writing about love, Khrais does not break with tradition but complements an established body of literature that celebrates love as bold, compassionate, and tender as the desert itself. The vivid description of love intertwined with a description of place is present in other Jordanian works. Tayseer al-Sboul, for example, ends his short story "The Rooster's Cry" with the following scene.

> She met him with a warm and wide celebration. Her body moved like waves, and a soft music played. They both closed their eyes and allowed the soft warm waters to complete the ritual, a free swing, soaring up high. The blueness of the sea was wild, and the sea had a white foam. It rushed toward them, shielded them, and washed over them with tremendous joy. His cries woke the dawn of the primitive earth. A man was united with a woman, and a woman was united with a man, perfect like two halves of a grain of wheat.[9]

Through drought, hunger, raids, births, love, laughter, and pain, life in the desert and the land around it continues. Within the rich tapestry of desert life, Khrais weaves the story of revolt, allegiances, resistance, bravery, and death that she pulls from the living memory of the desert's people and retells it in their voices. She makes sure that the reader realizes that the land and its inhabitants were there before Lawrence and the British troops came and continued to be there after they left. They are the ones that know it, love it, and depend on it for their livelihood. The land reciprocates. It

---

9. Tayseer al-Sboul, "The Rooster's Cry," in *You as of Today My Homeland: Stories of War, Self, and Love,* trans. Nesreen Akhtarkhavari (East Lansing: Michigan State University Press, 2016), 89.

recognizes the footsteps of it lovers and yearns for them as they yearn for it. Personifying the land, Khrais writes,

> The land spoke, only her lovers could hear her say, "Because I am the beginning and I am the end, because I was here before you, my flesh holds the memory of your footsteps . . . I know your scent and the heavy weight you carry. I kept the names of my lovers—the noble ones and the lowly amongst you; those who touched me with greed and malice, and those who gave their lives for my glory. I know the salty taste of your tears, how often it touched my thirsty lips; I soak it in, but I am never quenched."

With this in mind, Khrais describes the battles, analyzes military strategies, highlights troop movements, and exposes political realities as her people understood them. The leaders emerge, 'Auda, Prince Faisal, and all the other names that represented the Arabs' dream to be free from Turkish occupation, exploitation, and dominance. Khrais utilizes her extensive research and turns the novel into an alternative reading of history with elaborate explanations of not only the war's events but also the perceptions of the men that made these events happen.

Despite the many names that crowd the novel, Khrais manages to develop her main protagonists well. Prince Faisal emerges as the symbol of Arab nobility, refinement, and wise leadership. His effort to rid his people of Ottoman occupation after witnessing Turkish atrocities firsthand in Damascus turns his quest both political and personal. He knows how to collaborate with the British to meet their common goals and maximize support for his cause. Meanwhile, when the British try to sideline him by preventing him from winning more territory, he ignores their orders and moves forward. In spite of the difficulty of managing a diverse army, Faisal succeeds by surrounding himself with shrewd Arab politicians and military advisors that aid him in his effort. He also has the support and advice of his father, the orchestrator of the revolt. Khrais explains,

Faisal's job was not easy, even his father, the shaikh in Mecca, realized the difficulty in managing such diversity in one army. He warned him to keep the two rivals, Shaikh 'Auda and Hamad al-Jazi, apart, advised him to hold back on giving Ja'far high military titles to curb his ambitions, and brought Faisal's attention to the volatile emotions of el-Djezairi. Further, Faisal had to resolve numerous grievances from all parties, like the Syrians complaining that the Iraqis were better paid although Syrians were the first to support the revolt; at every step, there was a bomb waiting to explode. Faisal smoked his way through it all, kept the dream alive, realizing that it could not happen without managing all these conflicts.

'Auda, on the other hand, fights according to desert rules, with little or no compromise. His reputation, wisdom, and bravery are needed to unite the Bedouin volunteers and attract more of them to join the Arab Revolt. Enlisting under the banner of the sharif gives him a new understanding of war in which his leadership and responsibility extend beyond the limits of his tribe and its people. Prince Faisal knows the value of 'Auda and the importance of the Bedouins in winning the war.

'Auda does not concern himself with the rumors and the politics of war; he knows only the law of the desert and lives by it, regardless of what the circumstances are. His response to others' concern about a British conspiracy is simple.

> "What is not known today will be known tomorrow, and we will be there to ask for our rights. Look, Englishman, I do not want to ask you about what you write and say; we read nothing but what the land tells us, to pull out our thorns with our own hands. We will not allow the English to give and take. This is our land, and we know how to take it back."

Khrais does not totally dismiss T. E. Lawrence's role in the revolt and his aid to the Arabs. She rejects him at times and is sympathetic to him as a man and a leader at others. She portrays him as childish, occupied with taking pictures of women at the start of the novel, and rejects this through Mizna's refusal to pose for his pictures with the other women, angrily running away, dismayed. However, as the story develops, Khrais's characters became more tolerant of Lawrence.

> Sometimes he would walk over the thorny plants, a barefooted bum, and at other times, he gave orders with the authority of a Hashemite prince.

She even managed to bring out the personal and humorous side of his experience and the genuine affection of some of the Bedouins toward him.

> When the sun chased away the clouds and appeared majestically in the sky, Lawrence came out to the wilderness topless, wearing only a short trouser, pulling the lice that was holding tight to the hair under his arms, on his head, and on other places of his body.
>
> Al-Omari watched the action and said sympathetically, "I wonder where do the lice come from, it is winter!"
>
> Lawrence answered angrily in broken Arabic, "From the camels, from the goats, and from the Bedouins."
>
> Al-Omari laughed and said, "Tomorrow the war will be over, and you will return to your country and won't have to worry about lice."
>
> One of the Bedouins assigned to guard Lawrence interrupted, "May God not listen to what you say, son of al-Sham. Let the lice be! A man does not get rid of lice until he dies; may God make Lawrence live long and not deprive him of his share of lice."

Even 'Auda, who disliked Lawrence at first, became tolerant of him by the time they entered Damascus. He still questioned his motives, but for a moment, he felt that perhaps he had more in common with him as a person than he had with the politicians that were quarreling and plotting at city hall after the liberation of Damascus.

"I never heard you say it better! Brother, we are for the swords not the spoils. Let the others run after their interests. God's land is vast; nothing brings us happiness like the desert from which we came to the world. You should go back home, but I see you are coming back with us; in your eyes unquenched desire for gain, only God knows your real intention."

In addition to rewriting history, Khrais presents her readers with a genuine human encounter, real and imagined at the same time, with love—the glue that holds it together. Despite the harsh environment and the challenging life of the desert people, gentle love and deep compassion clothes the protagonists and their relationship with each other and their land. It helps them conquer their fear and practice their humanity. 'Alia's love for the sage as a child, makes her venture into the mysterious, dark cave to bring him food when no one else dares to do so. When 'Amsah doesn't think it is seemly to openly express her love for her son 'Auda, she asks his horse to watch over him and return him safely to her. Even 'Auda himself, the fiercest warrior of the land, falls in love with the infant 'Oqab as soon as he lays his eyes on him; he welcomes him to the tribe, declares that he is free, and entrusts him to the care of the sage, the wisest and most trusted man among them.

Keeping with true Arab tradition, especially among Bedouins who regard love and passion as a strength and not a weakness, the protagonists see no harm in expressing this love. When a friend tells 'Oqab that love is weakness and tries to sway him from thinking of his beloved so that he can focus on the battle at hand, he explains,

How mistaken are you, my brother. Men's hearts are their anchors; the fuel of manhood is a great love that makes a man rise above everything trivial and unworthy. How could love hold me back or weaken my resolve when I joined because of it! My lover did not ask for a treasure, or the eggs of a she-camel, or a sparrow's milk, she asked for water. My love is what sustains me, what makes my step steadfast, what makes the blows of my sword strong and swift. Men who do not know love are the ones that retreat. I forgive you for what you say about love; you just don't know.

The female protagonists in *The Tree Stump* are a source of power and inspiration to their men and the keepers of the dreams. Mizna is strong, wise, loving, and a source of wisdom, patience and power; 'Amsah is brave, honorable, and loyal to her people and traditions like Alia, 'Auda's sister, who was and still is the pride of generations of al-Howeitat tribesmen. This love is not only platonic but also erotic. It is never one-sided; it is compatible and reciprocal in all its forms. It is not timid but passionate at times and tender and holy at others; a romantic and noble love that lived in the imagination of Arabs since the beginning of time; a perfect union between two equal souls like "two sides of a grain of wheat"[10]; different from the images of savage Arab men, especially Bedouins, portrayed by most Western media and, in some cases, by Arab writers themselves.

Samiha Khrais's images are powerful and exotic without distracting from the substance. Her language is smooth, melodic, and powerful. The rich vocabulary she uses demonstrates her command of the Arabic language both classic and tribal. Her mastery of her craft is clear through the solid structure of her novel and the harmony of its characters. In addition to clarifying perception and highlighting Arab virtues without masking the many downfalls of traditional culture, the novel is filled with idioms and traditional Bedouin poetry written in the local dialect of the tribes. This makes the text highly authentic but also renders parts of it unintelligible to many Arab readers who are not familiar with the language, imagery, and cultural references embedded in these poems. This translation will make it accessible to many of them as well.

Khrais intended the work to be a reminder for her people of a time when they held onto a dream that united them, made them strong, and allowed them to be equal partners, conquering one of the most brutal

---

10. Ibid.

world powers in history—the Turks. It is also a reminder that they are today part of global events and that their mere existence depends on the role they choose to play. Khrais hopes that her work will reach a wider audience in the West as it did in the East and that the perceptions of her people and their way of life will become more familiar to others and that their side of the story will be more widely accessible; a link to our common struggles for freedom, security, and the pursuit of happiness; a testimony of the nobility and endurance of humankind.

About the Translation

Translating *The Tree Stump* was a joyful and painstaking task. This historical novel was written in Modern Standard Arabic with parts of the dialogue in Jordanian Bedouin tribal dialect (southern dialect in particular). It also includes significant references to local and regional mythologies, sayings, and poetry.

I enjoyed the author's style; mastery of the language; elaborate imagery; melodic tone; and the cultural, historical, and linguistic references that it carried within its pages. The desert, especially the Jordanian desert, is a familiar and intimate landscape for me. Like the author, I have visited most of the places mentioned in the novel, so describing them in English was a joy. Even though I am well versed in classical Arabic and tribal dialect and was able to understand all dialogues written in dialect, a few references to specific regional traditions in some of the poems made them challenging to translate. Through research and, in some cases, consulting tribal elders from the region, I was able to provide accurate translations in context that convey the intended meaning of these poems. The technical military and equestrian language occasionally proved challenging but forced me to learn new terms including words for the sounds horses and camels make when happy, angry, anxious, and annoyed in both Arabic and English.

My philosophy in translating literature is to preserve as much as possible the original structure and imagery of the translated text without hindering the reader's understanding or distorting the content and intention of the author. Most of the text in translation reflects the tone and elaborate images rendered in the original text. In a few cases, such as the falcon hunt, I found it necessary to restructure the text to provide the sequence required to visualize the operation so that a Western reader could clearly understand the steps of the hunt.

The novel's historical content made it necessary for me to revisit the history of the Arab Revolt. Because the novel included references to numerous characters who were historically significant but did not necessarily play a critical role in the story itself, I decided to introduce these figures to Western readers to achieve the effect that Khrais intended by including them in the novel. Thus, I provided brief information about each of them in the footnotes. This distracted me at times, because I found myself consumed with restudying these characters in order to better introduce them to the readers, and in many cases, to refresh and deepen my own understanding of the revolt's history through the new lens the novel provided.

Even though the original novel included forty short notes, which is not typical in Arabic novels, l found it necessary to expand some of the notes and add many more to the translated text that were not included in the original to further explain the historical, religious, and political context of the text. I omitted notes from the original text that were irrelevant to the translation because they referred to the meaning of uncommon Arabic words that the translation accommodated.

Further, as mentioned before, the novel included numerous religious quotes from the Quran and the Bible. These quotations had to be located in translation when available to ensure the authenticity of the text as intended by the author. In many cases, I was tempted to edit the already translated quotes, but to remain true to the author's purpose, I included the original texts as available in the translated scriptures.

Translating *The Tree Stump* was a challenge and pleasure at the same time. Like a historical dig, it unfolded layers of history and life, bringing with it the excitement of discovery and presentation. I am very pleased that we are making this exceptional historical work available to the English reader. Its value is not only in its contribution to the increasing body of Arabic literature in translation but also in providing an alternate understanding of history and a testimony of the struggle still alive in the memory and heart of the nation that cradled them.

The TREE
STUMP

Stump: The part of the plant, especially a tree, that remains attached to the root after the trunk is cut.

This is the definition used in the title of the novel. *Stump* has additional meanings in both Arabic and English. In Arabic, when used as a noun or a verb (*to stump*), it also means:

- to peel
- to teach an infant to take a bite of solid food
- the dough that sticks to the inner part of the clay oven
- an animal stud spared from work and riding and used instead for breeding; also refers to a powerful and genuine man
- tree that grows in seawater

It also means in English,

- the basal portion of a bodily part remaining after the rest is removed
- rudimentary or vestigial bodily part
- one of the pointed rods stuck in the ground to form a cricket wicket
- a place or occasion for public speaking (as for a cause or candidate); also, the circuit followed by a maker of such speeches—used especially in the phrase *on the stump*
- (of a question or problem) be too hard for; baffle
- walk stiffly and noisily

1.

....

Wisdom has built her house. She has hewn out her seven pillars . . .

—Proverbs 9:1

Happy is the man who finds wisdom
And the man who gains understanding; . . .
She is more precious than rubies,
And all the things you may desire cannot compare with her . . .
Her ways are ways of pleasantness,
And all her paths are peace.
She is a tree of life . . .

—Proverbs 3:13–18

Like a column of smoke, he stepped with his splendid figure out of the darkness of the cave into the glaring sunlight; his eyes did not blink. They thought that he must have lost his sight after spending long years in the darkness of the cave; otherwise, how could he withstand all this brightness without batting an eye! Nothing made him leave his seclusion, and now a strong inner calling was bringing him out.

His appearance surprised the crowd at the camp and made them wonder what happened. A man whispered in another's ear, "Nothing brings the sage out of his cave but trouble!"

The sage retreated to the cave in protest when the soldiers detained three of the town's brave men and took them away to Istanbul prison following al-Shobak[1] revolt against the Turkish gendarmerie[2]. At that time, the men climbed up the walls of the castle like Jinn and instructed the women of the tribe to stop providing the soldiers with water.

The story of the bravery of the three young men and the sage's stand with them continue to be retold until this day. The men who were young boys when the event took place, relayed, "He bravely climbed to the peak of the mountain and walked to the rift inspiring the fighters. When the soldiers took them away shackled, he walked with steady steps into the cave, in protest, and stayed there. When he first entered, the cave was flooded with light that no one knew its source. The slimy, gray, ghostly creatures that occupied it fled as if they had been struck by lightning."

The women swore that they heard the creatures' screams while their bodies scrambled escaping through the entrance, leaving behind the place they occupied for ages for the sage who chose to dwell in it. Soon, the voices and the strange figures disappeared, and the sage was no longer roaming the wide desolate place they called home, teaching wisdom to its people, or stretching out his hand to bless the newborns; the same hand that often blessed the brave men, 'Auda, 'Ali, 'Abtan, 'Atash, Sobieh, Salem, 'Eid, Hamad, and al-Arshaf on their way to battle. It had been years since the sage came out and blessed anyone.

With his absence, men were worried that without his benedictions, their newborns would not grow to be strong fighters; the women were afraid that their sons would not become the glorious men they hoped that they would be. The midwives frequented the entrance of the cave seeking the blessings of the sage without daring to enter. They pleaded, "For God's sake, do not send us away empty-handed!"

---

1. This references the tribal revolt in the city of al-Shobak in 1905 against the Turkish forces who required Bedouin women to carry water for the soldiers all the way from the wells to the garrison. This revolt was proceeded by another in 1900 by local Bedouin tribes against Turkish occupation and their cruel treatment.

2. *Gendarmeries,* used by the Turkish army, refers to a military force with jurisdiction in civil law enforcement.

The sage heard them but did not answer their calls. Only the shaikh's sister, 'Alia, was brave enough to enter the cave. She brought him food to keep his body and mind alive. The little girl with the big black eyes carefully walked into the dark cave looking for him, and when she saw his shadow in the dark, she stopped. When his hands touch her braids tenderly, she knew that she found him. She left the food her mother cooked for him next to the worn out mat he sat on and said with unfailing enthusiasm, "'Auda begs you to come back."

The sage continued to smile but did not answer or oblige.

What magic could unravel the secret of this wise man and bring him out of his seclusion to bless the brave men again?

Dayoud said, "This is only in God's hands. It is going to take a miracle."

Did such things ever happen anywhere else on earth?

The sage came out of his cave that morning when the sun was ascending the spacious sky; the women were elated and spread the glad tidings. The children ran out to see the legendary man that their mothers told stories about. He was over a hundred years old. He lived longer than God meant for humans to live and was still walking with the steady and confident steps of a young man!

He traversed the stretched rocky terrain, ascending Mount Meshhaq, his body covered with a long goat-hide coat over a black shepherd thaub,[3] leaning on his staff when the road turned rugged and the descent was too sharp. Behind him walked a small curious, anticipating crowd.

When he reached the stretch of black gravel at the bottom of the hill and approached the endless desert, his figure intertwined with the shadows of the mirage over the scorched land, a desert not like any other. The shaikh motioned to the crowd to stop.

The sage was moving consciously and confidently with steady steps to his intended destination. The crowd stopped. The sage heard the clatter of the sharp volcanic rocks under the footsteps of his old leather sandals;

---

3. *Thaub* is an Arabic word for a man's long garment. The word is also used in some regions for women's traditional embroidered dresses.

he walked, guided by a strange mysterious force. Amid the haze of the boundless glaring desert, he saw a cloud. The clear blue sky stretched serenely over the horizon with a single cloud pushed gently by the wind. The sage placed his hand on his chest feeling the pulse of his eager heart, supporting his trembling feet with the steadiness of his staff planted deep in the desert sand beyond the thin layer of dark flint gravel.

The caravan approached, the camels moving slowly, and the summer cloud cast its shade over the heads of the walking men and beasts—three men, four camels, and a mare. The sage stood motionless, and the caravan drew closer to the man that seemed planted in the middle of the hazy desert; the sound of their movement echoed through the desolate land.

"Whose dwellings are these, brother?"

"God's dwellings."

"Blessed be God."

The strangers covered with the dust of Sinai, fatigued by the long journey, slowed down by the heavy load on the backs of their camels, approached. The sage watched with great curiosity the movement of the cloud chiming with the steps of the riderless blond mare, just a heavy saddle on her back. The joy on the faces of the travelers at the sight of the sage showed their hope that they might have reached their destination after the long journey.

"Is this the dwelling of 'Auda, brother?"

Without saying a word, the sage walked toward the mare, touched her neck tenderly. Dazzled, he looked at the cloud and then into the big eyes of the mare, and said, "Purebred?"

"Yes. From both sides. We know that she is only worthy of a true rider."

It was the practice among some of the traveling merchants to go directly to Bedouin camps to trade and sell their products to avoid sharing their profits with an intermediary. The traders usually traveled alone, unless the journey was long and dangerous, then they would take a companion, a friend to help them deal with the hardship of the desert, and the terror its dwellers spread. Three men came all the way from Egypt and crossed the harsh terrain of Sinai loaded with goods, with their guns secured close to their chests, ready to be used, if needed, to protect them and their merchandise.

Joy flooded their exhausted faces when they came closer and saw the dignified old man, confident that such a man would not be out alone, in the open, unarmed, unless he felt safe. They had traveled enough to know that they were at the border of al-Jafar, the territory of 'Auda Abu Tayeh, the shaikh of al-Howeitat tribe. They were delighted to have reached their destination safe and went on congratulating each other. Meanwhile, the sage continued to stroke the neck of the sweating horse with the palm of his hand. While doing so, his hand touched the saddle. He looked inside, became consumed with emotions, and tears flooded down the creases of his aged face. His heart was pounding; a chill ran down his spine, and when he managed to catch his breath, he asked about the infant lying in the saddle of the purebred horse.

The three men nervously exchanged glances, seemed concerned, then one of them jumped next to the sage and said, "By God, we did not steal or commit any crime; we are not slave traders. Listen to what we have to say. It is up to you to believe us or not. It is the truth. Three of us left Egypt together, a merchant, a guide, and a peddler. We filled our bags with flour, sugar, and salt."

The peddler added, "We thought that, if we can catch falcons, we can sell them for gold."

They explained that, since the supplies were plentiful and the camels were young and strong, they moved through the desert toward al-Jouf leisurely, stopping as they pleased, enjoying the scarce sudden breezes that wafted by randomly. They stopped where they thought they could find falcons. To hunt, they set a net trap between two large rocks and covered its edges with mud after staking their pet crow and a dove as bait under the net, with a long string tied to the crow's foot. Then they hid behind the rocks and waited. They knew that the falcon had entered the trap when they heard the loud caw. They quickly pulled the long string attached to the crow's legs leaving the dove to its fate. As soon as the falcon dug his talons and sharp beak into the harmless dove, they pulled the rope to release the net over the sky-rider and trapped him. They caught three rare falcons and considered this a sign of a good and prosperous journey.

While traveling deep into al-Jouf, they met a caravan from Najd in the Arabian Peninsula. The shaikh of the caravan looked curiously at the four falcons. He examined them with great interest, looked at their curved beaks, and checked the sharp eyes shielded by small leather masks. He made an offer, but the peddler cunningly bargained, "They are not for sale. We are keeping them for Shaikh 'Auda; he will no doubt pay eight gold coins for each."

The Najdi shaikh raised his price, and the peddler continued to bargain realizing that the shaikh was in love with the falcons. Eager to get them, the shaikh quickly declared, "I will seal the deal with a thoroughbred horse."

The shaikh pointed to his men, and they brought out a horse with beautiful white stockings. The peddler took a deep breath and whispered to the merchant that he had no doubt that the horse was thoroughbred and that it was more valuable than all the falcons in the area put together. A deal was made. The Najdi shaikh believed that he tricked the merchants by giving them the horse, which had suddenly started sweating profusely, and he thought it was too sick and weak to make it all the way to Egypt. That is how the horse joined the caravan of a merchant, a guide, a peddler, and four camels.

"And the boy?"

"I am getting there, honored one. It is a story the like of which has never been told; and an event the like of which has never been seen; magical, like a dream at Laylat al-Qadr, the Night of Destiny.[4] Our experienced hunter was the first to spot the falcon roaming the wide sky."

---

4. Muslims believe that this night is when the first verses of the Quran were revealed to Prophet Muhammad and that on the anniversary of this night the blessings and mercy of God are abundant, sins are forgiven, supplications are accepted, and the angels descend to earth and receive their orders.

"My eyes never fail; it is a free wild tiercel, no doubt a great prize."

The merchant explained, "We were happy to see him but were surprised that he was flying so low. The hunter thought that there might be prey close to the surface that he was trying to catch, but the bird was not attacking and swiftly swooping down on his prey like he normally hunts. He was swirling over a designated area, not hunting. When we got closer, we saw a falcon, peculiarly lying on the bare ground."

The guide added, "I was sure that the falcon was no doubt sitting on her eggs!"

They further explained, "We were happy thinking of the price the rare birds and their young could fetch. That evening, the horse was out of control; it sighed and neighed violently, scaring us to death.

"We wondered what was wrong with her, and why she was sweating excessively. The peregrine tiercel flew away when the female bird rolled over her eggs. The men were shocked to see among them a large egg that looked more like an ostrich's egg shining under the bright orange sun.

"'This is not a falcon's egg.'

"'It is something only God knows what it is . . .'

"The falcon lying on the egg moved a little, and the tiercel continued to fly high over the scene."

Then, the merchant explained, "A cloud appeared, and the horse started neighing nonstop. We did not know if she was happy that the cloud appeared and was shading us or frightened from the sound of the eggs breaking as if they were made of iron. The falcon flew away joining her mate and disappeared in the wide blue sky leaving the nest behind, unattended. Miraculously, under the cloud and between the shells, we found this infant. His first cry made the camels stand still, and the horse nickered and came close as if it were a tamed goat. We wondered what a blessing we received, or perhaps what a curse! What should we feed him? What should we give him to drink? Believe it or not, the cloud never left, and it is still here, testifying to the truthfulness of what we say."

The sage held the horse's reins, wrapped the young body with his abaya,[5] pulled it close to his chest, and led them toward the camp.

'Auda cried with affection when he saw the boy and fell in love with the horse. He paid plenty of gold for the horse, and sternly announced in a thundering voice, killing any hope the merchants had to negotiate, "A free man can't be bought, and the boy is not a slave!"

The sage pulled the infant close to his wise heart and 'Auda went on saying, "Leave our land with your gold, the gold is no match to the thoroughbred horse, and leave the son of the falcons, the free can't be bought; this is the gift of the Almighty to our sage."

He then looked at the wise man and said, "This is your son, God's willing!"

Rain fell from the summer cloud that accompanied the newborn at the camp and left a bright rainbow behind. The sage looked at the infant's calm face and said, "Blessed are you, my son 'Oqab."

The sage carried 'Oqab to his cave showered by tender looks from the crowd. Shaikha 'Amsah,[6] 'Auda's mother said, "Watching him melts the soul, not just the heart. Find out who among the most honored women of the tribe is with milk and ask her to go to the sage and feed the newborn."

The mother of every brave man in the tribe went to the sage; even those who were dry started to lactate, and the scent of milk filled the air in the campsite.

The shaikh watched his mother walk to the mare stroking her wet bangs and smiled, "Mother, al-Asilah is a thoroughbred horse. I leave her in your care, honor her like you honor my horse, al-Saqlaweyah." The status of the horse rose because the shaikh left her in the care of his mother who he entrusted with caring for his most beloved horse, al-Saqlaweyah.

'Amsah brought the mare out, walked with her through the crowd of gathered riders and called in excitement, "Glory be to God! Glory be to Him!"

---

5. A cloak or loose over-garment worn over the thaub by men.

6. The Shaikh's immediate female relatives (mother, wife) receive the titles Shaikha, the feminine form of the word "Shaikh."

Al-Saqlaweyah shook her head aggressively, and 'Amsah laughed and said, "Why are you jealous? This will be the bride of al-Abjar, your son."

That night, the brave rider Za'al returned riding al-Abjar, who rode like a lightning bolt despite Za'al's attempts to slow him down, scattering the gravel under his hooves all the way to where his mother was. He calmed down for a moment and then raised his head high again, sighed and groaned. His mother returned his call.

The poet, Abu al-Kabayer said, "Congratulations, Shaikh. Soon you will have al-Asilah's colts."

The shaikh was amused by the recent events that took place in his camp including the sage's coming out of his seclusion, the strange appearance of 'Oqab, the summer cloud that rained, the dry breasts that gave milk, and the body of al-Asilah constantly sweating and shinning like a bright jewel. All of this did not derail his plan to raid Bani Sakhr at Wadi al-Sewagah. The tribe knew his plans and were getting ready with their bravest men to face al-Howeitat, metal meeting metal.

A full moon rose above the dark horizon accompanied by the Pleiades.[7] 'Amsah looked at the sky and sighed, then walked toward the horse stalls, guided by her familiarity with the path, watching with tenderness the tent of her son, the shaikh. The fire was still burning; the night breeze carried to her the voices of the gathered men. Her heart was full of love for her son; she wished to hold him tight, bid him farewell, and ask him to take care of himself.

How could she show her emotions now, when she had held them back all these years, even when he was a child? She recalled how she stepped on her heart when he was a mere child, put on his goatskin coat, tied it around his slim body with a wide belt, and sent him out to bring back the tribe's herds that had been stolen during a raid. She had to do that to save the tribe, prevent a famine, and make him a man. She had no choice. His

---

7. The Pleiades, or Seven Sisters (Messier 45 or M45), are an open star cluster containing middle-aged, hot B-type stars located in the constellation of Taurus. It is among the nearest star clusters to Earth and is the cluster most obvious to the naked eye in the night sky.

father, the shaikh, lay sick in his bed, crying over the death of his other sons, with no hope to be there for his remaining young son, 'Auda. She ignored her maternal instincts and told him, "If you come back without the herd, I will kill you with my own hands and cut off the breast that fed you."

That night, 'Auda came back with the herd, his coat soaked with blood. He became a man, a brave man, a shaikh in his own right, so how could she call on him today after he passed his forties and became a true hero, a feared shaikh, to tell him that she was worried about him? How she longed to embrace him and kiss his shoulders before he left for the raid? She held back the tears flooding her heart and reached inside a saddle hanging from a pole at the entrance of the stables for some of the food she prepared for al-Saqlaweyah. The horse walked closer and affectionately rubbed her head on the woman's head. 'Amsah held out a piece of the dough made of ghee, sugar, and flour, and the horse bent toward the tender hand to pick it up.

'Amsah filled with emotion sang to the horse, "You are in my care, and your rider is in God's care."

At dawn, al-Saqlaweyah plodded behind the camel that 'Auda rode; horses were spared the weight of a saddle and a rider to be strong and ready for battle. 'Auda rode surrounded by his brave men and a caravan of camels and horses and marched toward Wadi al-Sewagah.

Abu al-Kabayer stayed at his tent tweaking his poems, and Dayoud, the teacher, called with a loud voice, "Gather the young ones, we will be telling the tale of Abu Zeid al-Hilali."[8]

The children ran elated. When the adults were around, they rarely had a chance to hear the storyteller that the shaikh brought from Yemen to share the tales of Abu Zeid, 'Antarah, and *One Thousand and One Arabian Nights*. They sat mesmerized, listening.

---

8. *Sirat Abu Zeid al-Hilali,* also known as *Taghribat Bani Hilal,* is an Arabic epic recounting the tribe's journey from Najd to Tunisia and Algeria via Egypt and the conquest of Algeria. It is created based on historical events that took place in the eleventh century. The epic is folkloric and mainly oral. In 2003, it was declared by UNESCO as one of the Masterpieces of the Oral and Intangible Heritage of Humanity.

The sage stood at the entrance of the cave watching the flood of men, lovingly looking at the infant's face glowing under the bright morning sun. "These brave men are the fuel of war, and you, the son of the free, are here with me. I will teach you how to handle the sword; it is a mighty responsibility."

He then added, "'Oqab, you are the essence of wisdom hidden in the book, the dawn of tomorrow; your body is the living water of the free tiercel who soared high and never came back. You are the return of the echo of all yearning calls traversing over the vast desert, gushing through the paths of the streams and the rivers and the shedding of tears. 'Oqab, you are the focal point of insight. Watch the edge of the horizon and see how the sky becomes the mirror of earth, and how it chooses from among the living the ones that turn into stars that burn and fall, killing all evil. Son, watch the edge of the sky and learn that truth is a treasure that can't be sought. It shines inside you, suddenly born, like a piercing comet, like a flooding water that you can see in the echo of the wind and the dripping of the raindrops. When the sky opens its gates, do not stand still contemplating; turn inward to your inner self at this moment of exciting discovery, and you will find that it is full and overflowing. Then, you will see the face of truth, and you will meet inside your tender self with your soul, and when your soul yearns for knowledge, you will know. You will be born anew, as you were born in eternity. Into you, wisdom will manifest itself, and the conscious horse becomes your true ride. Wherever you place your hand, the land will turn green, and your palms will hold the rain of time that has stayed dormant for long. You will shake it and it will rise."

He continued, "Now, they are going to war, my son. O long night disperse.[9] We cry with our own eyes and fight with our own swords.[10] Do not let your sword fall and let your rusty heart glow like a sharp blade. Let

---

9. From a poem by Abu al-Tayyib al-Mutanabbi (915–965 CE), one of the greatest and most influential Arab poets. The content of the line referenced is "O long night disperse and be replaced by a bright morn, one like which there is none."

10. Ibid.

your bright light shine wherever you go and carry your sword with honor. Raise it away from the spotlight. Do not become too proud and arrogant; you were entrusted with this gift, no one else. The wind chose you and the paths opened for you. Blessed are your watchful eyes, and blessed are you, 'Oqab, the tiercel of the sky. You are the free tiercel's son, from his bones and heart. Lift your gaze high, look within you, examine what you see with your mind and your heart. Rise beyond time to reach the wisdom asleep within its cave. Push forward, you will find it; it is there, it is there."

The sage placed his hand on his heart, and mysteriously, with a similar gesture, the infant raised his hand and placed it on his chest above his heart and listened; his eyes opened wide when he heard the fast pulse of his throbbing heart.

2.

....

With you in my life, between the tender touch and
the fleeting storm, I became a perfect man.

—Samih al-Gassem

Ramla said to her husband, "I relieve you from your bond to me.
Take a second wife; I will bear that to see you have children."
Al-Hareth pulled his abaya over her body, pulled her close to
him, and said, "My honored wife, we cannot escape fate. This is our destiny.
I am happy with what was prescribed for me in this life."

It had been five years since they married, and Ramla's womb was
still barren, with no sign of a boy or a girl. She hoped for a child after
each time they made love. She waited for her man every evening,
with her feet adorned with henna,[1] in their small cave at the bottom of
Petra,[2] washed, her bed of woven palm fronds ready, waiting for him. She
offered her body, pure, eager, and fresh; he approached her with much
love, longing, and desire. Years passed without a sign of a child. She had

---

1. A dye prepared from a plant used since antiquity to dye skin, hair, and fingernails as well as
fabrics including silk, wool, and leather. It is still used today.

2. A historical and archaeological city in southern Jordan, half-built and half-carved into rock,
inhabited since prehistoric time and established possibly as early as the 4th century BC as the
capital city of the Nabataean Kingdom. The Nabataeans were nomadic Arabs who built Petra
as a major regional trading hub for its proximity to trading routes. It was designated UNESCO
World Heritage Site in 1985.

often told him, "Marry another one." He would always wrap her in his abaya and ease her mind.

This time he said, "Let's go to Ma'an. Perhaps God will help us with the blessings of Um-Jeadah?[3]

The couple tied up their scarce beddings and meager supplies and headed to Ma'an. On their way, Ramla bought kohl and henna, and al-Hareth bought some ghee, and they headed to the shrine seeking its patron's blessings.

The shadow of the tall trees towered over the dunes. Al-Hareth slowed down, a scream echoed inside his heart, "O Provider. Thou art the Generous and we are Thy servants."

Ramla made her way through the narrow paths; her heart trembled at the sight of the big silent, round rocks where the saint was buried. Her feet wobbled as she leaned next to it in supplication, weak and afraid. She put down her humble gifts and mumbled few words, unable to speak. She circumambulated seven times around the holy shrine, her tears flowing and her lips uttering disjointed letters that she was unable to form into intelligible words. Still, she was confident that God knew what was in her heart and cared not for how she said it. She had faith that Um-Jeadah in her mighty grave understood what she came asking for. When she could walk no more, she threw herself over the holy rock and wept. Upon hearing her own cry, a mysterious sense of calmness filled her heart with strength and determination. She was certain that, if what she wished for did not happen, it would never happen; if she did not hold tight to the rock with all her mind and madness and force it to make her dream come true, it was the end for her. She rubbed her back and her belly desperately on the smooth surface of the rock and cried profusely; in her hands, she held the secret. She rattled it; it responded.

In their way back from their sacred journey, al-Hareth and his wife

---

3. A shrine of a woman saint still frequented by people seeking blessing and asking for wishes to be granted.

silently watched the bright moon on the horizon, led their camel in front of them, and quietly rode their mules to Ma'an to rest.

One full moon passed. On their way home, Ramla rode close to al-Hareth's mule, bent a little, and whispered, "I had no period since our trip, my love."

Al-Hareth jumped off his ride nervously, flattened the sand with his hand, spread his abaya over it, raised his head high, and cried, "O God, I pray to Thee, accept my supplication."

He prostrated himself praying. Ramla heard his elated sigh and joined him in his cry of joy.

He then said to her, "May He give us a brave man that all Arabs praise his name."

"What if He gives us a she?"

"A mare, protected. We would be grateful for His generosity; she will be the pride of men."

To protect the seed in the fragile womb from the treacherous journey back, Al-Hareth led the mule and the she-camel of his wife to al-Jafar instead of the long journey back to Petra.

They pitched their tent close to Shaikh 'Auda and his mother's tent. After they rested for few days and Ramla was sure that she was pregnant, al-Hareth told her that when he prayed on the desert sand, he asked God for His Mercy, and made a promise to visit the Holy Kaaba in gratitude before the child sees the light.

"If time came and I did not fulfil my promise, I worry about what might befall us."

Ramla who knew the hardship and the danger of such a long journey to Hijaz, passionately held tight to the garment of her husband in desperation. She then let go thinking of the wrath that might befall them if he did not fulfil his promise! Thoughts and feelings flooded her mind and heart. She convinced herself that the safety of her pregnancy depended on al-Hareth's safe arrival to the blessed land. She held back her tears, thought of begging him to take care of himself, and of giving him a prayer to say there on her behalf when he arrived, but decided not to and was content with a tender quietness and the soft loving look that comforted her worried husband and eased his fears.

'Amsah stood next to her, consoling her, and pledged to watch over her and give her the support and protection of the tribe, making him feel a little better leaving her alone with a child in her womb.

Ramla went on counting the days and nights, watching the fullness of the moon come and go, one, two, three, four, five, six times . . and no sign of her beloved. She constantly prayed to God to protect him and return him safe to her. By the start of the ninth month, her heart grew heavy with longing and anticipation; she stopped counting and left her affairs in God's hand convincing herself that she would be happy with whatever he ordained.

The intense heat split the thirsty sandy desert ground and inflamed the volcanic rocks that spread over its terrain, making them impossible to step on; the herds of goats and camels stood silently waiting for heaven's mercy.

Ramla felt the intensity of the contractions. She bit on a piece of cloth and moaned in pain; then thought of al-Hareth's absence and wept.

'Amsah whispered, "O God of the dawning day, make her wish come true." She then looked at Ramla tenderly and added, "Have faith, my daughter, the absent has his excuse."

Her pain intensified, she tore the piece of cloth with her teeth and felt the torment of Hell. A young slave girl was sent to call on the midwife to help with the difficult birth.

The girls congregating outside the tent whispered, "Ramla is not going to give birth until her lover returns."

'Alia added, "Her child is held back like the water of the rain."

Dayoud said, "The raining season passed; no rain in the sky, not even one drop."

Despite this, the sage said, "I sense a scent of rain in the sky."

The girls gathered in the middle of the camp, surrounded by tents; gazed at the barren thirsty desert and the faces of the tired men; raised eyes lined with kohl toward the blue, wide sky with no sign of a cloud; and watched the men walk to the tent of the sage. Then, they saw the sage pointing his staff straight to the sky, guiding the men in a serried line, prostrating in prayer, asking for rain, and the safe deliverance of the pregnant woman and her child. They saw the midwife pull her skinny and thirsty donkey close to the tent where Ramla was giving birth. She was quiet at that point; her uterus had closed, and her body went into shock.

'Amsah turned her face away to avoid watching the midwife carry out her procedure, then the midwife yelled anxiously, "She is close like a virgin who never been penetrated."

The midwife ground a wild bitter herb called the "palm of Maryam," placed it in the boiling water over the fire, filled a small clay pitcher, and forced Ramla to drink a little. She then took some of the liquid in her hand and rubbed the entrance of the womb, placed her hand inside it, feeling it, and tried to stretch it to make a path for the baby to come out. Ramla's pain increased; she could bare it no more. In her heart, she said her prayer and was ready to meet her maker.

The midwife screamed, "By God, I can't find it. Where is it?"

Ramla heard the midwife's disappointed cry, pulled herself together and said, "It is in me. I feel it with my heart and soul. I felt it since the day al-Hareth placed it there; I feel it in me."

'Amsah hated to see the midwife search through the womb but asked her to look again, perhaps she could find something, "Do it again and I promise you a reward if you bring good news."

The rough, strong hand went back in searching for the child.

The singing of the girls became louder. They continued to dance moving in a circular motion with their hair down, decorated with small pieces of desert ferns, tracing the motion of the sun, from east to west.

O mother of plentiful rain, water our sleeping harvest.
O mother of plentiful rain, by God, rain on our crops.
O mother of plentiful rain, O savior, fill our dried streams.

Fill them with gushing waters.

Quench the thirst of our meadows and dreams.

'Alia noticed a limping fawn near the camp, left the circle and walked close to where the playful fawn stood. She stroked her back. The fawn did not run away, prevented by an injured leg.

A doe suddenly appeared, and the young girl backed off and said, "A deer! Evil will disappear!"

The two beautiful creatures, 'Alia, Shaikh 'Auda's sister, and the doe with her beautiful big eyes, looked at each other for a moment. The deer turned away nervously, then stopped, turned back and circled around her fawn. 'Alia understood and returned to the crowd. She watched the doe rub her large body on her little fawn, smiled, and joined the girls in their singing.

The men left the sage's cave and went back to camp. He came out and stood with his staff stretched in front of him holding 'Oqab's hand. 'Oqab let go of the sage's hand and followed the men with steady and confident steps. 'Auda though about turning him back but did not when he noticed that the sage himself did not stop him.

The midwife stood up and said anxiously, "No hope. I leave her in God's hands."

'Amsah covered her face with her hands and rubbed her tearful eyes, "Blessed be God."

'Oqab passed the young girls singing, asking for rain and went into the birthing tent. 'Amsah and the midwife were shocked to see him walk into the tent but were terrified to do anything about it. Their lack of action to prevent the little four-year-old boy from entering the tent perplexed them. The boy walked to Ramla, looked in her eyes. She barely saw him; her soul was struggling, trying to leave her body. He then kneeled next to her big stiff belly, touched it, and passed his hand over it. The contractions became strong and frequent. The boy stopped, looked at the women, smiled, and left the tent as calmly as he entered it. Ramla opened her eyes and let out her last scream, and the womb dropped its load. The two women heard the cry of life coming from the newborn, saw a flash of lightning, heard thunder split the heart of the sky, and the rain dropped in torrents.

The sky was generous that day, the place was filled with a sweet scent like musk, and the girls kept singing and dancing in the rain with great zeal and joy.

The sage prayed in supplication at the entrance of his cave, and 'Oqab entered with slow, confident steps. 'Alia noticed the doe pulling her injured fawn to safety; meanwhile, the earth was taking in the generous flood of water pouring down from the sky, filling the cracks and creases of the thirsty desert. The herds of goats, sheep, camels, and horses happily jumped around, indiscriminately making all kinds of noises.

'Amsah held the newborn in her arms and muttered, "What a perfect child! Glory be to the Creator!"

The midwife pulled the opening of the tent and said in a loud joyful voice, "Watch people, this is Mizna, al-Hareth's daughter. She brought you the rain."

A smile appeared on Ramla's exhausted face; between life and death, she whispered peacefully, "Mizna!"

Just before her soul left her body, she looked at 'Amsah begging, "I leave you Mizna . . . please protect her and show her kindness."

'Amsah closed her eyes and wept. The news that the stranger child, 'Oqab, has a blessed hand spread, and the women swore that the newborn was the one who brought the rain and caused mushrooms to grow plentifully in their camp. The orphaned newborn with her beautiful scent like a wild tulip, refused to drink the milk that many of the breastfeeding women of the tribe offered her with joy. She rejected all the nipples that they generously placed in her rosy mouth, closed it tightly, turned her head away, and refused to drink. They were worried that this stubborn child would vanish like her mother and absent father. 'Alia knew that she would live; she wet her fingers with the doe's milk and placed it in the little infant's mouth. The little girl sucked it with hunger and appetite, and from that time on, Mizna was feed from the doe's milk. 'Amsah wanted to tie the doe to the stakes of her tent to keep her around but quickly realized that the doe was not going anywhere. She always came back when it was time for Mizna to feed.

'Alia was crazy about the newborn girl, and whenever she came near her, she smelled the scent of musk, was filled with joy, and said, "She has a sweet scent, mother! By God, she has a sweet scent!"

3.

....

A horse is "a blazing rock that passes through the land like a flame of fire that mesmerizes those who watch. If called to battle, she runs with her rider on her back catching the falling stars. She has narrow hips, pretty legs, and a broad nose, beautiful inside and out. She has a royal lineage, and her bangs are like a bright crescent fashioned by the Almighty God. A horse raised by the proud Arabs as if she were the pole of a moving orbit, her rider is safe from the sword strokes of enemies or stubborn jealous rivals. Among all Arab horses, there was no horse better or faster than she was; no one saw any like her. The wind was formed by her gallops, the thunder by her neighs, the morning stemmed from the shimmering of her bangs, and darkness from the glow of her bright dark eyes. Her presence caused the sun to rise and stirred the wind of destiny. She was void of any imperfections and was beloved by all hearts."

—from *The Biography of the Princess with Intention*[1]

Dayoud passionately touched the horse lying on the ground. She felt his tenderness, closed her eyes, and surrendered. Then, she groaned in pain, trembled, and snorted as if she was catching her breath. Dayoud sat next to her and stroked her back. His hand was wet with her sweat; he wiped it on his thaub and thought about calling on

1. The biography of an Arab princess warrior from Hijaz, who lived and fought during the Umayyad and Abbasid Dynasties, and is said to have conquered the Byzantines in Constantinople.

someone to help with the delivery. Suddenly, the horse became quiet, so he decided to wait. She then turned on her side trying to stand, stumbled, and then stood straight. He heard her abdomen make a loud noise, and immediately after that, she gave birth. Dayoud swore that a lightning strike hit the sky when the foal was born on the eve of that hot summer night. The foal slipped out of al-Asilah covered with her mother's blood, standing. Her legs did not crumble under her and her body did not bend. She stood straight like a sword pulled out of its sheath, bright like its sharp golden edge, and looked at Dayoud with big eyes lined with thick lashes. He was enchanted by her beauty. She turned her head around, shook the fresh blood off her young body, and looked back at him.

Dayoud shivered with joy when he saw the white star stamped on her forehead, and cried, "Praise be to God, the Creator!"

Al-Asilah reached out to her foal with tenderness extending her udder for her to drink. The foal raised her head and latched to the nipple and gracefully began to nurse.

'Amsah was the first to see the foal after Dayoud. She looked at it through the light of a burning stick she carried from the hearth and fell in love with it. Dazzled by the magic in the beautiful lined eyes, she said, "The colt of al-Asilah and al-Abjar, we will call her al-Kahilah,[2] the one with the beautiful lined eyes."

The shaikh warned the children not to bother the newborn foal. "I better not hear that any of you have touched al-Asilah or al-Kahilah. You will have to answer to me."

The shaikh ordered the slaughter of many sheep in celebration of the new birth and asked his men to mark the belly, the feet, and the foreheads of al-Asilah and her newborn with the blood from the sacrificed lambs. The people of the tribe had plenty to eat that day in honor of the blessed birth.

The children heeded the warning and stayed away. They watched the

---

2. A description of a female with beautiful lined eyes, either naturally or with black kohl. The expression is also used to describes animals like horses and deer.

foal with her strong arched back like a crescent and wished they could ride her but did not dare come close. She circled around her mother with pride and arrogance, watched the children play, and snorted angrily if any of the adults tried to touch or saddle her.

The shaikh said, "Leave her alone; she is still young. She will be tamed when time comes."

Only 'Oqab was allowed to handle the horse. He walked around her like a gentle breeze and looked at her with eyes full of passion and adoration.

The keeper called on him, "Come close."

'Oqab went closer, stretched out his trembling hand, and touched her back. She jumped back surprised and let out a short neigh, then moved away with arrogant steps, watching him. The boy's eyes teared with excitement.

Al-Kahilah started wandering farther and farther looking for pasture.

The shaikh said, "She had enough time to grow. Tie her up; she is a prize that would no doubt be sought after by others."

Four man surrounded her; she circled around, then she ran with eyes beaming with anger into the inner circle they formed, sending a storm of dust into the air. They went on trying, and when they held her feet and put the chains, the harness, and the saddle on her, she cried like a wounded woman. Her mother groaned and put her head down. 'Oqab cried when he saw her struggle with fear in her bright eyes. The crowd watched her fight, jump up and down, kick her feet violently, then drop on her right side and roll through the sand trying to get rid of her shackles.

Dayoud screamed, "Fear God; let her go. She is going to kill herself!"

The shaikh yelled, "Let her go before she cracks her neck or breaks her legs."

The chains were removed from her legs. She rose like a flame, straightened her strong body, and ran like a straight arrow. The rest of the chained horses neighed, the camels grunted, the women stayed inside their tents, and the children watched from behind the tent poles.

Through the blinding sandstorm her angry hooves left behind, the men yelled, "If this horse is gone, she can never be replaced. Catch her!"

The shaikh was caught by surprise, and called promising, "Catch and tame her, and she is yours."

Through the thick rising dust caused by the riders' rushing after the rogue horse, 'Oqab caught glimpses of her tail at times and her proud face at others. His heart panted, and his soul longed to touch her. He wanted to scream, "Leave her alone; she is not yours," but said nothing.

For hours, al-Kahilah ran back and forth while the riders pursued her, resting and taking turns, with no rest for her.

Dayoud clapped his hands with despair and cried, "They will kill her before this cursed night is over!"

'Oqab walked calmly through the thick dust and with steady steps stood in the middle of the commotion ignoring the horse running toward him.

A woman cried, pointing to the boy, "He is crazy, he's crazy . . ."

In the wide-open space, the boy was barely seen through the thick rising dust. The men lined up behind al-Kahilah, so she ran forward like an arrow, a storm that can't be stopped.

In a blink of an eye, a man yelled, "Move, boy, before she crushes you."

The boy did not move, and the horse was startled to see his slim body in her path. She reared; he was straight in front of her, totally at her mercy. She dug her hind hooves into the hot slippery sand leaving a trail behind her; she groaned and danced in the air, moving her body in all directions, then she slowly calmed down and started coming down with all eyes staring at her with astonishment. She bent her left side a little and landed calmly next to the boy. He stretched his palm and touched with tenderness the hair on her sweaty body. She shifted, then relaxed and reached out to him with her head. The people held their breath, watched him stretch out his arms and hold her; she rested her neck on his shoulder. He stroked her forelock. She closed her eyes, so did he; she sighed tenderly, and so did he.

The shaikh kept his promise, "Who tames al-Kahilah keeps her."

Dayoud commented, "Al-Kahilah is his sister. The boy drank her mother's milk."

Mizna was captivated by the events that took place and smiled in admiration. Her fingers nervously played with her thick braid untying the black hair that ran over her back, shoulders, and her young breasts. When 'Alia pulled her into the tent, she looked back and gave 'Oqab a dreamy look that unveiled the flood of feelings bottled inside her.

'Auda proclaimed, "Boy, the horse knows its master, and the mount chooses its rider."

....

Al-Kahilah was the point of adoration and envy of all the tribe's young riders. On 'Alia's wedding day, the horse and its rider were elevated, as if by destiny. The men of the tribe strutted into the wide-open space where the wedding was taking place, aware of the beautiful black eyes of the young women watching in admiration the sculpted bodies on horseback.

When the sturdy camel stood up balancing on its back the heavy colorful hawdaj[3] of the bride, the men's excitement escalated. They circled the hawdaj, raced around the camel and its precious load, called to each other with pride, their long hair and loose abayas floating in the wind, eager to catch the attention of one of the pretty girls in the wedding party. The girls sang, and the men became more animated. As the camel with the bride approached, 'Abtan's horse appeared. His eyes were full of yearning for his bride, a love he did not bother to hide. Today, his lover 'Alia, the pride of the Tayeh tribe would be his. His brothers, the sons of al-Jazi drew closer, demonstrating their skills, as if their actions were a challenge to al-Tayeh men to match their performance.

The camp turned into a stage and a beautiful carnival when 'Inad, the son of Shaikh 'Auda called, "Bring al-Saqlaweyah."

Everyone realized that he was initiating the crowd's favorite game, the

---

3. A bed carried on the back of a camel, usually with a cover over it, used for carrying brides or women of affluence during travel.

rider and the flag. 'Auda laughed cheerfully and announced the start of the game. He then carried the flag in his right hand, mounted al-Saqlaweyah, tapped her slightly, and she understood. She bolted past the line of riders and climbed the hill where the cave of the sage looked like an old hump, then stopped. 'Auda bent down, planted the flag on top of the hill, and rode down to where the riders gathered.

They heard his voice call, "Who will bring the flag in today?"

The men moved on their horsebacks like the waves of the sea; the horses were excited, and the camels were tied behind the tents. The riders lined up, noble and proud, and the girls came out with their hair spread on their backs, dancing, and stealing the men's hearts. 'Alia looked from behind the crack in her hawdaj's silk curtain. Mizna who was with her, clamored to look out, could not wait, slid her slim body down the camel's side to the ground, flying like a colored butterfly. She caught 'Oqab's attention, jumping out of the hawdaj with her hair flying in the wind. His heart fluttered, and suddenly he could hear it pound through his chest. Mizna stood on the soft sand like a wild gazelle. Their eyes met and sparkled, and 'Oqab holding the reins of al-Kahilah suddenly became very interested in the game. As light as the wind, he mounted the horse, which no one had ridden before. Al-Kahilah was startled a little but felt the boy's excitement and became excited too. He led her to where the riders lined up, and the men stared at the wild, stubborn horse standing next to al-Asilah with surprise. 'Inad, the rider of the mother, laughed and said, "Is this the day of al-Asilah or her daughter, 'Oqab!"

'Oqab said in his heart, today is your day Mizna, the most beautiful of all women, the wild desert flower. The riders looked at the boy whose eyes were fixed where Mizna stood and realized what made him ride, smiled, and remembered the torment of their first love.

'Auda announced the start of the race. The horses galloped and the volcanic gravel covering the desert ground scattered under their hooves leaving a trail of sand behind. They approached, the bright prize flag calling to them, waiting for its bearer. The girls could no longer identify the horses or the riders.

'Inad realized al-Asilah was passing the crowd, and when she reached the dune, he turned and bent to pick up the flag, but a small, strong, steady hand snatched it out of its place. Al-Kahilah turned around, to the astonishment of the rest of the men, with the flag in her rider's hand.

The boy dismounted the horse, patted her neck, and quickly planted the flag in front of the mat where the shaikh was sitting. The pole parted the gravel, pierced the heart of the land, and stood straight and firm in its place. The flag swayed with the breeze, and the shaikh commented, "A true rider 'Oqab."

'Inad looked at the flag that the boy snatched right under his nose, recalled the boy's infatuated glance and said, "You are a true lover, 'Oqab!"

4.

....

Heed my advice, O friend, I say.

I warn you from evil deeds and say,

Your friend that is loyal and near today,

when the tables turn on you,

don't blame him for what comes your way.

The arrow of death reaches you even if you hide,

but the wrong arrow never touches you

if you watch your way.

—from traditional desert poetry

The drought spread throughout the region.

The ground cracked, and the herd starved and died. The shaikh's eyes were fixed on the sky, watching the sun whip the barren desert with its flaming rays. As if the land forgot that we are her children, it drowned in her agony, and tossed us out!

The shaikh said, "Load your belongings and get ready to move."

Those who were able loaded some of their household goods on their camels' backs. The men silently pleaded with 'Auda through their desperate glances, "Let us raid, Shaikh!"

Bedouins, accustomed to the desert's harshness, settled and moved, like migrating birds. They knew well the fear they spread when they raided the villages to gather their spoils from the farmers who harvested and stored their crops and feared nothing but the Bedouins' raids and the Turks' taxes.

A man lamented, "The drought consumed the herds and dried up the land. What's the harm in planting crops like the sons of al-Jazi?"

The others scolded him, mocking his sentiments.

'Inad said laughing, "What's wrong with you? They plant, and we raid."

That evening, 'Auda stared at the four coffee pots balanced on the open fire inside his tent, inhaled the freshly roasted coffee's penetrating aroma, percolating and mixing with the firewood and sage, and recalled his many raids that ranged all the way through the Levant and reached to Shatt al-Arab.[1] He then looked at his men, and thought: if the drought left somewhere green in this wide desert, he would have not sought to raid his cousins, but the generosity of heaven did not reach the Bedouins and favored the peasants this year. He thought about the Jazi clan who turned to farming and thus were spared the famine. Their land is not too far! Then, he thought about his sister, 'Alia, the bride of the tribe whose name they proudly invoke in peace and war. Her marriage to 'Abtan, the son of al-Jazi, signaled the end of the cousins' feud. Her presence among them now was a dagger in his heart; he hated to ruin her life by raiding her husband's land.

'Auda reasoned with himself, 'Alia's heart will break, but 'Alia accepts the tribal laws and customs; they drank it with their mother's milk. He made up his mind, "We will raid at dawn."

He then called his nephew Za'al bin Mutlaq to 'Amsah's tent. She silently watched, worries tearing her heart apart. 'Auda asked him to go and secretly bring 'Alia back this evening before the raid.

When he reached the Jazi tribe, 'Alia was happy to see him, so was her husband 'Abtan who warmly embraced him. Za'al laughed nervously trying to conceal his mission; his curious eyes looked around noticing that they were in much better condition than the devastation that overwhelmed his

---

1. A river formed by the confluence of the Euphrates and the Tigris in southern Iraq.

tribe. This helped him justify the raid to himself, and he planned to use it when explaining 'Auda's decision to 'Alia. That night, the tribe celebrated with a dance. He joined for a while, then took advantage of the commotion and went to 'Alia's tent. She knew that he came to her with news.

"What is up?"

"Please understand 'Alia, the tribe is devastated, the shaikh plans to raid your husband's tribe before dawn. Please get ready now; he wants you to bring your child and return home before the raid."

The shaikh's sister looked down with a broken heart, then raised her head up, held back the tears in her big eyes, and said, "I will not go back with you; I will return with 'Auda when he wins the raid. I will wait here until the morning."

Za'al hesitated and nervously looked around not knowing what to do. She stood up with confidence, opened the entrance of her tent, signaling him to leave.

"Go with God's protection."

Za'al had no choice, and when he stood up ready to leave, Mizna tugged on the hem of his abaya. He laughed trying to take his mind off his worries and said, "I know what you want to know. The men will arrive at dawn. The boy 'Oqab will stay behind. He went back to the sage who is filling his head with words that are stopping him from becoming a real man."

She looked at him reproachingly. He tugged on her braid tenderly and said apologetically, "Don't worry. Believe me, he's a real man even if he does not join the raids."

The moon disappeared; and 'Alia laid down consumed with torment and concern. 'Abtan came to her, touched her loose hair, and caressed her tenderly. She sensed his desire but pretended to be asleep. The drumming of war echoed in her heart, and she heard the men invoke her name in pride. "'Alia's brothers!" What could 'Alia do when clear skies turned gloomy? A hot tear fell down her face; she quickly wiped it up with the goat fur she laid on. 'Abtan embraced her, and the lover in her obliged; she generously made love with a trembling soul. As he calmly fell asleep, she quickly buried her fears and turned back to being who she truly was, the proud daughter of the desert.

She told herself while moving quietly between the sleeping bodies, "The ground trembles under the tormented sky, my brother!"

Preparing the way for 'Auda's raid, she collected the keys that locked the horses' chains to the stakes, lifted the edge of the rug that Mizna slept on, dug holes with her bare hands, placed the keys in the holes, smoothed out the ground, and covered it again with the rug. She knew that the men would be of no use without the horses.

The sun had not risen yet; 'Abtan was still asleep. She could not see his beloved face but could vividly recall it. She whispered silently, "It is not betrayal, my love, but the call of a brother. You will understand, excuse, and forgive!"

'Alia cried when she heard the horses approaching and was sure that the raiders were in the camp. 'Abtan woke up startled. She turned her back to him; he rushed out of the tent. As soon as he left, she untied her hair, placed her child in Mizna's arms and asked her to hurry and take him by the safest path to 'Auda's camp.

'Alia quickly climbed up her camel's back into the hawdaj her brother and his men knew well and rode toward them. Seeing her, with her long dark hair untied, risking her life to support them, filled them with pride and determination. 'Abtan and his clan could barely get to their camels before the raid started. They knew who the raiders were when they saw 'Alia on the back of her camel cheering them as if she wasn't one of them last night. She called out, so her brother's men could hear, "Abu 'Inad, my pride, when people see you, they stand."

'Auda replied proudly, "I am 'Alia's brother!"

The invaders grabbed sacks of wheat and supplies and led herds of goats and sheep in front of them past the women's tents. 'Abtan sense of loss intensified when he saw 'Alia riding to support her brother's invasion! Her hoarse voice stabbed him in the heart, but he knew her well enough to know that she could not but be there to support her brother!

He wanted to tell her that he understood with his mind, but not with his heart!

'Abtan pulled his gun and fired without thinking who he might kill, but soon his own body fell to the ground dead. Witnesses saw the killer; it was 'Auda's son 'Inad.

The desert has its laws that people know well.

'Auda put out his fire and lined up his empty coffee pots in mourning of his dead son and thought about the raid that turned into death and the fire that turned into ashes. He saw 'Alia's tears, felt the pain in her eyes, and could not look at her child.

Earlier, when 'Inad tried to speak, the shaikh turned his face away in disapproval, and whispered with a hoarse voice, "We shall never speak."

That day, the sage said, "The desert rises early and eats her own children."

Others quietly repeated what Dayoud said trembling, "The killer will be slaughtered, no matter how long it takes."

'Inad wept, heartbroken that he angered his father. "What should I do with myself, pour ashes over my head? Nothing left for me to do but cry and weep . . ."

The following night the situation escalated; al-Jazi men entered 'Auda's land. The men fought back and returned carrying 'Inad's body. Dayoud hid regretting his prediction that came true. 'Alia stayed in her tent dealing with the conflicting emotions that drowned her soul. 'Auda looked at his slain older son with anguish and a bleeding heart. He had hoped that he would be the head of the tribe one day.

The wind suddenly gusted, stirring the grains of sand. The men sitting in 'Auda's tent blinked when flakes of the burning sage flew in the air and landed by their feet and on their clothes. They silently put it out with their hands. In anticipation, they watched 'Auda pull his son's dead body close to the fire and place it as a shield to prevent the sparks from reaching the men who looked at each other, stealing glances at 'Inad's body lying still next to the fire. With hearts filled with sadness, they watched their shaikh move about with a strange calmness, pick up a small animal that someone had hunted and killed, and throw it in the fire. The stench of the burning flesh permeated the tent. The shaikh lifted his head, looked at the body of his son stretched on the floor, then looked at his men, scratched his throat, and with a voice he intended to be strong and clear, said, "Why are you dumfounded? The raid ended. We invaded, and they attacked back. 'Inad is a cub that our house lost."

'Auda added putting an end to the feud and preventing more bloodshed, "A man for a man. Raids are what Arabs do, and the world continues to turn."

....

The horses starved, the cows' udders dried, and the people ate barley, which was normally used as feed, if they found it. They even tried lizards and snakes; even those disappeared under the scorching heat. The land seemed to punish the desert dwellers, and the agony stretched from the dry land to the hearts of its people.

The sage made a fist, pointed to his heart, and said, "'Oqab, nothing purifies the land except this, . . ." and then pointed to 'Oqab's swords and added, "and this." He then said, "'Oqab, the sword in its place is pride and honor, and a rival facing a rival is nobility.[2] 'People are like a breath of air; their days are like a fleeting shadow.'[3] Proud men should not waste their days in unworthy pursuits."

'Oqab never joined a raid. "The sword in its place" used only at the right time for the right reason; this is what the sage taught him. During the hot summer nights, when no breeze wafted, the boy looked at the sky and yearned for the familiar Eastern Star. "How hard it is to reach you! But the heart continues to try."

---

2. Adapted from a famous verse in a poem by one of the most prominent Arab poets, Abu al-Tayyib al-Mutanabbi (951–965 CE): "Placing a dewdrop in the mighty place of the sword is harmful, just like placing a sword in the place of a dewdrop."

3. Psalms 144:4.

When people in the tribe said sarcastically, "The boy is not made for war."

'Auda shook his head in disagreement and said, "You don't know what you are talking about, 'Oqab will have his day."

The drought continued to tighten its grip over the desert land. 'Auda moved east with his men seeking the spoils of raids of the shores by the two great rivers, and on dry winter days, he yearned to be wet with rain. The land cracked, and the sun was white and bright; at night, it was cold and dry.

The children of the tribe were busy looking at a strange woman riding a camel that was carrying on its side water and supplies. The woman wore a small hat and trousers like men. Her eyes were hidden behind dark glasses, which she took off only when she used the big binoculars tied to ribbons, dangling over her small chest. Her camel walked beside the camel of the Englishman who was taking pictures of al-Howeitat women by the Bayer's well from which the women were pulling with difficulty the little stagnant water left at its bottom. The women laughed, untied their hair and posed for the pictures as instructed by the young blond, blue-eyed man. Mizna ran away refusing to be part of what she considered a degrading scene orchestrated for the stranger's lens.

Ms. Gertrude Bell laughed saying, "Are you having fun, Lawrence? Wasting your time taking pictures of women!"[4]

"Their eyes are beautiful, aren't they?"

"Yes, they are; but this is more important."

She pointed to the Hogarth map she was holding, and spread it open

---

4. Gertrude Margaret Lowthian Bell (14 July 1868–12 July 1926), an English writer, traveler, political officer, administrator, and archaeologist who became highly influential in British imperial policy-making due to her knowledge and contacts established through her extensive travel in Greater Syria, Mesopotamia, Asia Minor, and Arabia.

Thomas Edward Lawrence (16 August 1888–19 May 1935), a British archaeologist, military officer, diplomat, and writer, best known as Lawrence of Arabia. Deployed in 1916 to work with the Hashemite forces in the Hijaz. He played a significant role in supporting the Arab Revolt against the Ottoman.

on the desert floor.[5] Lawrence bent to look at it, laughed and said, "Don't forget to take my picture with these desert gazelles."

She shook her head consumed with looking at the map and added, "You are too romantic my dear!"

Mizna ran away, her heart angrily pounding at the site of the stranger taking pictures of her people and combing the face of her dry, sandy desert.

....

Three months passed since anyone saw a flower or a green plant. In the spreading drought, even the scorpions stopped coming out of their holes. 'Auda's raids went farther and farther, and each time he returned with fewer spoils that barely kept the tribe alive. The shaikh favored his sister 'Alia with the best. She would thank him graciously, fighting her mounting pain.

"Thank you, my brother."

She was drowned in her memories but never complained. The shaikh knew, and to make her happy, he dismantled a portion of the British railways that passed by his land and used the wood to build an additional story over his concrete house in Ma'an for her to live in. She watched the stretch of the barren, dry desert from her balcony but could not force herself to be happy.

"Sister, as soon as the year ends, you will not be alone. You could have the most handsome man in the tribe if you wish, God willing."

'Alia knew that her brother was referring to al-Dehaylan, offering to mend her heart with youth and beauty!

Then he added, "Dear sister, why don't you go to Petra, and enjoy yourself."

He knew that her heart was still mourning her late husband, but if he had asked her, she would have denied it in pride; regardless, she thought

---

5. Maps of the region sketched by David George Hogarth (23 May 1862–6 November 1927), a British archaeologist, were of great help to the allies in World War I. Hogarth knew T. E. Lawrence and Gertrude Bell and recommended them to the British army during the early stages of the Arab Revolt.

the trip might do her good. It might help her shed off the bitter sadness that had consumed her since his passing. If she admitted to herself that she needed new space, she might find some happiness. 'Alia lowered her gaze, and said, "Whatever you suggest, brother."

He immediately ordered, "Prepare the horses and the supplies."

With little enthusiasm, the servants wrapped a few loaves of grain bread and a container of camel milk and tied the supplies to the hump of a strong camel. Meanwhile, 'Alia mounted al-Saqlaweyah, and Mizna al-Asilah, and they went on their way. Two strong men were assigned to guard them; they rode some distance away to give the women their privacy. The caravan also included two chatting female servants who spoke softly so as not to disturb their mistresses' silence.

Mizna touched al-Asilah's sweaty neck with the palm of her hand; her heart fluttered, and a strange yearning filled her soul. The scent of the horse reminded her of 'Oqab. She touched her dry lips and felt her body tremble. She tried to recall the story told by 'Amsah when she was still a child about the boy that was saved by al-Asilah's milk, but the details became jumbled in her mind.

In the afternoon, the caravan arrived at the entrance of Petra; the rosy rocks told the city's story, and the top of the mountains pointed to the locations of the ancient Nabatean guards and snippers. Desolate posts, empty open mouths in the face of the mountains.

The two women in love sensed the flood of memories that filled the place. The Nabateans lived here in the past, Arab armies spread over these hills, and nations came and went, and the mountains remained, rosy, standing as a witness of endless time, holding in their core the souls of all those who passed by and are now gone. A giant witness that baffles minds and hearts.

'Alia closed her eyes and recalled the image of 'Abtan. Then she realized what she was doing and stopped herself; she came here to forget, not to remember!

In the presence of the majesty that surrounded the glorious rock city, the sun veiled the horizon with its glorious colors; the rocks shined, red like glowing embers, a flame of fire, and a bundle of light. The horses calmly carried the women though the Siq,[6] the narrow pathway that led to the heart of Petra. 'Alia told herself, "I won't remain sad. Enough! It is time for me to let go of my love for him. It's time for the woman inside me to get back to living."

Meanwhile, Mizna was realizing that a different love was growing inside her like a bright dawn. Petra's beauty and the radiance of the stones carried her to a mysterious and magical world. Her heart was racing, her breathing became irregular, and she was flooded with memories of past times. When al-Asilah passed through the Siq and stood in front of the Treasury, a masterpiece chiseled in the rock and transported through time like a story, the scene consumed her soul and erased all else. 'Alia was next to her admiring the large vase and columns carved by the early Nabateans. She thought about the Bedouins who believed that it held a treasure and tried to shoot it down with their rifles, to no avail. Meanwhile, Mizna's eyes jumped to the colored caves. She noticed in the distance the Prince's Palace[7] sitting high on top of a faraway mountain. She felt as if she were traveling through time, to a distant memory that lived within her. Her soul clambered in search of the familiar. That feeling scared her. Was this the first time she had stepped in this land? Why did it seem frighteningly familiar? She seemed to know the paths that led to the palace on the top of the mountain, and to recognize the colors of the rocks. She was familiar with the type of flowers that grew shyly between the red, green, and purple pebbles and knew that the beautiful black iris filled the pathways.

A mysterious force guided her steps and made her see past times. The horses seemed other horses, and she was not Mizna, and her companion

---

6. A natural dim, long, narrow, winding gorge that forms the main entrance to the ancient city of Petra ending at its most elaborate ruin, the Treasury.

7. An ancient palace and temple at the city of Petra dating back to the first century BC built using blocks made of juniper wood and stone, in contrast to the rest of the city that was carved out of a large rock. It said that it was built for one of the ancient Arab goddesses, while some of the Arab tribes believe that it was built for the pharaoh's daughter, Isis.

was not 'Alia. The place that her mind conjured was from a different time, crowded with people with colorful clothes and turbans, alive, moving only in her imagination, calling, "O Hareth,[8] we are thirsty, hungry, and the Kingdom of Judea is raising its swords against us; should we fight them?"

Al-Hareth appeared riding his horse, his voice soaring through the sky, "If they raise their swords, we will raise ours, and when they put theirs down, we will continue the fight. This is the only way to protect Petra and be safe from Judea's plot. This is how we will keep our rocks free and make sure that the city will never kneel. She is in our protection now and throughout time."

Al-Hareth's daughter heard the cry of the mothers and wanted to dry their tears but to no avail. Their voices echoed, "Water, princess. Our children are dying of thirst."

She looked at the brave men, and walked with a broken heart back to her palace, stopped at the gate, and said, "Here I will die alone. I will hold back from you my glory, my light, and my face. My death will be your shame, and loneliness a curse of your manliness, until a man rises, swings his sword, and beats the land to create a sea and pulls water from the aquifer into our thirsty city. Only then, the women's eyes will stop crying. Is there a man who will break the face of earth and help fill our streams with water? I will be his lover and lawful wife. He will have my admiration and the yearnings of my flesh, and I will shower him with my tender love. Is there such a man? Is he out there?"

Mizna suddenly called from the bottom of her heart, "Water, water, 'Oqab!"

The women were startled by the sudden cry, noticed a shadow and saw 'Oqab on the back of al-Kahilah standing in the place of the guards. Mizna noticed him first and was filled with joy; she did not regret her call that echoed through the place. 'Oqab held up his bright sword and waved its

---

8. In reference to the Nabataean King al-Hareth and the wars led by Herod, beginning in 32 BCE, against the Nabataeans during the reign of King Malichus II in which Herod cut the city's water supply.

sharp blade high in the air. Mizna's heart fluttered, and the sword's blade glittered, followed by lightning in the sky, then thunder, and chill in the bones. The rain fell in sheets.

'Alia and Mizna returned with their caravan through Wadi Musa, guarded by the blades of the riders. The caravan passed the long road between the stone statues carved into the mountains of solid rock. The statues watched the women entering the heart of the colored wadi beaming with the shades of a rainbow that the rain painted skillfully over the horizon. At the site of the stunningly green, lush land at the center of Wadi al-Qamar, Mizna stopped, filled by a renewed yearning, consumed by an overwhelming love, in awe of the glorious scene. It was a piece of heaven that God no doubt had left at the bottom of this wadi. The green patches surrounded Moses's Springs where God became angry at the Israelites and called on his prophet, "Climb to the top of the opening and raise your gaze to the west, to the north, to the south, and to the east; look with your eyes, but you will not pass this Jordan."[9]

Her eyes followed the pathway constrained by the branches piled through time, and at the far shoulder of the rocky mountain, the patches of green were carefully planted with date palms as if no road led to them. Her yearning soul soared toward that desired piece of paradise and wished ardently that she could be there with 'Oqab.

When they returned from their blessed trip, the rain fell, and in celebration of the long-awaited rain, 'Auda arranged his sister's marriage to the handsomest man in the tribe.

---

9. In reference to the Biblical verses regarding God's warning to Moses, "But the LORD was angry with me on your account and would not listen to me; and the LORD said to me, 'Enough! Speak to Me no more of this matter. Go up to the top of Pisgah and lift up your eyes to the west and north and south and east, and see it with your eyes, for you shall not cross over this Jordan" (Deuteronomy 3:27–28).

5.

....

From the distant past, crowds appeared,
Constantly searching, looking for the truth.
They moved steadily, rushed to the future,
They felt the strength in their bones,
They kept traveling, beyond death's homes.
In heaven, God's eternal call sounded,
"Do not stop; keep going, cross the borders far."

—Tagore[1]

T he wings of two soaring black birds flapped making a whishing sound. They dove down a little in search of a place to hide in anticipation of the coming storm. Their black wings glittered in contrast to the gloomy gray sky. A shepherd and his herd occupied the cave at the bottom of the hill. The young shepherd lay silent in the dark wet cave, scared, mumbling, "O God, protect me from the two Jinn brothers with their two hammers, one smashes the head and the other crushes the feet."

He then stretched his small covered head and saw the two black birds, the only sign of life around. They landed nearby flapping their wings, and then flew again. He cheerfully said, "Lucky who spots two crows in the sky."

---

1. Rabindranath Tagore (7 May 1861–7 August 1941), a Bengali polymath who greatly influenced Bengali literature and music, as well as Indian art in the late nineteenth and early twentieth centuries; the first non-European to win the Nobel Prize in Literature in 1913.

The birds disappeared flying around the dunes. He came out of the cave feeling fortunate to be alive and went on leading his herd. The goats hurried past him, and he went back to gather the slow young sheep and bring them back to the fold. The sky was still clouded, and the cold wind pierced his skinny body wrapped with a coat made of sheepskin. He hoped to reach his tribe's camp before the rain poured down and soaked him and his herd.

The young shepherd and his animals jumped around trying to avoid the sticky spots where the rain soaked the sand turning the hard ground into quicksand traps. He looked at the gloomy sky wondering when it would rain again and, to keep his herd safe, watched nervously for the quicksand. He randomly slapped his hands cursing the stubbornness that led him to leaving the safety of the camp on such a day. He felt that, if the herd did not die from starvation, it would probably die now from the cold.

The optimism caused by seeing the two crows slowly vanished as he fought to rescue his young herd from the quicksand that filled his way. Then he suddenly stopped, so did his herd.

He listened carefully and heard with his expert ears the sound of strange horses' hooves, echoing. Many horses and riders. The shepherd laid on the ground and placed his ear on its muddy surface, unsure if he would hear the coming steps through the wet land. He heard them again, slapped his head, and said to himself with confidence, "Ah, I fear that the big war reached our land!"

He knew that it was the sound of the warriors who left Mecca and traveled to al-'Ala. He rushed toward the source as if he were looking for a carnival, without paying attention to his animals. They followed him, and many ended up stuck in sand traps. He looked back and saw their shadows moving like a wave in the fog of winter, or like a painting of a mirage. He stopped, panting; his throat was dry, and his eyes were full of tears.

As they drew nearer, their voices became louder, mixed with the howling wind and moving with its gusts. They came wrapped up in January's fog . . .

The young shepherd jumped in the air hardly containing himself, "By God, O Lord, it is the Prince!"

Faisal, the son of the sharif of Mecca,[2] was leading his army to al-Wajh, a glimpse of the spirit of the revolt that started in Mecca and spread north. The young shepherd had a hard time figuring out the number of fighters as well as the horses and camels they had with them. The horses were in the front, followed by the mules, followed by seventy camels loaded with weapons and supplies that the fighters had captured from a Turkish caravan headed to the battleground. They were moving to al-Wajh on the Red Sea to support the British Army in Palestine. It was World War I, in which the Arabs choose to fight their Turkish occupiers after hundreds of years of submission.

They approached slowly. The rain confused the sheep and slowed their movement. The shepherd waved his arms and ran toward the caravan leaving his herd behind. The men around the prince realized his move, thinking that he is too simple to figure out which one was the prince, but when he came close, they stood ready to block his way. A slight move from a skinny hand stopped them. Breathless, the shepherd held to the neck of the prince's horse. With his eyes fixed on the rider and his throat dried, he yelled with excitement, "Sir, Sir, Fai . . . Faisal!"

He suddenly felt dizzy and fell. The men ran to him, gave him water to drink, and held him up. When he regained his balance, they bombarded him with questions about the terrain and the closest caves that they could use. The boy answered with his eyes fixed on the thin Hashemite rider, admiring the beautiful Hijazi outfit the prince wore, a buttoned vest over a green velvet rem, turned darker by the rain, its sleeves closed by a different set of buttons. His looped dagger sat in the middle of his wide leather belt

2. Hussein bin 'Ali al-Hashimi (1853/1854–4 June 1931), a Hashemite Arab leader, who was the sharif and emir of Mecca from 1908 and, after proclaiming the Arab Revolt against the Ottoman Empire, King of the Hijaz from 1916 to 1924. He unified Arab forces in their fight against the Ottomans. He was later ousted by the British after refusing to ratify the Treaty of Versailles, in protest of the establishment of British and French mandates in the region. His sons Faisal and Abdullah who led the Arab Revolt and were instrumental in winning the war, were made rulers of Iraq and Transjordan respectively in 1921.

set with shining silver decorations. He also wore a silk keffiyeh, wet and dripping, that was held in place with a Hijazi iqal decorated with golden and silver threads.[3] Glamor befitting a prince.

The shepherd was not able to look directly into the prince's eyes. His gaze shifted like a frighten bird looking at his clothes and landing on his long thin, pale fingers holding the horse's bridle with strength and determination. Every time he tried to say something, he trembled and could hardly speak. He was so nervous the men had to pry the information out of him, and when they finished, he gathered his strength and managed at last to look at the prince's face. The prince's eyes captured the shepherd's soul and filled him with great amazement. He had never seen such beautiful eyes. The prince was so pale that you could almost see the bones through his skin. Behind the thin face, the full beard, and the commanding, beautiful eyes, the shepherd detected a sadness that reached out and filled his heart with sadness too. But the prince looked at him and smiled, filling his soul with limitless peace. The shepherd was convinced that the prince favored him with his love and kindness. At that moment, he decided to follow him to the end of the world and dedicate himself to his service.

The men led the shepherd to the back of the troops and had him ride behind a Hijazi Bedouin, who did not mind. Even if he could not see the prince directly, he was content to be among his troops. Despite losing his herd to the storm and having what was left of it added to the troop's supplies, he was happy.

The caravan passed the mud traps to al-Haif where the shepherd claimed there were many caves suitable for shelter. The further they moved, the thicker the clouds became, and at last, they saw the openings of the caves and rushed toward them exhausted. Then they heard Shaikh al-Balawi warn, "Beware of snakes, light the fire!"

---

3. A Hijazi iqal is an accessory, usually worn by Arab men, made of a black cord, worn doubled, that is used to keep a keffiyeh (head cover) in place. It is traditionally made of goat hair. In certain regions of Hijaz, some are made of cotton or silk and decorated with gold and silver threads.

At the entrance of each cave, a fire was lit, and the cracking of the wood burning was heard. The men entered looking inside; the snakes slithered out and a small wolf ran out in a hurry. They took the mules and donkeys into the caves to keep them warm; the horses shielded themselves behind the rocks, and the camels sat down nearby. The men stretched over the caves' wet floor, covered their bodies with their abayas, and the world fell silent.

Hajras picked a slightly wet sack of dates with his strong arms and shook it to get rid of the water. Faisal laughed calmly and said, "Hurry up, Hajras. The men are hungry."

Nasib al-Bakri, who had known the prince for a long time, knew that behind the laugh hid a thought, so he asked the prince about it.[4] Faisal told him that he was thinking about his father, the sharif, and his wise advice not to carry too many supplies, which he did not understand at first. Now, upon seeing all the spoils of the Turkish caravan that they had acquired, with the shepherd's herd added to their supplies, he could see the wisdom of his father's advice.

They laughed, and Faiz al-Ghusein added, "The lucky stumbles on his fortune."[5]

Ahmad al-Balawi[6] responded jokingly, but intending to deliver a message at the same time, "Stumble, not at all! It is not nice of you to say that, city boy; we did not stumble on the Turkish caravan by luck. We were surrounded by soldiers. Each of us carried his soul in the palm of his

---

4. Nasib al-Bakri (1888–1966) was a Syrian politician and nationalist leader who helped establish an underground organization which sought the independence and unity of the Ottoman Empire's Arab territories. He became a close aide to Prince Faisal during and after the Arab Revolt.

5. Faiz al-Ghusein (1883–1968) was a shaikh from Horan who aided the Arab Revolt and served as the secretary of Prince Faisal as mentioned in his memoirs *Muthakarati 'An al-Thawrah al-'Arabiyyah* [My memoirs of the Arab Revolt] (2 vols. Damascus, Ibn Zaidoon Press, 1939/1970).

6. Egyptian historian who joined the Arab Revolt and was among Faisal's close circle of companions.

hand when the bullets flew all around us! We were not aware that death was a joke among city boys."

The rain continued to pour down, beating on the stones above the caves. It swept into the caves and flooded parts of them. Faisal's two servants, Hajras and Tafs, made sure that the men received their share of dates. When the sun went down, the men slept, except for a few who gathered in Faisal's cave around the dim fire where Faisal sat, the glow casting a copper light on his face. The faint light from the fire was shining on the men around him, Nasib al-Bakri, Faiz el-Ghusein; and the doctor, Hassan Sharaf.[7] They wore urban pants and shirts common in Damascus and Palestine and wrapped their cold bodies with their abayas to stay warm. They were joined by Ahmad al-Balawi, who was wearing Hijazi clothes, Ali al-Najdi in his Bedouin thaub and long black braids, and officer Mawlood Mukhles in his blue military uniform.[8] Lawrence, the young Englishman, stood out with his bright blue eyes and wet shirt and trousers. A Bedouin noticed him and offered him a thick coat made of sheep wool to keep him warm. The two black servants, Hajras and Tafs, squatted by the entrance of the cave adding wood to the fire, waiting to serve the prince. The prince rarely asked them for much, except for his cigarettes. His constant smoking left yellow traces of tobacco on his thin brown fingers.

With enthusiasm and pride, the men talked about their Arab alliance after centuries of occupation and oppression by the Ottomans when being an Arab was a taboo. Mawlood Mukhles recalled the name of the Arab men executed by the Turks in Damascus. Mentioning their names, one by one, filled his heart with courage and determination. Al-Bakri described the square where they were hanged and the friends that he lost that day, Muslims and Christians, all proud Arabs. More names clamored like a riot in Mawlood's mind and brought back painful memories of

7. Hassan Sharaf served as Faisal's physician and helped form the regular army.

8. Mawlood Mukhles was born in Mosul in 1885 and received his education at the Imperial Military Academy in Istanbul, then joined the Arab Revolt under Prince Faisal's army, which he helped form, leading numerous battles. He also served in key political positions in Faisal's administration after the war.

the victims of Mesopotamia. The men's tales that night painted a trail of pain that stretched from sea to sea, a wounded Arab body tormented by decades of Turkish tyranny, of torture, and pillaging, and so much more. The men at Faisal's tent felt a hidden force stirring up their emotions and pouring fuel on their already burning fires. They enthusiastically recited the revolutionary pledge in unison as if it were being invoked by Tariq[9] or Salah al-Din[10] and pledged to rise first thing in the morning and march to the city of al-Wajh, set camp, and get ready for the fight. Every night, they renewed their pledge as if they were making a promise to distant souls that came, and shared their evenings by the cave's fire each night.

Tired and sleepy, the men walked to their caves, and stretched resting on the damp floor. Tafs moved slowly, looking to see if the prince needed anything. To avoid attention, the prince faced the wall of the cave and wrapped himself tight with his abaya. He pretended to be asleep, but his eyes remained open, staring into a void. The fire by the entrance turned to ashes, Hajras made sure to put it out before he joined them in the cave. Then the two black giants sat down with their backs resting on the cave's wall next to the prince and went to sleep sitting down, the wall holding their bodies up, preventing them from sliding and lying down.

Faisal fell asleep and hell returned holding him in its grip. How can he get rid of the nightmares of what he witnessed? The scenes continued to haunt him. He could vividly see the military cart approaching. Faisal watched himself in the dream, consumed by worries, carrying a big secret in his heart. He was standing next to Jamal al-Safah, who combed his mustache mockingly, his face bloated.[11] Faisal lost his color, felt sick, but stood still.

---

9. Tariq bin Ziyad was a Berber Muslim commander who led the Islamic Umayyad army; he crossed the Strait of Gibraltar from the North African coast, consolidating his troops at what is known today as the Rock of Gibraltar (named after him).

10. Salah al-Din al Ayyubi was a Muslim of Kurdish ethnicity who led the military campaign against the Crusaders in the Levant; he was the first Sultan of Egypt and Syria and the founder of the Ayyubid Dynasty.

11. Jamal Pasha, born Ahmed Djemal (6 May 1872–21 July 1922), a Young Turk and member of the Three Pashas who brutally ruled during World War I, known among the local Arab inhabitants as al-Safah, "the Blood Shedder," was one of the most brutal and influential

The cart stopped by the edge of al-Marja courtyard that had been turned into a stage; the whole city of Damascus had been turned into a theater that displayed the atrocities of the Turks. The wooden poles lined up like vertical stairs, and from the tip of each pole, a rope dangled. The circle of gallows swung like a door to hell, the crowd's faces turned pale, their hearts were full of fear, their hands trembled, and their feet wobbled. Silence, broken by a few soft whispers, filled the place. The procession arrived, young, bright men, like fresh poppy flowers, their heads uncovered, their feet bare and thin, some in trousers and shirts, and others skinnier in their thaubs and gumbazes.[12] With sparks in their eyes, they walked steadily and steadfastly, not rushed by their executors. Faisal stood in the military cart, next to the Butcher.[13] His soul trembling with agony, Faisal felt that the eyes of the men calling him; he thought of reaching out to them, his mind churning, why did he have to pretend to be neutral? Why couldn't he stop the weeping inside him? Why couldn't he do something?

The men walked to the gallows, carrying on their chests a rectangular white paper with their sentences written on it. They broke into unexpected chant! Their voices choking, trembling, but sincere, "Decorate al-Marja, al-Marja is ours, al-Sham is a site to see when it is decorated!"[14]

The whispering of the crowd became loud, and the place was pulsing with life again, stirred by the magic of singing. Jamal Pasha spat in disapproval; Faisal's eyes watched the spit land not too far from his military boots.

The men's heads were placed inside the nooses and the sentences were read consecutively. The executioners pulled away the platform, and the

---

Turkish military commanders. He played a major role in fighting the Arabs during the revolt and is said to have had a role in the Armenian, Greek, and Assyrian genocides. He was responsible for the hanging of many Lebanese and Syrian Shi'a Muslims and Christians wrongly accused of treason on 6 May 1916 in Damascus and Beirut.

12. A type of trouser with wide crotch worn by Syrian peasants under their thaub.

13. A title given to Jamal Pasha.

14. In some cases, *al-sham* refers to Damascus and *Bilad al-Sham* refers to the Fertile Crescent, which includes modern Syria, Lebanon, Jordan, the State of Palestine, Israel, parts of southern Turkey, and the western half of the southeastern Anatolia.

men's bodies dropped one after the other. The bereaved audience heard a devastated women's ululation breaking the silence of the crowd. The last one to hang was a twelve-year-old boy who walked to his death like a man, placed the noose around his neck, and smiled. When his skinny feet were dangling in the air, his body was still jerking inside the noose, which did not break his skinny neck as it should have. The crowd heard him take his final gasp, and someone in the crowd called, "Allah'u'Akbar! God is great!" The bloody mucus seeped out of his nose and mouth, and the world turned dark in Faisal's eyes; he could hardly see the courtyard, everything around him became foggy, and his legs could barely hold him up. He heard the Butcher standing next to him, irritated, cursing the Arabs—the traitors; the words stopped in Faisal's throat, every drop of blood inside him was boiling, and his soul was screaming, "It's time to do something, Arabs!"

Faisal's body shook, and tears filled his eyes.

6.

....

We swear by Almighty God to hold back when
you hold back, and to move forward when you
move forward; never to obey the Turks; to be
kind to all those who speak Arabic; and to make
independence a priority over our lives, our families,
and our wealth.

—The Oath of the Great Arab Revolt

Shaikh 'Auda Abu Tayeh was aware of the fate that led him to join
the fight. He had experienced the lure of gold, and understood the
power of its seductive glitter in the Turkish soldiers' hands. They
used gold to please him when he turned their lives into a living hell with
his raids, and threatened him with their weapons when he refused to pay
the taxes that they called "government right" imposed on their subjects.
What government? 'Auda saw the world as an open sky and endless land,
paths for his horses, and pastures for his herds. Nevertheless, he had tasted
the sweetness and bitterness of gold. With his tongue, 'Auda touched the
cold, smooth golden surface that covered his teeth, a gift from the former
Turkish governor of Ma'an before he was ousted by another leader who
took over the city, announced himself a prince, and forced the small
Turkish regiment to pay him for the right to stay in the city. 'Auda knew
how to manage gold, turning it to a master that aided him as he needed,

and a slave that he disposed of when his pride gave him the illusion that he was the most powerful and generous prince in the region.

If it wasn't for gold, how would the shaikh justify his journey? He convinced himself that the scale was leaning to the young Hashemite prince's side, so he was joining the revolt, but his soul realized that this had nothing to do with gold or capturing territory, it was something lofty, something he never experienced before. He was not fighting for control or seeking wealth. He was not hungry; he was thinking of freedom, a desire to lift the heavy burden placed for years over his land and open it to the wide sky again. This was what really made him come out, silent, contemplating.

A line of poetry crossed 'Auda's mind, "I have no money or horses to offer."[1] The shaikh spoke to his heart while thoughts and ideas flickered in his mind trying to take shape, "So, it is not about gains; it is about a dream that lives in my mind. The prince has no treasures that I desire; it is fate pushing us to march together on a thorny but attainable path."

....

Hajras slightly moved the curtains covering the entrance of the shaikh's tent, attempting politely to wake up his master. Faisal closed his eyes and pretended to be asleep. Tafs walked quietly toward him. Faisal slightly moved, opened his eyes, and stretched pretending to be waking up. He wanted to convince his servants who worried about him that he had slept and had had a much-needed rest, but his red, tired eyes revealed the traces of another sleepless night. Hajras's large body bent with nimbleness picking up the many cigarette butts around the small Persian rug that the prince sat on, and thought, "My Master would have needed the whole night to smoke all these cigarettes."

Tafs carried in the container of dates and the plate of cookies and

---

1. From a famous verse in a poem by one of the most prominent Arab poets, Abu al-Tayyib al-Mutanabbi (951–965 CE), translated as "You have no horses and no wealth, so let your words be happy if your affairs are not."

spoke directly to the prince, "Master, you should have breakfast today; the mistress sent these cookies."

Tafs placed the metal plate full of small homemade cookies next to the prince; Faisal recognized his mother's cookies. They reminded him of the many times he sent written messages from Damascus hidden inside the cookies the women of al-Bakri family made for that purpose. The tender thought of his mother in this faraway land placed a sad smile on his tired face; he stretched his hand reaching for the cup of black coffee that Salem had made, and took a deep puff from his cigarette, a signal to the three guards that it was time to let the others in.

Faiez al-Ghadeen came in first with his dagger fastened tightly around his waist. The prince noticed through the opening in the curtain a group of beggars looking for the prince's favor and said tenderly to his men, "Don't let them wait. Be generous with them."

The friends from the night before gathered around the fire that Hajras had started with fresh wood and grass, enjoying the aroma of the fresh coffee brewed over the open fire. Faisal picked up one of his mother's cookies, took a small bite, a sign for the men to eat theirs, and took another encouraging them to have as many as they liked.

Mawlood spoke enthusiastically about the first batch of volunteers in the formal army, soldiers and officers that deserted the Ottoman army and joined the resistance, six hundred men left their families' fate in the hand of Jamal Pasha, the Butcher, and accompanied Nuri Al-Said to meet Prince Faisal outside Hijaz.[2]

Mawlood complained, "The men are here, but the weapons and the food are not enough, and the British have not delivered what they promised."

They looked for answers in Faisal's confident face, and saw the glow

---

2. Nuri al-Said was born in Baghdad in 1888 and graduated from the Imperial Military Academy in Istanbul. He served in the Ottoman army, and later was arrested and exiled for his ties to Arab leaders. After the British gained control of Iraq, he was sent to work with the Arab leaders in Egypt, then joined Prince Faisal's army and accompanied him in his political career, serving in key military and political positions.

in his eyes when Shafeq al-'Eir's small body and white face announced, "Master, 'Auda, the shaikh of al-Howeitat, has arrived!"

The men backed off making space for the large figure that blocked daylight from the tent's entrance, to come in. 'Auda walked in, holding the hand of an eight-year-old boy. Faisal stood up, even though he often welcomed dignitaries from Najd and Hijaz seated. He was excited to greet the shaikh who carried the weight of a whole tribe. The two giants embraced, and the men felt that a new era had started. The shaikh greeted Faisal with a statement that stunned all, as if the desert opened wide to a new era, "Peace be upon you, Prince of the Faithful!"[3]

History was awakened, and the ashes that the Turks left behind with their swords, heavy boots, whips, and turbans for what seemed like eternity, were scattered. The men quivered, and 'Oqab closed his eyes letting hope churn the fire burning in his soul, listening to 'Auda's powerful voice reciting the revolt oath and enlisting in the revolutionary army. 'Auda's voice trembled, "We swear by Almighty God, to hold back when you hold back, and to move forward when you move forward; never to obey the Turks; to be kind to all who speak Arabic, regardless of whether they are from Baghdad, Aleppo, or Damascus. I swear that independence will be more important to me than my tribe and wealth."

With his eyes still closed, 'Oqab thought of the word "independence."

"What is above the tribe and the pleasures of this world? What is it, if it was not life itself? Independence, where dew sets and the sword speaks, this is what the sage has waited for all these years and has made me wait for all my life."

Standing by the entrance of Faisal's tent, 'Auda removed the gold from his mouth and swore not to eat with the Turk's golden teeth again. The men outside the tent cheered and shouted, "Praised be God."

'Auda shrugged his shoulders and thought, "They are pleased with the performance while in my heart storms rage!"

---

3. "Prince of the Faithful" is a title that implies political and religious leadership over the body of believers as the head of the nation, or caliph.

Faisal and 'Auda sat together, reminiscing and dreaming; and when they had a tender moment, they playfully rubbed the head of Muhammad bin 'Auda, who sat quietly by his father, then quickly returned to their conversation.

'Auda humbly said, "I will take back 'Aqaba."

'Aqaba, the quiet village with its tall date palms at the tip of the gulf, where Wadi Araba stretches, flashed like a dream in the consciousness of the Bedouin. Meanwhile, Mawlood suggested, "The British are in al-'Arish. It will be easy for them to take 'Aqaba."

"'Aqaba is ours! We know the way to it, and for its sake we would lay down our lives and the lives of our people. We will take back 'Aqaba." The war proved that 'Auda's enthusiasm was backed by his fierce fighting. He knew the desert and its tricks and knew what to do to own it.

"What about the feuds of the past and the pains the raids have left?"

"These we can handle, but not the wounds inflicted by our cousin. That is a different matter." 'Auda realized that the agony of losing his oldest son, 'Inad was still fresh in his soul. When he found out that the tribe of his cousin, al-Jazi, had joined the revolt he accepted that they would both serve the same cause, and was willing to work under the same banner as long as they did not meet; "The desert is big enough for both of us," he declared. Faisal understood and took precautions.

In the coming days, the desert witnessed the meeting of giants. 'Oqab and al-Howeitat fighters watched the commotion at al-Wajh camp that accompanied the arrival of the Iraqi officer, Ja'far al-'Askari, and saw the enlisted soldiers crowded by Faisal's tent to watch their leader with his loud laugh and khaki outfit take the oath of the revolution.[4]

In a tent made of palm husk and dry fronds, three men drew over the sand a map that they were willing to give their lives for. Ja'far drew a map

---

4. Ja'far Pasha al-'Askari (September 15, 1885–October 29, 1936) served in the Ottoman army during World War I until he was captured by British forces. After he was released, alongside his brother-in-law Nuri al-Said, he joined the forces of Emir Faisal and became an ardent supporter of Faisal throughout his political career. He held several important cabinet positions in Iraq.

from 'Aqaba to Damascus. Faisal's eyes teared up, and 'Auda erased the map with the palm of his hand and redrew it with his finger turning to the west, and said, "This is what we promise."

The men agreed, "Whoever frees a land, it is his."

It was our land, but during that same year, two other men drew a different map on paper . . . Sykes-Picot, sealed with gunpowder and gold and the blood of those who did not know what they gave their lives for.[5]

Al-Howeitat fighters spent some time at al-Wajh camp watching Ja'far organizing his soldiers and lining them up in uniforms worn-out by the harshness of the desert and the rush to escape the Turkish soldiers. The men raised their rifles in the air ready, and when their leader's loud voice called, they respond in unison, "Yes Sir."

Al-Agailat tribesman were learning how to plant explosions supervised by the English captain, Garland, who was wearing Arab garb.[6] Meanwhile, the tribesman of al-Sharart and Howeitat participated in target shooting competitions, complaining about standing in line waiting for their turn.

Za'al said, "I like to do things my way."

Ja'far responded laughing, "I also like to do things my way, but this does not work in a real war; this is not a raid."

Ja'far was having a hard time organizing the Bedouin volunteers. Seven hundred fighters from the Jahina tribe, wearing white thaubs and red keffiyehs, waving palm branches, were accompanied by hundreds from Anza not accustomed to following military orders; they were joined by three hundred fighters that came with Sharif Muhammad Abu Sharyan in

---

5. The Sykes-Picot Agreement (May 1916) was a secret convention made during World War I between Great Britain and France, with the assent of imperial Russia, for the dismemberment of the Ottoman Empire and the division of Turkish-held Syria, Iraq, Lebanon, and Palestine into various French and British-administered areas. The agreement took its name from its negotiators, Sir Mark Sykes of Britain and François Georges-Picot of France.

6. Major Herbert Garland (1880–2 April 1921) was a British metallurgist and army officer, who served as the Superintendent of Laboratories in Egypt, then as an officer with the Arab Bureau. In September 1916, he was assigned to train T. E. Lawrence and the fighters of the Arab Revolt on explosives. His mines were used against the Hijaz Railway and in many operations against the Ottoman forces. He became director of the Arab Bureau after the war and was involved in postwar negotiations for the future of Arabia.

their bright orange henna-colored garments under their black abayas. The colors mingled forming what looked more like a carnival than an army. Ja'far was grateful that 'Auda was leading and organizing the Howeitat.

Faisal's army was composed of two branches, military battalions with soldiers and officers, and a carefree group made of Bedouins who followed the directions of their tribal leaders. This worried the British officers. Colonel Newcombe doubted the usefulness of the unorganized, loudly speaking men, who were constantly singing and ululating;[7] he felt they would be more trouble than the Turkish Army itself. Even if they caused no harm, he worried about securing the needed supplies to sustain them.

Prince Faisal and Ja'far ignored Newcombe's concerns; they were confident that the army would not be able to move through the desert without the Bedouins' help.

The Howeitat fighters rushed their horses and camels into their camp, ready for a mission only 'Auda knew. They rode out without fear, calling, "We are Saleha's brothers, we are 'Alia's brothers; we are a sight to behold." They stopped to watch the two Rolls-Royces drive toward the camp accompanied by a frightened she-camel ridden by a short blond man with a large head, proud, boasting. He waved his hand in greeting but did not get a response. The Englishman rode in their direction; 'Oqab recognized him from his perplexed bright blue eyes. 'Auda said to himself, "A red man with blue eyes, may God protect us from this bad omen!"

The Englishman said softly to 'Auda, muttering broken but comprehensible Arabic, "You must be 'Auda."

The shaikh shook his head laughing, "Good, you are our brethren, the English Orance,[8] we recognize you."

Lawrence was elated; the shaikh that he longed to meet had heard about him!

---

7. Lieutenant Colonel Stewart Francis Newcombe (1878–1956) was a British army officer commissioned in the Royal Engineers, who later served with the Egyptian army. In 1913 and 1914 he was engaged in strategic survey work in the Sinai Peninsula, and at the end of 1916, he was appointed chief of the British Military Mission in the Hijaz.

8. One of the ways Arab tribesmen pronounced *Lawrence*.

The two cars drove into the camp, 'Auda gestured to his riders, and they followed leaving the camp behind. Al-Kahilah stared at the strange metal frames driving over the desert sand, 'Oqab felt her agitated moves, as if she were contemplating turning around and checking the rears of the soulless figures, but felt too proud to do so and went on in her way.

7.

....

Nothing stops me from going to Him,
No matter where He is.
When my song hovers with both its wings,
I push the closed door of my mind,
It opens into a mystic home.

—Tagore

'Auda looked at his men and waited. Some understood and said doubtfully, "'Oqab will no doubt join us!"

He had joined the fights defending the tribe but never accompanied them in their raids; he did not support raiding. They wondered if he would join them in this war.

Then they saw him, standing with his tall figure, which suddenly seemed taller, dispelling their doubts. He said, "I am coming with you."

"What about the sage? Will he stop you? You are like a ring on his finger."

"If his feet could carry him, he would have been here."

The shaikh smiled and rose to welcome him, "We gain a fighter like none other."

The shaikh's praise sent a trace of jealousy into the hearts of the men, but they knew that he was right. 'Oqab said, "I have a favor to ask before the war starts."

'Auda looked at him tenderly and said, "Mizna?"

"Yes, Mizna"

Dayoud laughed and said, "'Antarah, 'Antarah and 'Abla!"[1]

The shaikh patted the young man's shoulder and said joyfully, "We will not betray you like 'Abla's family did with 'Antarah. Mizna will be yours before we head out to war."

'Alia combed the bride's hair with almond oil, perfumed her body with incense, and lined her eyes with kohl. 'Amsah held the young bride's hands, while the women tattooed with a thin needle a design called the "drip" from the bottom of her lip to the edge of her chin. Mizna was happy despite the pain the needle caused. Meanwhile, the men were preparing 'Oqab. They tattooed the "lover's bracelet" on his wrist, and the "lover's pillow" on his arm. The whole tribe came out to the main square of al-Jafar to celebrate 'Oqab and Mizna's wedding. They sang,

Here comes the bride,

with eyes like a deer,

long pretty neck,

and a thin waist she bares.

Day sleepers rise,

wake up to hear,

'Oqab caught a deer,

like her you'll never see.

The sage joined 'Oqab and Mizna's hands together and blessed their heads. Mizna looked at her lover's face, gathered her courage, and whispered

---

1. 'Antarah bin Shaddad (AD 525–608) was a pre-Islamic Arab knight and poet. He is one of the poets of the Mu'allaqāt, the collection of seven "hanging odes," the most prominent in Arabic pre-Islamic poetry. He is famous also for his chivalry and his love for his cousin 'Abla who was the inspiration for much of his poetry. 'Antarah's family refused to allow him to marry 'Abla because of his black complexion and the status that he inherited from his slave mother, a former Ethiopian princess. He won his freedom after a long struggle through his bravery, fighting records, and the eloquence of his poetry.

with the shyness of a new bride, "I would like for us to consummate our marriage in a place that my heart chose before it met you."

"It will be wherever you choose." They moved far from home, with their supplies tied to the sides of al-Kahilah, their sole companion in their travel. Their imaginations soared as they entered Wadi Rum, the Valley of the Moon. Their presence startled the small wild animals that scurried down the slopes of the rocky mountain surrounded by seas of colored sand. The partridges looked at them curiously, and then flew high into the air.

Hand in hand, they crossed the valley and watched tenderly the thorny plants and the acacia flower growing stubbornly in the sand. Just before sunset, Mizna raised her hand and pointed to their anticipated paradise; the green spot reflected the rays of the sun setting and seemed like an island in a sea of desert, a moon in the sky, and a heart in a body. They drew near, their steps synchronized, walking toward their dream that rested in the heart of the yellow sand, glowing orange, touched by the reflections of the rays of the setting sun; the whole valley, a burning torch, and the island, the refuge, the oasis.

She leaned on his shoulder, overwhelmed with emotions. The path left the past behind and pointed to their new life; they entered heaven, the promised Eden that no feet had trampled before.

"They say the she-ghoul lives in these caves."

"Let them say what they want. We alone know that only you and I are here."

The colored rocks glittered in the sun and the mysterious whooshing of rushing water hidden in the distance between the volcanic rocks reached their ears. Carefully, they untangled the branches, intertwined, blocking the path to the palm trees. Mizna swore that she heard the soft whisper of the palm trees while passion crept slowly filling the pours of her thirsty body with pleasure. He moved a thorny branch out of her way clearing the narrow path. They walked breaking the dry sticks and bending the green grass under their footsteps. Was this their first time there! Everything looked familiar, the palm trees and their fronds, the valley with its pebbles and gravel, the bending of the road and the shade of the trees at the end of the path. They knew where the sparrows hid and were able to point to the cracks from which the finches poked their heads. Where did all the birds that were not startled by the two lovers' footsteps come from?

She noticed the huge tree and said, "'Oqab, this is not an ordinary palm."

It was taller, stronger, and straighter than any palm they have ever seen; it had a wider canopy and more dates than one tree can carry. They laid down under its shade, alone, surrounded by the charming black desert iris, as if it were carved from the flint of the barren land.

The evening fell upon them like a cover emblazoned with stars, and the scent of wild violet nearby filled the land. The shadows and the shades disappeared, her face glowed, and his shone. His mind raced with thoughts and his heart flooded with emotions, he thought, "I am going to war, but for now I am here, a pillow to hold your dream and make you feel safe; my body your bread, and my blood your wine. I am here for you, a sacrifice, the generosity of the universe, my arm your pillar, and my rain your drink, close to you like your life's vein. Heaven opened its doors, and we are almost there to reap its fruits."

She basked in his scent like a doe sensing her partner and touched with the tip of her fingers the hair on his chest. His soul soared when he slid over her silky body; he wondered, how could the desert hold within its midst all this soft luxury! Their breath intertwined, two in one. The place tenderly carried the echo of their whispers and witnessed their passionate love, sweet like honey, tender at times, and wild at others, pulsing with desire, burning with longing. They drank its wine and melted into each other. 'Oqab realized that she was the cloud that shaded him at the time of birth, and she realized that he was the rain that was held back waiting for her arrival. They discovered with a spontaneous simplicity that earth and heaven are one universe. The land burst with colorful flowers and became their soft bedding; they held each other in a long embrace in their private space, beyond all that surrounded them. They softly talked, kissed, and were intoxicated with love. The flow of their conversation quenched a different kind of thirst, a yearning for a companion soul, hidden and then drawn near, unmasked and returned to its source. They felt that life could move on while they continued their warm majestic embrace that they were not ready to break up. The early signs of dawn wrapped them in a sweet calmness lulled by a pure tenderness as if they were two leaves floating over a shimmering body of water. They wove their passion into a song and turned the rays of the morn into crowns that adorned their bare heads. They hummed the sad melodies that they learned in their homeland with joy flooding through their trembling voices, occupying the distance of this stretched land. They blossomed against all odds, like the rare flowers of the desert, breaking its bareness. With joy, they danced, and their songs turned to garments that clothed their nakedness. As if she were the Nabataean queen, standing at the entrance of her palace, thirsty, with her voice echoing throughout the desert, "Water, water, dear 'Oqab . . ."

....

Back at the tribe's camp, she opened the flap of her tent and waved to him. He was riding al-Kahilah, galloping to where the men gathered. She could hear the echo of their voices singing, while crossing the path between the two mountains, Meshach and Tawala.

> The fire of war is ablaze,
> who could quench its thirst?
> The horses with their riders came,
> looking for revenge.
> Woe to the tyrants' rule,
> our swords make them quiver.

The voices faded in the distance, and the lover kept her smile and proud posture but her soul was torn by yearning. When she could no longer see them, she sang with a voice, soft like a breeze,

O dove high on the mountain peaks, sing,

I never thought my love wouldn't hear my plea.

O dove high on the mountain peaks, cry,

I never thought my love would go so far!

8.

....

When Omar became a caliph, he ascended the pulpit and said, "Listen to my words and feel secure because of them; Arabs are like a proud camel who follows his leader. Let the leaders watch where they lead them. As for me, I swear by the Holy Ka'ba, I will carry you over to the right path."

—Al-Tabari [1]

Riding north was difficult . . .

A flame in my heart rooted in the south desert led me with its light to the north, to a place called Damascus. Between my roots stretched deep in the womb of the land and the bright target in the distance, there was an endless, harsh, and silent land. My body glued to yours, as if it were part of yours. Constantly you turn your head, waving the locks of your reddish mane. Sitting on your strong, solid back, I glimpse your big eyes; I know that you wish that you could turn your head around and look at me. Kahilah, you remind me of my love. Like you, she is warm, wild, with piercing eyes. Mizna, you and I, are one!

My body shivered with gratitude when she waved goodbye. She must have realized what it meant to join a great war. Her smile has accompanied me throughout my journey. She is part of my soul; she knows that it longs for the blue sea, an old dream I have had since I first heard 'Aqaba's name.

---

1. Muhamad bin Jarir al-Tabari, *Tarikh al-Tabari, Tarikh al-Umam Wal Muluk* (Dar al-Kutub al-'Ilmiah: Beirut, Lebanon, 1407), 2/355, http://islamport.com/w/tkh/Web/2893/918.htm.

My soulmate knows how much I hunger to taste 'Aqaba's dates and sit under the shade of its tall palm trees. She knows of the passion that rages through my veins; a passion that consumes my soul, grinds me down, and then scorches me with its holy fire, and makes me whole again.

I could not stay behind. When I was young, the sage said something that became imprinted in my mind, engraved on the tablet of my heart. I saw the light, but I did not exactly understand its source to fully comprehend the sage's words, "The sword in its place is pride and honor; to place it anywhere else is a shame." I, the free, the son of the keeper of the sky, will never live in shame. My sword is resting, ready in its sheath, next to al-Kahilah's body, and my rifle holds me straight.

The shaikh inspected us laughing and shared proudly and boastfully what other shaikhs said about him consulting his men, "This is not our way. A shaikh never asks his men what they want to do! Why is he doing that? Is he the shaikh or not!"

We were told that our strong, strict, but joyful shaikh responded with fire in his eyes, "If your men are sheep, mine are purebred horses."

Did you hear that al-Kahilah? He was talking about you. All around me are brave men of al-Ghayer brigade, the heart of the army organized by a fearless general who never lost a raid. They are all here, with their horses, al-Maharam, al-Amtheir, al-Mnayekh, a string of jewels. I know them well; they are the warriors of the tribe, we raced together, we fought and defeated raids on our tribes together; and they know me too. They came to accept my refusal to join their raids on other tribes; they know that my father, the sage, taught me that the sword in its place is where the sword should be, and they realized, as I did, that now was the time for my sword to be drawn. They are my brothers. Their mothers breastfeed me. The taste of milk came back to me, my heart pounded, and I knew that I was willing to lay down my life for them.

I was eager to fight. When the scouts went, I wished I was with them, light, brave, and alert like they were. When the front units moved to engage and distract the enemies from discovering the movement of the troops, I wished I was there. When a regiment stayed behind to set a trap, I wished I was with them. How can I split myself and be at all these places at the same time?

I walked with al-Ghayer fighters led by 'Auda mounted on his camel. I love being with him; I watched Ghazal, the camel of the Hashemite, al-Sharif Nasser trudging behind Na'ma, Lawrence's camel. Za'al noted that riding a horse is not customary at this stage of a desert raid and that horses are spared until the raid starts to ensure that they are rested and ready for battle. I was the only one riding a horse. But you are not like any other horse; you are al-Kahilah!

Za'al commented sarcastically, "A stubborn horse and a stubborn rider."

I know, my love, that a stubborn fighter shows up inside every man when danger strikes; I also know by instinct that the fighter is uplifted when the battle is sacred. Today we are not fighting for a raid or food; we are here for things that we cannot touch or put a value on, a war we are willing to give up our lives for. Water is scarce in our deserts, and the Turks devastated our villages and stripped our land as locusts do, forcing people to join them through bribes and threats. The prince does this too sometimes; it happened when we fought the English ships loaded with supplies in the water by 'Aqaba. But we did not come for that today, neither did the soldiers. How handsome they looked with their neatly cut hair! They came from Syria, Iraq, and Palestine, and jumped on board the ships that led them to 'Aqaba. I wished I was with them, but I moved forward on land with my companions taking a different route. All the dreams led to liberated deserts and land, but all the fires that raged inside our hearts pointed to Damascus.

How can I explain the longing of the Bedouin for a city! I desire no roof or door, I dream of a sea and a river where I can stretch the giant that was awakened within me, his feet in 'Aqaba and his head in Damascus. A spark propelled me to come out in such a drought with a certitude that made me follow an unusual shaikh who chose to enter 'Aqaba through the land of Sarhan, extending the journey. 'Aqaba was on the western borders of his land, but he planned to take us east, and then turn north. At first, I did not understand, but I realized his intention when I saw our troops increase in number as we traveled on the path he charted through the winding, harsh, and dangerous desert. Bedouins from different tribes and clans joined our troops in tens, then in hundreds. Every time we moved a little, a new group joined; they would approach, look at the royal Qurayshi's face for confirmation, and then turn to 'Auda looking for the promise of victory in his eager eyes.

Did the lure of gold move the dormant troops in the stillness of time? Were they moved by the same dream that filled me with life? What brought out those who often sought refuge from the dust of storms and the cruelty of the desert sun in their tents and caves where they used to stay, play their melancholy tunes on the old rabab,[2] listen to the echo of their souls, and try to purge themselves of a yearning that they could not comprehend? Was it a concealed desire for a future that they had waited long for that made them move? Was it the lure of gold that made them engage in this global war? How global was it? The world was fighting, the paths varied, and the purposes tangled. Gold and drought, famine and injustice, greed and dreams. Was there something different altogether awaiting them? A place under the sun, a rock to climb, a limitless horizon! I heard the men's footsteps and the echo of their songs. My soul rejoiced; how beautiful was the sword in its place!

> The one who picks a fight with us was made to leave,
> Like pulling a thirsty man from his drink.
> No doubt if he did not go,
> he would've been eaten by wolves.

Twelve harsh days, the shaikh watched us like an eagle, harsh on men and beast alike. His commanding voice made the animals move and

---

2. A rabab is a basic lute-like musical instrument used by the Bedouins. It is usually accompanied by reciting or singing poems in local dialects.

motivated the men beaten by the scorching sun. The heavy red boots with metal spurs added to their agony; some replaced them with shoes made of camel hides tied together with leather strips. When their feet touched the bodies of the horses or the pebbles of the desert, they felt scorched by hell's fire. Their feet blistered. I felt a crack between my toes, sharp like a knife, and ground my teeth trying to endure it. The heat spun the heads covered with keffiyehs and whipped the body.

Thirst was another haunting killer. The shaikh enforced a strict and nonnegotiable ration of water that we followed despite our thirst and access to the small water pouches at the side of our saddles or the large containers tied to the hips of the she-camels. He knew from experience that our supply was hardly enough to get us to the land of Sarhan. We alternated between riding slowly at first, then trotting, to avoid tiring the men and camels. Despite the long treacherous journey, the shaikh was full of energy, even on the last day. This helped us pull ourselves together and move on.

When I saw the small groundhog appear, then run back to his hole startled by al-Kahilah's footsteps, I realized that we were at Sarhan valley. My thirst went away, my soul calmed down, and I no longer felt the pain between my blistered toes, as if Mizna were casting her shade over me in God's wide-open space. "What are you doing now, Mizna? Al-Kahilah and I crossed the path east. The battle hasn't started here yet."

I felt the warmth of the horse's breath and heard her panting, our passion fused. "Come close, al-Kahilah. You will soon rest; allow me to hold and stroke your neck and the lucky star that crowns your forehead, and to rest my head on your beautiful mane. Like me and my love Mizna, you and I know our path well and know where we are heading!"

The Shalan men approached, welcoming. A raging storm started up inside me. I could feel it grow, expand, then spread its madness over the limitless barren space, turning the face of earth upside down, plowing it, baptizing me, celebrating a new birth.

....

The Shalan men welcomed the visitors with great respect, led them to the tents prepared for the guests after placing their camels and horses in their stables. The men whispered, "The shaikhs recognize other shaikhs."

When the camels kooshed, 'Auda was the first to set foot on al-Sarhan tribe's land after twenty days of exhausting riding. He then waited for Sharif Nasser to get off his camel, and they walked together to the tent of Shaikh Nuri al-Shalan, the prince of al-Rwala. Shaikh Nuri rose and welcomed the guests showing respect. They were then greeted warmly by the rest of the men in the shaikh's tent, "Your visit is a blessed moment."

They were invited to sit on the mats lining the parameters of the tent in a prominent location facing the entrance. They comfortably sat down resting their arms on the large hard pillows placed strategically over the mats.

The shaikh sat wrapped in his 'abaya warmly greeting them with a bright glowing face like the sun, a nose like a hawk, and piercing eyes searching out their thoughts. He called with a hoarse voice, "Coffee, coffee."

The young men standing ready to serve, responded, "The coffee is ready, uncle."[3]

The smell of the fresh coffee filled the place, the sound of the beans popping in the skillet intertwined with the rhythmic beats of the mehbash[4] crushing the freshly roasted beans and the added cardamom and saffron. The singer's beautiful voice moralizing time with his poems, tuned his rabab, warmed its strings up by the fire, and played melancholy and heartwarming melodies.

"I warn you, son, don't befriend the roasters.

If you stay with them, you soon will crow.

Don't marry someone that takes you away from your charge,

---

3. "Uncle" here is used to indicate respect and does not necessary suggest direct blood relationship.

4. A mortar-like instrument made of wood and a long stick used to crush coffee beans that creates rhythmic sound at the same time.

even if she is as pretty as the sun and the moon.
Gossip and backbiting are not worthy of you;
be wary of the bite of an ignorant friend."

The poem made the men elated, and they asked for more. The singer continued,

Your enemy who has been a foe for a long time,
if your feet tarry from the straight path, he'll tell.
Be kind to your guest, if he came to see you,
make him your friend and beloved and dear.

Excited by the poem and its melodies, the men continued to shake their heads and ask for more.

The black slaves moved around carrying hot coffee pots in their left hands and small cups in their right hands. They started by pouring coffee for the sharif, then for ‘Auda based on the subtle instruction of their master, and after that for the rest of the guests.

The prince of al-Rwala motioned to his servants, and they quickly rolled the dried tobacco cigarettes with trained fingers, lit one, and handed it to the prince, who took a deep drag with pleasure, carefully thinking about what he will say after he completed his first puff.

Za‘al fidgeted in his place listening to the sharif's lengthy oration about the sanctity of the battle. ‘Auda looked at him reprimandingly. He settled down, but still hated to see the sharif spend all that time talking about what he considered frivolous.

Nuri replied carefully, "Be positive. As you know, if you try to straighten a crooked branch, you will break it. Remember my distinguished guests that my tribe's supplies come from Horan; would you want me to cut my tribesmen's access to that land? Let today come and go; if you capture ‘Aqaba, we will talk."

Al-Bakri, the shaikh's relation by marriage, expressed his concern,

"Shaikh, I came to you two months ago and you said, 'Capture al-Wajh and we will see!'"

The prince ignored al-Bakri's insinuation and admonition. 'Auda redirected the conversation by pulling a bag of gold from his belt and calmly piling its contents in front of the prince, "The gift of the emir to Shaikh al-Shalan."

Nuri did not look at the pile of gold; he disregarded it, fully aware of how skillful and calculating 'Auda was. He knew the weakness of the desert men. Instead, he addressed the sharif laughing, "Gold is nothing for us but dirt on the hands. You know that we are the first who said, 'We are your men,' and you know the story of the 'blond horse,' the secret word between us and al-Sharif Hussein; we were his messengers between Mecca and Damascus! We are still, as we were before, his men, but I must secure the safety of my men. Here I tell them, whoever chooses to follow the prince, he is free to do so.

'Auda cleared his throat and said, "The sun can't be covered by a sieve, and the stand of the brave man is remembered. True men seek each other, and we are seeking your favor, Shaikh. We want to pass the valley peacefully."

Nuri scratched his head and contemplated what to say. He was a shrewd politician, not easily swept by emotions. He knew how to calculate his risk, how to plan carefully and make sound decisions. He thought that if he accompanied the army of the prince, he would lose the Ottomans and their flood of supplies, and if he did not, he could be the loser in the end. He knew how to hold the stick in the middle, how to choose sides, and when. "Talks are not binding, and the war is not just talks; airplanes need airplanes to stand against them, and cannons need cannons to stop them; the Turks are manipulative. They asked for my son Nawaf as a guest! They were planning to hold him hostage, a tactic we know well; I sent my nephew Trad instead as a delaying tactic. Despite all of this, if you pass through and return winners, things will work out. Honorable guests, this is a major war, not child's play; if you had skirmishes in al-Azraq, you will distract their attention, and pass."

'Auda answered enthusiastically, "This is easy; tomorrow Za'al and Lawrence will go to Wadi al-Delail and tamper with the railroad and return. We will meet them by 'Aqaba."

Nuri nodded his head, looked at Lawrence, and said, "That would be good. Arabs are annoyed by seeing the English; who could believe that the lamb plays with the wolf!"

Despite Nuri's use of a local idiom, Lawrence understood, was annoyed, but said nothing. Then, the men gratefully plunged their hands in the rice and meat dishes the shaikh of al-Rwala invited them to and said, "May God reward the hosts, and keep them victorious."

Others added, "Good laughter and good food."

'Oqab bent over Za'al's shoulder and whispered, "I hoped the Shalans would support us; they seem to be with us and yet not with us."

Za'al looked at the bright innocent face and into the eyes of the young lover who understood more than the rest of the fighters did but was still unable to decipher al-Nuri's strategy, and said, "'Oqab, you cannot tie two horses to one hitching post."

The fighters left the camp, and the bags of gold stayed behind at the rug of the shaikh's tent. In their hot treacherous ride, the men briefly talked about engaging the Turks in al-Azraq, referred to Lawrence and Za'al's assignments, and did not say much after that. A strange feeling filled their souls.

'Auda was concerned when he noticed the absence of wild animals in their path; no deer, or rabbits, or birds, except for the crows that followed the camels and pecked on the herds' backs leaving open wounds behind, startling them and annoying the foot soldiers who had to constantly shoo the birds away.

The birds disappeared for a couple of miles, but soon returned. These subtle signs told 'Auda that there was no water except the water tied to the side of their camels. He almost doubted himself because he knew that there were large wells in the area, but a few days later, his predication came true. They soon discovered that the Turkish forces intentionally poisoned all the wells in the area. Fear spread and some men complained, "It is taking long . . ." but they had no choice but to be patient.

Far to the north, the troops met with Lawrence and Za'al after they finished engaging a small group of Turkish soldiers in skirmishes by the railroad north of Azraq. Lawrence was tired and felt dizzy. Thinking that he might be suffering from heat stroke, they stopped to rest. He wrapped his head with a light white keffiyeh, laid on the ground with his large notebook, and went on writing. Meanwhile, the Bedouins watched laughing at the swift awkward movement of his pen, from the left to the right.

The stop bothered 'Auda, but he found it an opportunity to consult about the plans with Sharif Nasser, "Should we rest or attack! The first option would make the men realize how hungry they are, and the second would help us win and get closer to 'Aqaba's supplies."

"Starve! I thought the men just came out of a famine where you ate barley and millet."

"Here, there is no barley or millet; we have only our rides. If the men starve, they will eat their rides, and there will be no war."

'Auda realized that his men are more tired and disappointed than they were letting on. He knew that their legs were blistered from the long ride, and allowed them to rest their camels a little, but soon he was excited again and got up calling, "The warriors are used to being tired. Come on, men!"

The men got up enthusiastically and jumped on the saddles of their horses, joyfully chanting. The sharif, surprised by their reaction, wondered, "What makes the men jump and follow him like devils?"

Za'al replied proudly, "'Auda is a shaikh that other shaikhs draw strength from being his friends."

During the short breaks, 'Auda kept his eyes on 'Oqab and al-Kahilah hopping around like a fog, deep in the front lines. He suddenly noticed the quick turn al-Kahilah made, running back with her rider, his braids floating in the air without taking time to fix the cover over his head, screaming with a trembling voice, "The Gendarme are by the edge of the valley, uncle."

'Auda's face lit with a sudden excitement; meanwhile, the baffled Lawrence quickly collected the papers and notebooks around him. 'Auda poked him with the back of his rifle and said, "Come on, get up, and watch how the Howeitat fight."

The blood rushed in 'Auda's veins and he yelled, "Welcome death, welcome!"

His call gathered the men who jumped on the backs of their camels and horses and moved with him to meet the Turkish regiment. The Turks were shocked to see the desert fighters rushing down the hill toward them like Jinn singing, laughing, and screaming. With their abaya's floating in the air like the wings of flying bats, they sang,

> The call came, we fought, and 'Auda's name was held high,
> he returned the way he went, triumphant and strong.
> They shouted, we shouted, and we all realized
> Azrael was there waiting, that angel of death!

The Turks often saw the sight of the tribes rushing to fight each other but seeing them run down like a torrent, with colored flags and flowing thaubs, targeting them, was something they had not faced before. The surprise allowed the Bedouins to infiltrate the Turkish troops with ease. 'Oqab's horse flew, passing Lawrence and leaving behind a cloud of dust mixed with the yellow cloud produced by the burning gunpowder. The dust made the Englishman cough. Lawrence watched the battle, and his mind raced looking for words to describe the scene.

He thought, "How would I describe these flying men? What would I write?"

The dust of the battle settled; the desert fighters captured a hundred and sixty prisoners. They boasted, "Our rifles knew how to shoot."

The sharif counted the prisoners and put Nasib al-Bakri in charge because he was somewhat concerned when he saw the Bedouins' enthusiasm and pride counting the bodies of the three hundred Turkish soldiers they killed, then checking their men and pointing out that they lost only thirteen martyrs.

When the battle was over, they calmed down, but 'Auda was still full of energy; his excitement and determination escalated. He called, "We won't put up with hunger for more than three days; hooray to the braves!"

The men marched forward. 'Oqab was mounted on al-Kahilah, sitting straight as if he was standing, and she lead him to the front line. 'Auda muttered, "I like this boy; he is never thirsty or hungry . . ."

'Oqab was very thirsty, but he was good in hiding it. He was eager to reach the sea.

The scouts confirmed that Abu al-Lissan was fortified by the Ottoman troops, and that the checkpoint had a mounted cannon by the water hole. In spite of that, 'Auda decided to attack. The riders approached from the left side of the wadi while the sun was setting in their direction; this turned them into images instead of clear targets. The cannon emptied its ammunition arbitrarily without being able to aim clearly. The Bedouins infiltrated the Turkish troops, and screams filled the air. When night fell, the silence of the dead bodies spread all over Abu al-Lissan. 'Auda moved around encouraging his men and pushing them to move forward, aware of the burden caused by dragging the large number of captured soldiers behind them; something they were not accustomed to in their former raids. These were new rules of a new war; the men heard his voice loud and clear, "The captured should not be touched or killed . . ."

Tired and hungry, they attacked al-Quwaira, Khadra, and Kathar. 'Auda showed up in his black iqal and red keffiyeh, his sleeves pulled back exposing his muscular arms, looking from a distance at the sleepy port city by the Red Sea. Closer than life's vein was 'Aqaba.

'Auda looked back at his men and yelled, "Ibn Jad!"

The shaikh, Ibn Jad, came forward, and 'Auda waved his arms inviting, "There is 'Aqaba, go get it."

The heart of the brave man 'Auda chose to lead the troops pounded. He looked at the fighters and saw traces of envy in their eyes, but they followed him racing the wind, filling the air with their screams, 'How sweet is death!"

'Auda led his regiment from the other direction; his call was the loudest, "I am 'Alia's brother, and I am coming!"

'Oqab tapped al-Kahilah's neck encouraging and thought, "For your eyes, Mizna, I fight!"

All in the field, including al-Kahilah who was not comfortable being ridden, even by her beloved 'Oqab, felt the sanctity of the battle where the sword was meant to be. She sensed the excitement of her rider, and drew from his soul her strength, aware that the flowing of the blood in her veins intertwined with his pulse in the heat of the battle, aware that she was born to do this.

The Turkish soldiers scattered fighting back the attacks that closed on them from three directions. They fought in hand-to-hand combat; the Bedouins jumped from their horses stabbing the enemies with their daggers, aiming at their neck. The ones who managed to escape ran into the clay houses, hid between the palm trees, or took refuge in the mosques, and watched with despair the sea paved with English ships. Having direct contact with the Bedouins frightened them; one of the Turkish soldiers swore that he saw a bullet hit 'Auda, but it did not faze him, he stayed on the back of his horse, flying.[5] The Turkish officers ran to the mosque, terrified, leaving their horses behind. Za'al's voice called warning the men, "Do not rush to the spoils of war. Our leader gets his share first, the white horses and the camels with blond backs."

The camel riders reached the battleground after the horses. To Lawrence, the scene seemed like a dream from a distant time. Fascinated, he watched the men ravaged by the fever of war, and felt the blood in his veins rage, instigated by the shouts of the Bedouin and their calls. His soul soared. Uplifted by the ferry of the battle and its clamor, he bent and kissed the hump of his she-camel; his chest pounded. Excited, he raised

---

5. Different sources provide different accounts of what exactly happened to 'Auda during this battle; some suggest that he was grazed a couple of times but was otherwise unharmed.

his gun in the air shooting, as they do. His aimless bullet ricocheted and hit the leg of his camel Na'ma causing her to thrash, kick, and spit.[6] Her bellow startled the rest of the camels. She fell, dragging Lawrence's skinny trembling body under her, rendering him unconscious.

The soldiers heard shots from the sea reaching the old mosque causing its clay walls to collapse. Fifteen Turkish soldiers appeared through the wide gap of fighters with their hands in the air, the final remnants of the Ottoman army in the area.

Nasser's soldiers surrounded the seven hundred prisoners to protect them; meanwhile, the Bedouins gathered the bodies of the six hundred killed. By that time, Lawrence woke up from his fall and was astonished that only four Bedouins were killed in the battle.

A Bedouin ululated with excitement, "By God's name, 'Aqaba is ours now. It is ours!"

'Oqab heard the sea whisper, "'Aqaba was ours from the beginning of time . . ."

Thoughts rushed through his mind, "At last, O beautiful sea, here, the blue green spreads, and the waves crash; the corals colored by rainbows, a tremble in the heart, and a sacred moment. With the water that flows between my fingers now, we will paint the desert."

Al-Kahilah stood perplexed in front of the sea. She closed her eyes, and then opened them, trying to understand. 'Oqab dismounted and walked down the beach, soft sand and shells rattled under his feet. He walked carefully to avoid stepping on the beautiful shells and gathered some to take back to Mizna. The scent of the sea filled the place, warm like the smell of birth; an aroma alive like nothing else he knew. The movement of the tides and the sound of the waves crashing on the sandy beach stirred the love in his soul. The water touched his feet as he walked closer. He stopped; his body trembled with excitement waiting for the next wave to arrive. He watched it approaching, forming, rising, slipping at the edge of the sand,

---

6. The tribal and other sources provide varying details of how Lawrence was injured during this battle.

spreading on the beach, tickling his feet again; and with tremendous joy, he celebrated. The sea called him for another embrace, and he joyfully yelled, "Water, here's the water, Mizna."

Like a naïve child, he ran into the waves, welcomed the sea with open arms, soaking his thirsty chest. Not bothered by the weight of his wet clothes, he threw himself into the lap of the warm and living sea. His soul rejoiced, and he knew that Mizna was there with him at that moment.

"Your beauty is my desire, and the sea is your scent, your kohl, and the henna in your braids; despite my heavy clothes, I feel like I am flying through a constellation. Like the joy of our first reunion in our isolated oasis, away from this world, is this reunion."

He danced with the waves. Elated, he felt the touch of the sea on his face and was surprised to taste the salt it left on his lips. The sea is salty, he knew that, why was he surprised!

"You, the water, and I, are one. I wish your eyes could see this, my father the sage, and witness my joy and the gladness that fills my heart."

Suddenly, 'Oqab felt that someone was watching him. He looked around and saw in the far distance the English barges. Instantly, his heart became heavy. He pulled his wet body out of the water, rested on a fallen tree, leaning on its burned trunk, annoyed with the sudden heavy feeling that took his joy away.

The prince arrived in 'Aqaba and stood by the sea, contemplating, watching the nearby shore of Um al-Rashash, and realizing that 'Aqaba offered a strategic position for the British, and that the battle had started.

Lawrence rode his she-camel, Na'ma, after he checked her slight wound and went through al-Naqab to the Suez Canal to file his report and double his effort to secure supplies for the army in 'Aqaba, which was growing daily. Meanwhile, Ja'far al-'Askari rushed back to Cairo to check on his family.

'Auda led his men through the mountainous path until he reached the highest and clearest point. He stood with his fighters on the top, watched the stretch of land below, scratched his head, and wondered, "Will the

Turks really leave and let the seed of freedom grow in this desolate and salty land?" He then turned to Za'al who walked behind him silently, and said, "Those who want to join us let them come to al-Quwaira. It is easy to win the land, but it is another thing to keep it. We are at a time that consumes all, the green and the dry; I want to devour time, chew it with my teeth and grab it with my hands." 'Auda and his men headed home.

The women rushed to meet the men, letting their hair down, singing,

> Welcome to the horses and to their riders,
> Abu 'Inad mounting, leading his braves.

Mizna sang with a trembling voice,

> Welcome to the horse that came when the pigeons cooed,
> mounting his horse, 'Oqab, the twin of my soul.

The sage came out of his cave, and sensing 'Oqab's presence among the returning men, his heart was at peace. Abu al-Kabayer recited,

> I start by mentioning the one above all,
> God of the land and all who dwell on it.
> Rise, 'Ali, you're an honor to every brave man,
> we saddled a horse that traversed lush land.
> Mounted by a boy with only good deeds,
> he used to cross valleys and harsh terrains.
> The horses groaned, tired, when he dismounted,
> from the battle of Abu Tayeh who never loses."

Dhaylan shoved him teasing, "For God's sake, this is an old poem. Don't you have a new one? Did your poetry dry up?"

Dhaylan's criticism did not dampen Abu al-Kabayer's enthusiasm; he replied, "These days are so great that the poems cannot describe, and the sound of the rababa cannot do them justice."

'Oqab's heart was searching for Mizna; he saw her walking toward him with steady steps. His soul fluttered, longing to be united with hers. Silence prevailed in the distance between them despite the chaos and clamor of the crowd searching for and meeting their loved ones. They met, walked side by side, followed by al-Kahilah that knew when to go and when to stop. In the tent, the fronds gave them the privacy they needed. They drew near, she asked, "Did you see the water, 'Oqab?"

"I saw it."

With his cracked fingers, he touched the locks of her hair, came closer, and smelled her. The scent of musk filled the tent; she basked in his scent and was lost in the sea of 'Aqaba. He braided her hair into small braids that rested on her trembling breasts; with her fingers, she untangled his long hair that had not been braided since he left for the battlefield. With the sense of a lover, she found between his locks the scent of the desert mixed with dust and ashes from his treacherous journey. Slowly, they melted into each other. He held her tight, and they became again, as they were in time before time—one. He embraced her, and they were intertwined. He sweated, and she trembled, and they became engulfed in multiple and joyful climaxes. She told herself, "He was a mirage when he left, and now returned a sea; he went a boy and came back a man." Meanwhile, he told himself, "She was a flower and became a full-grown tree; she was a girl and became a woman."

9.

....

The eye cannot be lent to someone to cry with, and the sword
cannot be handed to the enemies to fight with.

—from *The Biography of the Princess with Intention*

'Oqab sat on the floor, cross-legged, in the presence of the sage, "I rode behind them and felt as if I were in front of them. The desert opened like a wild lily that grew up inside me, like Mizna's eyes. I heard the waves clap, gush, and call to me personally. I heard every grain of sand in 'Aqaba call my name. Was I hallucinating, father?"

"The land does not trick its children. It owns their souls and they become eternal; it owns their blood and reveals to them her secrets. She opens her body wide and showers her martyrs with her sweet fragrances and scents. She covers the damned and abased with the scent of hyena's urine, and they take it with them to their graves, while the sincere and righteous ones walk toward light and life."

"How could we know in advance?"

"People do not know, but the honorable free ones know how to hunt the hyenas and how to make their bright gray hides into rababs to play melodies that tell of the pain of their longing . . . This is when the sun of your insight glows within you. It is a glorious moment that separates light from darkness, like al-Farooq, the one who distinguishes truth from falsehood.[1] It is this insight that held your sword back from participating in the tribal raids and left it free searching for the true cause."

'Oqab understood some and missed some of what the sage said.

The sage stretched his arm and said, "Get up, don't stay long in the darkness of the cave; wisdom is inside you, and the truth is under the sunlight. While you are between this and that, winning and losing . . . wisdom is outside, in the open, that is what it lends its voice to."

The change in 'Oqab's life was amazing. Since his marriage and participation in the battle at 'Aqaba, he was welcomed in the shaikh's tent and participated in the race for the medal. Full-heartedly he embraced the irony that marriage had turned him from a hermit to a man.

As soon as the desert sun rose, yellow and gentle at the start of the day, drying the dewdrops of dawn, 'Oqab and Mizna left their tent. Mizna left first carrying the milk pail and walked to her she-camel. She gently pulled the camel's calf close to the mother. He rubbed his head on her leg, and she moved to welcome him. With light pressure, Mizna's fingers gently pulled on the camel's udder; they flowed with milk that streamed into the pail. When the pail was filled with warm milk and a thick layer of froth, she carried it away and said, "This is for the sage."

She then milked a little more into a small cup and brought it close to 'Oqab's mouth to drink. He gently brought the opposite side of the cup to her mouth, and they drank together and kissed, licking the traces of milk from each other's lips. She gave him a keffiyeh, she wove its fringes while he was gone. He looked at her fondly and pulled her closer to him. She slipped from between his arms and gently sang,

"Leaning on your sword, you wounded me with your love;
your love divulged my secret, to all God's creatures!"

---

1. The title of Omar bin al-Khattāb (579–644), one of the most powerful and influential Muslim caliphs and a senior companion of Prophet Muhammad. He succeeded Abu Baker as the second caliph and was an expert and just Muslim jurist. This earned him the title *al-Farooq* (the one who distinguishes between right and wrong).

Listening to her sing made him insanely want her. He drew her to him in a passionate embrace, and when she gently resisted, he said, "Are you a Jinn or a woman?"

She replied, "I am a doe, o son of the free tiercel."

....

The sun came out shedding its light on the bustling life at the camp. 'Oqab carefully fixed the keffiyeh on his head and joined the men at the shaikh's tent. Something exciting was taking place today; the prince sent 'Auda a gift from al-Sharif Hussein bin Ali of Mecca. The men crowded, elbowing each other trying to get a good look at the gold-gilded sword ornamented with precious jewels. Even though 'Auda owned many rare Hijazi swords, Yemeni daggers, British and German rifles, and one of a kind guns, this was different. It was special. It filled him with pride. He held it up for all to see with love and pride. He then allowed his son Muhammed to carry it and raise it high; the boy's fragile body bent under its weight. The men laughed, and 'Oqab looked at the sword and was overwhelmed with a mysterious feeling of nobility. He thought to himself, this was not only 'Auda's sword, it was the sword of all the men in the tribe who fought in the war; it was his sword too. Mizna must see it. Wasn't she the one who sang this morning about him and the sword? He must bring her to see it; that would make her happy.

Za'al announced, "Uncle, you have guests."

The movement increased at al-Quwaira camp in preparation for the visit of the three shaikhs of the peasant tribes in the region. They had heard of the financial challenge 'Auda was facing in his efforts to gather fighters and were confident that they would succeed in their mission.

They told 'Auda, "You cannot compare a needle to a drill; war is a red death, we have nothing to do with it. We greatly respect the son of the sharif, but the land is for the caliph from the day we were born, and the Turks protect our villages and crops."

'Auda thought, "The peasants are ruled by seasons and have their crops to worry about, but he is the son of the open land and he owns the wide sky. Who could steal the sky from him?"

"What are you thinking, Shaikh?" asked Diab al-'Oran troubled by the shaikh's long silence, worried that they had offended him by mentioning the role of the Turks in protecting the farmers' crops from Bedouin raids. Hussein Krayshan tried to steer the conversation to where he thought he might attract the interest of the Bedouin shaikh, so he assured him that the Turks' supplies of money and food would never stop.

'Auda replied laughing, "The Turks feed the mouth so that the eye ignores what it sees. I don't think we want to be controlled!"

Shaikh Daifallah Abu al-Sqour realized that 'Auda was being facetious, and that by his comment, he had dismissed what they had to offer, so he looked for a better way to entice him, "We know that it is not about food, and we know that you could feed all the Arabs if you wished. It is about making you an emir and giving you an emirate no one would dispute. This is your day 'Auda, a chance to be the prince of the desert; no camel will rise or sit without your orders."

The shaikh finished his talk, meanwhile Muhammad al-Dhaylan fidgeted looking in Za'al's face for an answer or a gesture that could get 'Auda engaged. 'Auda was busy looking at 'Oqab's face and spontaneously smiled thinking that 'Oqab was the soul the sage planted among them to stop such offers. The shaikh looked at the three messengers of the Turks who often trembled at the sound of his horses during his raids and thought of the long history of animosity between them. They planted, and he raided and took. Today, things are different. He sees himself in a different light; he sees himself heading a great army out of the desert, spreading, bringing together cities, desert camps, and villages. He could see in his mind's eyes the backs of the Turks, retreating.

He stirred the sand with the jagged knife in his hand, slightly lifted the edge of the colorful carpet that he was sitting on and fixed a surreptitious gaze at its corner. The place was drenched in silence. Nothing moved except the dagger of the shaikh and the breaths of the men. When he realized that he was silent for too long with no reason for that, he whispered welcoming his guests, "God's blessings be upon the shaikhs."

'Oqab's heart beat like a hollow drum, and the men in the tent replied, "God's greetings be upon you."

The shaikh looked at the entrance of the tent where the poet usually sat, and called on him, "Dayoud, come close, and tell us of the story of the foxes and the dogs."

Dayoud beamed proudly; the shaikh was calling on him to send a message. In the details of the stories that he often told lay the answer to the visitor's request. He recited, "Praised be the Prophet, more praise upon him.

"Dear distinguished listener, from the beginning of creation, there has been animosity between the dogs and the foxes. Despite their common ancestry, they deeply hated each other. One day, the foxes grew tired of this. Their leader suggested that they write a call for peace and send it with the youngest and fastest among them, and say in it, 'There is no need for animosity anymore. Let us extend our hands to each other and bring about peace.' The foxes sent their letter and put their affairs in the hands of God.

"The messenger crossed the land and traversed terrains, and when he arrived at the dogs' camp, he raised the letter high and said, 'Rejoice. I come to you with good news.'

"The dogs barked, clenched their teeth, and looked with hateful eyes, thinking, 'You came to us with your own feet.'

"He knew that they intended to harm him, and yelled, 'Sons of a bitches, read my letter first, and judge my offer after that.'

"The dogs did not give him time to explain. They knocked him to the ground, cut his letter into pieces, scattered it over the sand, plucked his beard, and if it was not for his youth and strength, he would have not been able to escape. He went back to his people, swollen, bleeding, and with his tail cut. His people said, 'Mercy be on the soul of your parents, did you go there to fight or to bring about peace?'

"He said, 'How wasted is good among those who do not deserve it.'

"They replied, 'Why didn't you have them read the letter stamped with the seal of our shaikhs.'

"He laughed and said, 'When you sent me, wise ones, to the land of the ignorant, you did not know that they do not read and write, but to tell you the truth, they know well how to fight and bite and I suggest we learn their language.'"

'Auda's men signaled their approval of the tale told by their nods and short compliments. Dayoud sat basking in his friends' praise, "Blessed be your tongue."

The visitors fidgeted, and lost hope as they figured out the meaning of the story.

'Auda spoke, "Good men, if you searched my body, you will see what will astonish you. There is no place on it that does not carry the scars of a sword, or the stabs of a dagger. For a man that knows war well, I am surprised that death has not caught up with me. This land of ours is like a good body with no place in it left that the Turks have not wounded with their swords and actions. How could you forget?"

"We did not. We know that they would not even piss on a wounded sore [to help it heal]."[2]

"You see! Are we wrong to want to pull out our thorns by ourselves? By God's help, I mean to purify the land from their tyranny, a mission that I would not abandon if they gave me all the money in the world, and the treasurers of King Solomon. I desire nothing. I have promised the emir, and we do not break our promises." Then he quickly added, "Welcome to the guests."

The men left with a clear brief message; Dhaylan clapped his hands in approval, Za'al laughed, and 'Oqab hurried to Mizna for a long embrace.

"We do not know where water springs from, as if it is pouring out from my hands."

....

---

2. An old local Arabic saying.

Dhaylan sneaked into 'Auda's tent while he was busy training his son to ride, stole his seal from a leather bag hanging on the tent's pole, and wrote a short letter to the Turkish governor of Ma'an asking for enough gold to please his rebellious men and boldly stamped it with 'Auda's seal. He thought, "If the prince's supplies did not arrive, the Turk's will."

Muhammad Dhaylan did not intend to hide the matter from 'Auda. He delayed telling him for a couple of days to guarantee that the letter will go through. 'Auda was surprised by Dhaylan's confession and was angered by his action, but he stopped himself from punishing him for 'Alia's sake. Then, he thought about the matter and laughed when Dhaylan explained, "War is a trick, and we need the money."

Ma'an's Governor was surprised by 'Auda's letter, especially after he heard his reply to the shaikhs and his strong devotion to the rebelling sharif. He was first confused, and then decided that the greed of the Bedouin is stronger than his loyalty, which he was willing to sell for gold. He loaded two camels with gold and supplies and sent them, guarded by three of his men, to al-Quwaira, a gift to 'Auda, confident that his success where the Arab shaikhs failed would make him famous and raise his status in the capital.

'Auda was ready. He took two of his men with him, and they hid behind the sharp rocks, waiting for the gifts of the Ottoman government. As soon as they saw the caravan of gold and supplies, 'Auda ascended toward it with his two masked men yelling loudly. One of the guards yelled, "You will regret this raid, go back! These are gifts to a shaikh that does not forgive; they are for 'Auda."

The shaikh laughed and took off his mask; the men saw his face and ran away terrified. 'Auda stopped them.

The men moved the gifts and placed them on his camel. 'Auda ordered the soldiers to strip naked and return to the governor's camp. They thanked God and ran like a storm; 'Auda's men watched the soldiers run and dropped to the ground, laughing so hard.

'Auda returned with his spoils to al-Quwaira, and the Bedouins were entertained that night by the story of naked soldiers sent back to the governor of Ma'an. Meanwhile, 'Auda was getting ready to join the rebels that spread throughout 'Aqaba. Their numbers multiplied with the arrival of Nuri al-Said and his troops and the enlistment of Bedouins from the Rwala, Zawaideh, Darawsheh, Taqaiqa, and Zalbani tribes, and later by civilian volunteers from Damascus.

In the evenings at camp, on good days, the men sat around the campfire talking as if they were on a hunting trip, not at war. At other times, they were consumed by worries. Some worried about the English that Mawlood Mukhles had with him; Ja'far was concerned about the way the troops were organized and was angry over not receiving a military title. By constantly talking about it, he made the men anxious. At this time, Faisal sent Sharif Abdul-Muin and Mawlood Mukhles to set camp in Wadi Musa to monitor the way from Hijaz strategically. The dreams of the sharif stretched toward Damascus ignoring Allenby's orders not to move beyond 'Aqaba.[3]

---

3. Marshal Field Edmund Henry Hynman Allenby, First Viscount Allenby (23 April 1861–14 May 1936) was an English soldier and British Imperial Governor. He fought in the Second Boer War and also in the First World War in which he commanded T. E. Lawrence, and led the British Empire's Egyptian Expeditionary Force (EEF) during the campaign against the Ottoman Empire, capturing many territories including Palestine and the Jordan Valley and later with the support of the Desert Mounted Force and Arab troops, captured Damascus and advanced into northern Syria. He continued to serve in the region as High Commissioner for Egypt and Sudan from 1919 until 1925.

10.

....

Trod light, the clay of the land is made of nothing
but from the flesh of these bodies.

—Abu al-'Ala al-Ma'ari[1]

The land spoke, only her lovers heard her say, "Because I am the beginning and I am the end, because I was here before you, my flesh holds the memory of your footsteps. Those of you who touched my flesh with your bare feet, I know your scent and the heavy weight you carry. I kept the names of my lovers—the noble ones and the lowly amongst you; those who touched me with greed and malice, and those who gave their lives for my glory. I know the salty taste of your tears, how often it touched my thirsty lips; I soaked it in, but my thirst was never quenched. I know the sound of confessions, it seeped through my pores, and I take it in. I know the taste of blood when it gushes from the wounds, it runs in rivers into me; I drink it to my fill. I can distinguish between one blood and another. The blood of betrayal, I reject. I do not let it rest at my core. It nauseates me and I spit it out. On the other hand, the blood of great love makes me shiver, crave it, feel it, embrace it, and I let it root inside me.

---

1. Abu al-'Ala' al-Ma'arri (December 973–May 1057) was a blind Arab philosopher and poet. Al-Ma'arri held and expressed an irreligious worldview, which was met with controversy, but in spite of it, he is regarded as one of the greatest classical Arabic poets.

"I know you one by one, since I gave my glory to my son, but he betrayed me, tempted with desire. The head of the martyr was beautiful on the golden plate.[2] I spilled my hot tears over him. I offer you my tears; taste them. Since that distant time, you have been passing over my body, columns of horses and riders, your footsteps leaving cracks in my frame, thirsty, yearning for you. What death awaits! Tears, sweat, and blood. I am as I was at the beginning of time, the martyr, the martyrdom, and the witness; as I was before, I will always be.

"I love the hooves of the horses touching my side. I love this young man from Quraysh, and 'Oqab, my flesh and blood, the secret I placed in the womb of the falcon, watered from the vein of my life, and left in the care of my sage. Here he comes, my son, my father, my brother, and my lover, riding al-Kahilah, the pride of all brave men, I know him well.

"My body aches from the footsteps of strangers that came from far away worlds, moving their bodies with pride. They cannot handle my short temper and the harshness of my paths and do not know the secrets of my generosity. If they trod the path of my lovers, they panic, and I cast them off. I have no need for strangers. I have my lovers. 'Auda's eyes that adore me suffice; I rest on 'Oqab's arm, and he rests on mine. The dreams of the Hashemite matter to me, the anger of the Iraqi is about me, and the scream of the Syrian tells who am I and how I feel. To them, I make myself accessible and reveal my treasure; their blood is the thing I yearn for."

....

This is the time for longing and love, and the place where the horses and the riders rest. My eyes are on the sun, unblinking, and the sun that dried the chest of the desert will eventually give up. Summer wrapped 'Aqaba, and the scent of salt and corals wafted softly from the sea, mysterious, alive in the hearts of men that surged from everywhere.

---

2. In reference to the head of John the Baptist that was placed on a golden platter and presented to Salome, the daughter of Herod II and Herodias.

This is the station of love; the plants were not dry as before; they poked their blue stems through the piles of smooth rocks. I could no longer see the beautiful black iris growing between the flints; even the tender 'Aqaba grass that competes with the sand was not there anymore. The desert became a playground for the sun, the fighters, and love. I bent on my knee, touched the barrel of my gun, as if it were Mizna's soft body and her flowing hair. The smell of gunpowder made my head spin. I held my gun closer and was lost thinking of her.

Wadi Rum glowed like amber; al-Kahilah flew like a true thoroughbred horse, and the camels caught the fever of the race and ran. The sound of the metal rubbing the rails when the train approached al-Mdawara was melodic. When Salem carried the dynamite, the death sticks, as Lawrence called it, carefully between his fingers, death came close, but no one cared! We waited for Salem to plant the explosives under the crossing. It exploded and the place trembled. You could no longer hear the train or see the steam billowing in the air. Dust and black smoke were everywhere, the horses neighed, and the men yelled. There were sixteen of us there. The spoils of the raid were many. The prisoners raised their hands over their heads and walked through the columns of fighters, frightened. A Bedouin yelled, "We performed miracles. Ask the prince, where is the gold?"

The voice of the sage inside me warned, "This is not the point of the fight."

Lawrence was astonished at the sight of the colorful, ornately designed carpet that he looted; he had never seen one that beautiful. He took the best; its squares, triangles, arches, and colors befit only your body, Mizna, but this is not the place to worry about that, forgive me!

The sun was ready to set; Bedouins, Syrian, Iraqis, and others from lands we never heard of passed by; their clamor quieted down when the evening pulled its orange spread stitched with golden rays over the body of the sky. It made me think about the warmth of your bosom; my fingers touched the sand of 'Aqaba, and my heart gushed with love. Why did our river stop? Why does it not continue its journey through the desert to the sea of 'Aqaba? How sad it is when the rivers do not reach the seas! O thirsty river, drink from the flowing river of my soul. Only the North Star that shines in the far distance tempts me, pulls my soul to it, but the journey is hard to take. Al-Buraq[3] felt my agony and longing and permitted me to ride. I spread the wings of love, with my heart bleeding, eager for my Mi'raj and the end of my holy quest.[4] Suhail was my aim;[5] the sky opened its doors and bathed me in its light. In the silence of the night, the voices vanished, and the colors intertwined in the magenta sky. The wind howled in the quietness of the night; a song split the heart and lifted me to paradise.

A noise brought me back to the camp . . . From the summits of Auras Mountains?[6] Where are these mountains? Who is this newcomer with his companions roaming the camp and creating all this noise? I saw him, Abdulkader el-Djezairi,[7] riding his horse, standing above the crowd with his learned companions, al-Qarawiyyin,[8] chanting, and al-Qadry on his horse carrying a banner on a pole, waving it in the air.

My heart was forever full. I landed on Suhail, reached heaven, sat down and held my rifle, away from the feverish celebration, glued to the hem of the colorful flapping flag, my heart ponding, racing up the pole, reaching for the hoisted flag raised for the first time. History turned, brought back the memories of the ones we love and the ones we hate, the ones who lifted us, and the ones who brought us down. The sound of the horses echoed the stories buried long ago, and the colors of the flag spoke about us. The

---

3. A mythical creature from the Islamic tradition, a winged steed from heaven that is said to have carried Prophet Muhammad from Mecca to Jerusalem and back during the Isra' and Mi'raj or "Night Journey" as recounted in hadith literature.

4. The point of arrival in the holy journey of Prophet Muhammad to heaven and back.

5. Suhail is the Arabic name for Canopus (Alpha Carinae), the second brightest star in the night sky.

6. Mountains in southern Jordan surrounding the city of Tafilah.

7. The grandson of Abdelkader bin Muhieddine (6 September 1808–26 May 1883), known as Emir Abdelkader el-Djezairi, the Algerian religious scholar and military leader who successfully led the struggle against the French colonial powers in Alger in the mid-nineteenth century.

8. Referring the Algerian Islamic scholars and fighters who came with el-Djezairi from al-Qarawiyyin, the oldest mosque and university in North Africa.

white was pride that recalled the troops of Khalid and Omar raising the banner of the Umayyad Dynasty; the darkness in the black evoked the pain of al-Hassan and al-Hussein and what the 'Abbasids left behind;[9] the lush of the green waved Fatimid's melodies and the images of Cairo being built by its caliph. History was poured into a flag decorated with traces of my blood all the way back to the Kaaba; the star pierced my heart, burned me, then gathered my ashes in its seven corners, and I prayerfully recited, "In the name of God, the infinitely Compassionate and Merciful. Praised be God, the Lord of all the worlds. The Compassionate, the Merciful, the Ruler on the Day of Reckoning. You alone do we worship, and You alone do we ask for help. Guide us on the straight path, the path of those who have received your grace; not the path of the ones who have brought down your wrath, nor of those who wander astray."[10]

The past, the present, the future, the body, the soul, al-Jafar, Petra, Ammon, 'Aqaba, Ma'an, al-Sharia,[11] Saint George,[12] John the Baptist,[13] the flags of Ja'far,[14] Mu'tah,[15] Yarmouk,[16] our horses, palm trees, rocks, tents, dreams, Damascus, the sword, love, and worship; all that was and was

---

9. The sons of 'Ali, the cousin and companion of Prophet Muhammad, who were slaughtered by the Umayyad army in a brutal battle that came to symbolizes oppression and later became the impetus of Shia Islam.

10. Surat al-Fatihah is the first chapter of the Quran. It's seven verses are recited by Muslims as a prayer for guidance and an important part of the Muslim's obligatory prayer.

11. A list of cities and places in Jordan.

12. Recognized by Arab Christians and Muslims alike as a saint called "al-Khadr."

13. Known as Yuhana in Arabic scripture.

14. Ja'far bin Abi Talib (c. 590–629 CE), also known as Ja'far al-Tayyar, was a companion of Prophet Muhammad and his cousin. He was known for his courage and bravery, especially as the standard-bearer during the Battle of Mu'tah against the Byzantines. It is said that he fought until both his arms were cut off before he was eventually killed, still carrying the flag.

15. The Battle of Mu'tah was fought in September 629 CE near the village of Mu'tah, east of the Jordan River and Karak, between the forces of Prophet Muhammad and the forces of the Byzantine Empire.

16. The Battle of Yarmouk was a major battle between the Byzantine army and the Muslim Arab forces. It consisted of a series of engagements that lasted for six days in August 636, near the Yarmouk River by the Syria-Jordan border, and ended with a decisive victory which concluded Byzantine rule in the region.

meant to be; all that passed and what remained; the drops of my blood; all of me, all of us, everything rose and became part of the flapping flag.

I know now what resurrected me from my slumber. It was the flag; it baptized me in the scents and the ashes of the past, took me back to where I was born, where the free falcon held my body in hers, guarded me until I was found, in this place and at this time. My eyes beheld the image of this flag, and my soul soared to it; it is the scale of justice that stands the passing of time.

In the morning, I was able to see clearly the colors of the hoisted flag that Sharif Hussein of Mecca sent. All were gazing at it and absorbing its beauty; I, on the other hand, had already fallen in love with it when it arrived during the blurry night. I felt one with it. Al-Kahilah was like me, skipping in the stable, whispering to me. I understood what she meant to say. Like everyone else in the camp, we were entertained watching the game of horsemanship that el-Djezairi and Sharif Ali al-Harthy played.

11.

....

Since I was not ignorant, I realized from the beginning that if we
won the war, our promises to the Arabs would be dead paper;
but Arab enthusiasm was our tool to win the war in the East;
of course, I constantly felt bitterness and shame.

—Lawrence

The campground was filled with horses and riders. El-Djezairi kept
them occupied with the stories he told of the legendary heroism
of his grandfather who gave him his name, and his own journey in
exile that took him to Damascus, a destiny that led him to join the revolt.
He turned his back to the few blue-eyed English officers in the camp and
refused to deal with them. In the evenings, he warmed the hearts of the
crowd in Faisal's tent with his poems about the glorious past.

"Our deeds were righteous, high above all blame,
what I say is supported by the things we retained.
If we knew pure water could bring us shame,
we would've been patient, stayed thirsty, not complained."

The men at the camp liked to watch him race the handsome, joyful
Sharif 'Ali al-Harthy, bragging, "This is what my grandfather would do."
He touched the horse's shoulder with his chest, stroked her neck, and

stood on her back straight, like an arrow, flipping from one side to the other while she stood still.

When it was al-Harthy's turn, he gently kicked the side of his camel; it bolted like a dart. He raced wearing his Hijazi garb. Like a fleeting ghost, he ran parallel to his she-camel, waited for her to draw near, then jumped up and climbed her hump while the crowds cheered.

When el-Djezairi missed home, he raced his horse; pulled his feet out of the stirrups and stood on the saddle; then bent, pulled his rifle, aimed, and shot, hitting his mark no matter what it was while the horse was still running, showered by the crowd's awe and admiration. When the spectacle ended, he led his horse in a dance to the melodies of a flute played by a shepherd saluting the fantastic performance.

After the show, 'Oqab leaned and rested his head on al-Kahilah's chest, but soon heard 'Auda calling to practice shooting. The Bedouin sharpshooters stood in line taking turns firing; and at the other side of the camp, Ja'far was rearranging the troops.

The tent of the prince was busy welcoming his older brother 'Ali. Faisal's job was not easy, even his father, the shaikh in Mecca, realized the difficulty in managing such diversity in one army. He warned him to keep the two rivals, Shaikh 'Auda and Hamad al-Jazi, apart, advised him to hold back on giving Ja'far high military titles to help curb his ambitions, and brought Faisal's attention to the volatile emotions of el-Djezairi. Further, Faisal had to resolve the numerous grievances from all parties, like the Syrians complaining that the Iraqis were better paid although the Syrians were the first to support the revolt; at every step, there was a bomb waiting to explode. Faisal smoked his way through it all, kept the dream alive, realizing that it could not happen without managing all these conflicts. He figured that the presence of his well-respected brother would help in his plan to take al-Azraq away from the Turks by chopping trees to create a path in a terrain that was too muddy for the camels to travel on. Such plans required fortitude and patience, a trait many people in the camp did not have.

On the night before embarking on their mission, el-Djezairi publicly complained about the presence of the Englishman and looked at Lawrence with disdain when he saw him wearing the Hijazi outfit, dragging his thaub behind. The way he looked at Lawrence worried all, but Lawrence avoided a confrontation by quickly leaving the tent. The prince said calmly, "We fight with their money; war requires compromise."

El-Djezairi protested, "I will not serve with a spy."

Despite his objection the night before, el-Djezairi joined at dawn the expedition that included Lawrence and Captain George Lloyd, and for the first time, they were accompanied by an Indian troop led by Hassan Shah.[1]

By the borders of Bayer, the soldiers trailed behind; they looked weak, tired, and pale. Their morale was dampened by the scarcity of food and water. Their leader Hassan Shah stayed with them in Azraq, and soon they were replaced by Bedouins from the Sarhan tribe and selected men from al-Ziben tribe who were more accustomed to the harshness of the land.

The desert witnessed a strange crowd pass its land that day; they caroused wherever they went, their voices and movements intermingled when they sang. El-Djezairi commented, "If we knew that pure water lead to sin . . . !"[2]

Al-Sharif 'Ali politely smiled, 'Auda shook his head in disapproval, Lawrence fidgeted, held his camel back and left a distance between himself and the Arab leaders. Al-Kahilah fretted objecting to changing the pace; 'Oqab tapped her neck calming her down and promised to go faster. Suddenly, the horse was startled, 'Oqab's heart pounded, and the rest of the horses and camels stopped. They could see Bayer's wells from the distance, and the crowd of thirsty men and animals rushed to it. A great noise the desert was not familiar with roared in the distant sky followed by a big explosion that shook the ground and stopped them in their tracks.

---

1. The Indian troop led by Hassan Shah and accompanied by the desert fighters later liberated Haifa and Akka from Ottoman control.

2. This is part of a line from a famous poem by Abdulkader el-Djezairi who was a poet in addition being an Algerian rebel with experience fighting the French occupiers in his own homeland. The rest of the line states, "We would have endured thirst."

Lawrence laughed sarcastically, and when the sharif scolded him with his glance, he shook his shoulders and explained, "It is the sound of Allenby's machine guns in Palestine."

The British went in with all their might showing their military superiority. The sharif was pleased, and some cheered. This angered el-Djezairi who muttered with trembling voice, "Do not rejoice; these are the machine guns of the infidels killing the Muslims."

A strange feeling of dismay filled their hearts, the first real remarks that emphasized the ties between the Arabs and the Turks. The presence of the Englishman among them was awkward, and the Arabs' support of him became worrisome, but there was more to the matter. In seconds, the connection planted in the minds of the men by el-Djezairi's emotional remark dissipated when the fighters recalled the gallows, blood, injustice, hunger, deprivation, and the long trail of pain and slavery the Ottoman left behind despite their common faith. The religious ties were soon overshadowed by a dream of a homeland, and a hope of ending forever the tyranny of the Turks and the days of Safarbarlik.[3] Getting close to the water changed the men's attention. They rushed with their horses and camels to the wells. El-Djezairi's comments were lost in the commotion; this compounded his dismay and feeling of estrangement.

In the evening, 'Oqab found a place to be with al-Kahilah alone recalling the image of his beloved. He could feel her presence, watching his every move, holding his tired body, sheltering him with her tender glances, filling his soul with calmness and reassurances. He had no interest in spending time with the tired and weary fighters. Instead, he fixed his glance on the bright moon, a silver cylinder in the heart of the sky surrounded by a garment of glittering stars. He thought, "I long to be cuddled in the bosom of the universe and to borrow the skin of the silver moon to protect me in

---

3. Safarberlik is the forced migration orchestrated by the Ottoman government, especially during the Balkan wars and World War I, which displaced local populations and replaced them with military troops. This action resulted in a host of atrocities perpetrated at these times. One of these major operations took place in 1915 in Medina, on the Arabian Peninsula.

my travel, to give me the strength to capture the sunrays and turn them into beautiful, sweet dreams that light my nights. I wish it would lend me its glory and take away my heart, fill it with light, scatter it in the land like seeds, and water it with its pure glistening light, as the river gives life to its crops."

The men who dismounted by the camp of Shaikh Mifleh, the leader of Bani Sakhr, were pleased with the warm welcome they received, except el-Djezairi who was still frustrated by the incident that took place earlier. Meanwhile, the sharif was trying to underplay the argument that took place between the British and French officers in a language that the Arab fighters did not understand. This annoyed the leaders, but the Bedouins found it funny; 'Oqab laughed without understanding why that amused him too. This cheered him up despite the sight of Shaikh Mifleh's horse constantly digging with its front hoof the sand around the shaikh's tent. The men noticed and kicked the horse trying to stop her, but she kept digging. When they managed to push her away, she would calm down a little, and then start digging again. The men yelled at her, "By God's name, hold back your evil curse, horse."

'Oqab kept himself occupied watching the strangers' argument and the actions of Shaikh Mifleh's horse; meanwhile, the host's men generously prepared dinner for everyone. The guests gathered around the trays filled with rice and meat satisfying their hunger. 'Auda reciprocated by inviting the shaikh and his men to dinner in his camp, "To feed the men is a debt to be repaid."

'Oqab drank some of the yogurt broth the meat was cooked in and returned to al-Kahilah. Darkness wrapped the desert with its cloak, calmed his doubts and worries, and allowed his soul to soar to his beloved. He laid down, held his rifle, and touched the ground; it was dry and thirsty. To his surprise, he felt its sadness creep into his soul. Dry was the land, and so was his body, rifle, and horse. He did not like the way his moods swung. He was happy yesterday, and today he was lying on the bare ground, his heart's beats synchronized with the land, as if it were part of his own body; he sought its refuge from the midday heat, scorched by the wind of defeat. When the sun fully disappeared behind the horizon, he stared at the desert, became engulfed in its emptiness, and screamed, "Do I exist? In a land of absence, who am I? The desert of this land rebelled against us, so we sold the glory to Caesar, and gave him the pupils of our eyes, and then cried in sadness.

"How can we quench the thirst of this universe? What gifts should we offer? Our blood?"

The cry of the land intensified beneath the length of 'Oqab's body lying down, listening to her pain. He listened with all his senses; his soul longed for a deeper, farther, and sweeter place, a new day—tomorrow. The young man who slept holding his rifle, reciting softly, "O Thou revealer of mysteries, and dispeller of what is in the heart and souls,"[4] was visited in his sleep by friendly ghosts; thus he woke up with a trembling heart and the images of al-Kahilah's eyes, Mizna's braids, and the thirst of the land intertwined forming one universe. Next to where he slept, he noticed for the first time, a cactus plant, tall, strong, and proud; green in a sea of dreary yellow desert; decorated with sharp needles and thorns, branching out into three sections, like a beautiful painting. At the tip of one of its branches grew a delicate flower, stunning purple in color, like nothing of the desert colors around it. Where did it come from? What great roots protected the water in the core of the desert and sent it to the body of the cactus to grow and produce this beautiful flower!

In the blurriness of dawn, al-Kahilah's eyes were watching him. He felt his body's lightness and spontaneously said to the cactus flower, "Good morning."

....

They arrived at al-Azraq. The water they picked up earlier from Bayer's wells made it easier to continue their journey. The summer was in its final

---

4. Quran, Surat al-Nur, 24:35.

days; they felt confident about their mission and doubted the news that el-Djezairi was spreading regarding his plans to leave them and their allies, the English, and raise with al-Druze the banner of the revolt, leading it in a different direction. But, in the darkness of the night, el-Djezairi and his company left. The rest of the men continued their journey quietly. They were used to men coming and going into their regiment, which had no specific order; what harm would it do if a few more left? This is how they trained themselves to think to deal with the changes and uncertainties they faced. Lawrence showed relief, while 'Auda expressed his surprise, and 'Oqab tried not to dwell on the unpleasant things, and instead tried to be positive.

They stood in front of al-Azraq's rumbling waterfall as if they were in a dream; the water flowed generously in the heart of the desert.[5] 'Oqab could not see water, hear its sound, or smell its scent without thinking of Mizna. The men threw themselves into the waterfall with great joy, to be soon reminded that they must reach the checkpoint at the bridge on time, without attracting attention. Al-Zibn men, who knew the place well, vied with each other in leading the way, demonstrating skills and familiarity with a terrain foreign to many desert dwellers.

Mifleh and the other men dismounted their camels and horses, and the rest of the animals followed. Several men marched on foot carrying sticks and walked slowly counting on the rumbling sound of the waterfall to mask their movement. They reached the bridge and looked over the sleepy garrison ready to carry out their mission, but the Turkish regiment on the nearby hill spotted them. They quickly dropped the dynamite sticks they brought to blow the bridge and ran away.

The sound of the train approaching was heard from the distance. Lawrence had to accurately estimate the time to press the detonator. The retreat of the men from the troubled offensive on the garrison added to

---

5. An oasis in modern Jordan that was known for its streams, waterfalls, and wetlands that faced environmental crisis due to the over-pumping of its water sources, and recently became environmentally protected by the government with support from international agencies.

his stress; he pressed the detonator before the train arrived. The rocks shattered, and Lawrence fell; his left arm was covered with blood and Fahid al-Zibn's body flew into a ditch nearby. The men scrambled to get on their horses and camels, and chaos spread. 'Oqab led his horse in the direction of the explosion, "We have to retrieve the wounded."

The words of the young man and the sight of him riding his horse into the scene made Sharif 'Ali hesitate for a second, then ask the man closest to him, Turki al-Zibn, to kick his camel forcing it to follow al-Kahilah that lead al-Sharif's camel in the same direction. The rest of the men retreated, and the sharif was able to pick up Lawrence who was soaked in his own blood checking his arm; meanwhile the Turkish soldiers continued to fire in all directions. 'Oqab came close to the top of the hill exploring the place and saw Fahid's body moving, trying to climb the hill. He rushed down riding al-Kahilah, ignoring the flying bullets, and pulled the wounded man by his shoulders, placed him on the horse behind him, and climbed up the hill.

The Turkish soldiers returned happy with their victory after pursuing the attackers for a while and killing six of them. The Bedouin fighters who were used to victories returned to al-Azraq camp disappointed. As soon as they reached the old castle, they dropped off their stirrups, and laid on the soft green grass of the oasis. Lawrence also dismounted and laid on the grass with his wounded arm tied to his chest. He let his imagination soar back to the green, lush, and wide-open English plains, but he soon remembered where he was; this frightened him and made him wonder, "What did I come here for? I can taste a bitter shame!"

When night fell on the castle, the ghosts of the trained hounds of Bani Hilal, which had mysteriously died in this land many centuries ago, rose and stared the fighters in the face.[6] They did not disturb the courageous ones but fueled the terrors of the fearful.

The sharif entered the castle ignoring the legends; although 'Auda felt a little apprehensive, and Za'al closed his eyes sarcastically pretending

---

6. See n. 8, chap. 1 (pg. 12).

that he was waiting for the promised spirits, they did not encounter any and went to sleep.

In the morning, Hassan Shah and his Indian troops went on restoring the dilapidated castle using the clay and stones from the place itself, and then repaired the nearby mosque. They were transformed to crews of skilled laborers as if they had not just returned from battle. 'Oqab watched the change in the landscape and realized that the desert has many different faces beside the one he knew.

The place turned into a bustling camp. Shaikhs and leaders sat in the castle strategizing, civilian and military men were training, new delegations arrived, and Bedouin and Circassian's brought rice and bulgur to welcome the new occupants and fighters. There was also the strange Englishman, Lawrence, who spent his days wandering around, lying in a warm corner of the castle at nighttime with his pen and notebook, his eyes gazing into the distance as if he were somewhere else. He inquired, "How far is Der'a?"

'Oqab grew tired of the place. He sat by the scattered freshwater ponds, thought of Mizna's face, and lost himself in his love for her. He passed through groves of reeds and palm trees listening to the snaps of sticks under his feet like the sound of her anklets, music to his ears. The place turned to a paradise when her image was present. He stretched out his hands that perchance he might touch her small hand or wrap his arms around her crescent waist, but reached nothing but emptiness and returned to his sorrow and longing.

Za'al saw him and said, "I see your eyes wander as if you are far away. You love the water, the sand, and the heat of the sun. You are not like us. Sometimes I wish I was like you; I am tired of our hot sun, I hate the sand, and do not believe in the shimmering of the mirage. I see our lives as a constant thirst. I dream of a home in the city that has a door and a lock. I am tired of the desert. I swear that I will leave it and never step back here again. But the truth is, 'Oqab, when the sun turns to a red disk with beautiful colors and dissolves in the lap of the sand, I become enchanted again, my heart melts, I feel the urge to kneel on its ground, and only because I fear the mocking eyes, I hold back my tears. O God, it is hard to figure out the desert's magic and its spell!"

....

Everyone at the camp had his own world. Mine converged on the desert oasis; the summer gathered its remaining heat and dates, and moved back allowing winter to come through.

12.

....

Heads are balls
at the thrones and their courtyards.
The players perform,
their intentions are expressed
through obedience.
Heed, O tamed observer,
the desert of this madness.

—Adonis[1]

T he temperature in the desert dropped at night. First, this was welcomed after the grueling heat of the day, then it became unbearable. The frost intensified; you could hear men's teeth chatter beneath their winter coats. They wrapped their arms around their bodies like the wings of a bird, curling up, hoping that their flesh would warm up their bones.

The availability of supplies in the camp tempted others to enlist, especially with the arrival of the cold weather. The Arabs who deserted the Ottoman army joined the troops in Azraq in droves. Many Bedouins, Armenian merchants, and farmers from Horan headed by Talal al-Hardini

---

1. 'Ali Ahmad Said Esber (born 1 January 1930), also known by the pen name Adonis, is a Syrian poet, essayist, and translator who is considered one of the most prolific and influential Arab poets of the modern era.

also enlisted. Whenever the adequacy of supplies concerned the sharif, the people in the surrounding areas brought him more than the troops needed. Lawrence was uncomfortable with this influx of volunteers and insisted on taking the minimum number possible, but no one listened to him, especially knowing that such a request would offend many and cause unwarranted reactions.

The snow fell; this rarely happens in the desert. The oasis turned to a white plain that fascinated the Bedouins, most of whom had never seen snow before. 'Oqab raised his hands to the sky collecting the falling snowflakes, staring at them, feeling their coldness, watching them slowly melt, and enjoying the water dripping between his fingers. He was suddenly overwhelmed by a desire to wash with the pure water of the sky. He raised his hand full of the melted snow and wiped his face; the sweet water of the sky mixed with the salty water of the sea. Za'al watched with a discerning eye and said, "What's up? Are you thinking of your family?"

'Oqab did not reply, and Za'al advised, "You are still young, 'Oqab. The fatal part of man is his heart. Don't let your heart hold you back or weaken your resolve. You are lost in love!"

"How mistaken are you, my brother. Men's hearts are their anchors; the fuel of manhood is a great love that makes a man rise above everything trivial and unworthy. How could love hold me back or weaken my resolve when I joined because of it! My lover did not ask for a treasure, or the eggs of a she-camel, or a sparrow's milk, she asked for water. My love is what sustains me, what makes my step steadfast, what makes the blows of my sword strong and swift. Men who do not know love are the ones that retreat. I forgive you for what you say about love; you just do not know."

They were waiting for the winter to end in al-Azraq and Wadi Musa, but in 'Aqaba plans were being made to be implemented soon. Lawrence became increasingly tired of waiting in Azraq, so he moved to join the revolt leaders in 'Aqaba. He arrived about the same time the young prince, Zeid, Faisal's brother, reached 'Aqaba. Zeid came carrying a banner decorated with a star; he was seventeen years old, proud, leading an army of one thousand and six hundred fighters. The presence of additional soldiers meant the need for additional supplies. Prince Faisal relied on Lawrence's audacity to travel in such a bad weather to al-'Arish to secure supplies for the troops. He was surprised when he heard him ask for escort after the news spread that the Turks were paying a handsome ransom, twenty thousand lira, for anyone who brought back an Englishman's head. Thus, fifteen Arab fighters guarded Lawrence. He enjoyed chatting with them and learning about their lives and dialects, and when he was asked to accompany Ja'far al-'Askari and 'Ali ibn al-Hussein in their reconnaissance, he indulged himself by taking with him his escort. They stopped at Wadi Musa where Mawlood Mukhles camped with his soldiers. Times were difficult at the camp; the troops had to endure the frost of the desert, which was beyond human tolerance at times. When the sun set, many of the men huddled seeking the warmth of each other's bodies, and often woke up in the morning to find that they had held a corpse all night.

It was war, suffering did not mean much; things took place that would have been ignored under normal circumstances, but there, they were the fuel that made the men move and fight harder. It was a bitter winter, a jab in the body of the troops, but the war moved on and kept calling the men to engage. At Faisal's tent, they were ironing out the details of a plan they called, "the clamp." Colonel Joyce seemed concerned that Faisal had given the battle leadership to his young brother.[2] Meanwhile, Ja'far al-'Askari accepted that decision understanding his leader's shortcomings, but realizing that if he tried to spend his time fixing all transgressions, he might end up too busy to win the war. The plan divided the troops into five sections. The first three were al-Sharif Mastur leading al-Howeitat, headed by Shaikh Hamad al-Jazi; al-Sharif Nasser and Nuri al-Said leading the regular soldiers; and 'Auda Abu Tayeh leading the rest of the Howeitat and Bani Sakhr tribes. They were to move to Jarf al-Darawish station, then to Tafilah (this was the largest and most urgent mission), and then Sharif

---

2. Lieutenant Colonel Pierce Charles Joyce (1878–1965) served in the British Army and aided the Arab troops in their fight against the Turks.

Abudulmoin with the fourth group was expected to move to al-Shobak, followed by a small force led by Sharif Abdallah al-Ghafar headed to Ghor al-Mazra'a near the Dead Sea.

The three main convoys moved without supplies; the weather became increasingly moderate, and the men raised their voices with poems and songs. The Bedouins fired bullets in the air in celebration when the sharifs and tribal leaders placed their hands on top of each other, sealing the plan.

"To dig out the truth or bury it is the burden of those who know."

The crowd moved like a torrent, and the singing of the night travelers from Bani Sakhr tribe became louder.

> Two tied to eight,
> ten walking the night,
> the walkers will walk no more;
> they will become the load.
> The poet doesn't know what to say,
> his mind is perplexed, gloating,
> may God have mercy on their souls!

Traveling through al-Mujib to Shihan Mountain, and climbing 'Arar summit, left the men exhausted, hearing the echoes of their breathing. They recalled tales of ghosts in the wadi that appeared to the travelers as they passed through. They became silent and felt as if the ghosts had joined the marching troops. The two fearless Shaikhs 'Auda of al-Howeitat and Mifleh of Bani Sakhr exchanged pleasantries as their paths crossed descending with their troops south of Tafilah. Meanwhile, the enlisted soldiers carrying their cannons and machine guns climbed the eastern highlands. The two shaikhs, who were enemies in the past, grew closer as they drew near to their destination. Tafilah, the home of wild tigers, was resting in the heart of a wadi surrounded by mountains and high plateaus to the east, north, and south, with the west fortified by thick forests and harsh terrain.

The protected location did not ease the fears of the villagers who lived there, for they clearly remembered the painful raids and looting they suffered at the hands of the Bedouins. Their scouts returned with terrifying news about convoys of Bedouins, armed and united, descending on Tafilah. The news forced Shaikh Muhammad al-'Oran, who had a wavering relationship with the Bedouin shaikhs, to feel that he had no choice but to work with the Turkish garrison commander to defend the village. All, soldiers and farmers, men and women, rushed frantically to fortify the place. The women locked the doors from the inside and hid the supplies in holes they dug in the ground and covered with rugs, and the young men pulled out their axes and stood guard. Meanwhile, the frightened garrison commander distributed the guns and ammunition to the villagers, wondering if they would be used against him and his soldiers. Al-'Oran realized that and said assuringly, "All the people of Tafilah are with you, we will not let you down, Zaki al-Halabi." The commander remembered the city he was named after, Aleppo, and recalled the gallows in its square and wondered, how it could be that he, Zaki from Aleppo, was a Turk! How could he be a Turk, and what should he do with his Arab blood! He felt a lump growing in his throat, ignored it, and went back to being a disciplined military officer in a well-organized force, giving orders and placing the men, soldiers and farmers, in strategic places inside and outside the city.

Getting to Tafilah required passing by Jarf al-Darawish station. The stone bridge leading to the city was a tempting target. 'Auda realized that if they could demolish it, Tafilah would easily fall into their hands. The Bedouins split, members of the Sakhr tribe attacked from the north and al-Howeitat from the south. Before the sun rose that day, the machine guns of the regular army placed on top of the eastern hill covered the Bedouin's attack with heavy shelling. The soldiers in the Turkish garrison were not able to return fire due to lack of visibility at that time of the day. As soon as the sun rose further and the soldiers at the Turkish station could see the Bedouin fighters clearly, the Arabs' artillery on the other side of the hill went silent. Nuri al-Said lost his temper when he discovered that the machine gun stopped working; the enthusiastic Bedouin fighters were in their way climbing the hill, exposed to Turkish artillery. Fortunately, one of the officers, Rasim Saradast, calmly dismantled his handgun with skill and determination, as if he knew exactly what to do when in fact it was a desperate attempt to fix the problem. He pulled a piece out the machine gun and replaced it with a piece from his gun, then pointed the machine gun to the garrison laughing, "We will try. What can we lose?"

Nuri al-Said clapped joyfully when he heard the shells reach the station and watched the confusion this caused in the Turkish garrison. The Bedouins who were not aware of the technical difficulty were able to reach the middle of the station in large numbers, giving the Turkish soldiers no option but to surrender. The sight of the two trains full of supplies near the garrison was tempting. The Bedouins ran to the loaded trailers. 'Auda was devastated to see 'Oqab carrying the body of Mifleh al-Qaman, the shaikh of the Sakhr tribe, in his arms. The enemy of yesterday and the partner of today was killed in the heat of the battle. 'Auda frowned, and the rest of the men shook their heads in disbelief. Za'al whispered, "May heaven be his resting place. My heart told me this would happen as soon as I saw his horse dig next to his tent."

'Auda shook his hand dismissing and said, "Stop. It is not bad luck; he died in battle, a death that makes men proud."

'Oqab laid the body of the martyr shaikh on the back of his horse; members of his tribe gathered around him and decided to bury him there. While the men of the Sakhr tribe were busy burying their shaikh, the rest of the fighters continued to raid the train; 'Auda yelled warning, "Get the men together. You are taking too much time worrying about the spoils; if we are late, we will ruin everything."

'Auda, Za'al, 'Oqab, and the other leaders urged the men to stop, but they ignored them and went on looking through the carts checking the merchandise, laughing, and throwing bags full of dried meat to the soldiers, "This is pigs' meat."

The soldiers replied, "Pigs, monkeys, who cares. Hunger knows no religion."

The commanders seemed to have lost control over the Bedouins and the fighters who thought that the battle ended by having their hands on the loot. Nuri al-Said's worries multiplied when he arrived with the two hundred prisoners he captured and found out the reason for the troops' delay. He told 'Auda, "These are your men, Shaikh, your responsibility, make them move . . ."

Salem al-Zowairy jumped next to 'Auda and said, "I have a solution, uncle."

"What is it?"

In a moment al-Zowairy jumped inside the train looking for a specific cart, and as soon as he found it, he started moving small metal boxes and handing them to 'Oqab and Za'al who carried them away without asking what he was doing. When one last box remained, Salim opened its lid, and a strange familiar smell filled the air. He spilled the thick liquid on the floor of the cart, walked back, flickered his lighter and threw it in the liquid, which instantly burned. Nuri laughed watching the Bedouins come out of the carts running, mounting their horses, and awaiting 'Auda's orders. First, he freed one of the prisoners and gave him a strong camel to take news of the battle back to Tafilah.

'Auda knew that most of the leaders disapproved of his action, which prevented their army from using the element of surprise. Meanwhile, al-Sharif Nasser supported 'Auda's position and argued that gaining friends was more important than defeating enemies. The troops moved slowly allowing the messenger to deliver the message and come back with the answer.

They set camp in the evening and lit their fires. 'Auda watched the faces illuminated by the light of the campfires, full of excitement and anticipation, and said calmly, "Do you know what happens to the wolves when famine strikes their land?"

The men muttered; some knew the story and others did not, but all listened. 'Auda said, "The wolves were patient and put up with hunger; their hearts were made of stone. They roamed in their caves waiting, but hunger was stubborn. It persisted and did not leave them alone; it brought death close to their bones. At that point, the wolves came out into the open; stood facing each other, thin, sick, hungry; and howled. The wolves understood each other, their voices revealed their truth. The meek and weak had soft squeaky voices that did not carry far; tired, their voices quivered. The wolves knew who amongst them was the weakest. They became the packs' lunch and dinner at that time, when plagued by starvation. During war, people are wolves; raise your voices, let it thunder, the wolves will stand by you, but if you become weak, afraid, and hide, you will be eaten.

Nuri al-Said looked at 'Auda with beaming eyes and said, "Are you entertaining us, or scaring us, Shaikh?"

"Not this, nor that. I am telling a desert tale to kill time."

Nuri stared at the dying fire next to the shaikh's tent and remembered the Tigris and Baghdad, his hometown, that were so far away. They seemed so near to him now!

....

Diab al-'Oran watched with sympathy the enthusiasm of the villages, knowing well the strength of the approaching army. He felt helpless seeing a sad sense of submission draping al-Halabi's face. It seemed that their suspicion turned into certitude, and their confidence became doubt. Both were haunted by a feeling that they were not ready to share.

When 'Auda's messenger arrived describing the occupation of Jarf al-Darawish, they had no choice militarily but to surrender; al-'Oran declared, "Tell me if anyone ever fought 'Auda and won? I can't have my men slaughtered in a lost battle. We know how the Bedouins raid; all the wealth of Tafilah will not satisfy them if they enter as raiders . . ."

Al-Halabi agreed, but was conflicted as a military man who did not feel that surrender was a choice, "I will not surrender to the Bedouins; to the army, yes. Just as they sent a messenger, we will send one with our conditions."

Abdul al-Salam, the older son of al-'Oran, went as a messenger announcing that the village would be willing to surrender if they were guaranteed the safety of their children and belongings. The message was sent, and they waited for a response.

When the horses of the rebels came close to the village, the place was wrapped in silence. The fighters stayed behind while Nasser and 'Auda approached. The women looked through the cracks of their locked doors, and the children peeked from behind the trees and their other hiding places and remained there until they saw al-'Oran with two of his men come out to meet the fighters. When he came face-to-face with 'Auda, he hesitated, but 'Auda suddenly felt at peace and asked spontaneously, relying on the friendship he had had with the man in the past, "I hope your good coffee is ready, Shaikh."

Al-'Oran answered feeling optimistic, "Welcome, may God bless the guests."

The women opened their doors, and the men ran into the paths that lead to the guest quarters. The smell of the fresh morning coffee filled the place; rounds of drinks were served, and the people of Tafilah heard laughter inside.

Nasser said, "We guarantee the safety of the Turkish soldiers in the garrison if they give up their weapons and leave. We swear not to harm them."

Al-'Oran replied, "We accept the sharif's word, but Zaki al-Halabi is a stubborn army man; he will not surrender except to the army. These are the rules of engagement that he lives by. Honor him, honorable men. He is an Arab like us."

When the troops arrived at the village, al-Sharif sent two men with Lieutenant Muhamad Ali al-Ajloni offering the conditions of surrender to the soldiers holding up in the fortified buildings of the garrison. The

Turkish men came out with their hands up, while al-Halabi walked toward them calm and confident extending his hand to shake the hands of the victorious Arab leaders.

The people of the village were greatly impacted by al-Halabi joining the revolt. They had a great respect for the man and appreciated all that he had done to protect them in the past. They were overwhelmed by an impulse to want to belong to people like themselves. Their fear subsided when they saw that the Bedouin raiders restrained themselves and did not loot their village, and in the afternoon, Bedouins, peasants, and soldiers stood together on the plateaus, surrounded by green plains, watching the Turkish soldiers leave on their way to al-Karak.

A farmer said, "Every night, before dawn, we hear the swords of the Muslims rattle. There, by the edge of the wadi, the battle of Mu'tah was fought.[3] As if the souls of the martyrs are still present, haunting the place, we hear them and feel them.

Then, a Bedouin commented, "Good, then the wadi will carry the sound of the camels of the Turks leaving for al-Karak, and their men weeping on their way back home."

Another corrects him, "You are above being wrong, brother, but al-Karak is not their home! It is part of our homeland."

Al-Karak's time would come. It was hard for the fighters to think about the boundaries of the land they had won, and that they had to work on securing it. 'Auda knew about battles and was aware that this was not the end of the war. He explained, "The future will not be easy. They will not let us keep Tafilah without a fight. Tomorrow we will hear and see."

Early the next day, 'Auda gathered his men and headed home. Tafilah had become crowded with the arrival of Sharif Zeid, Hamad al-Jazi, Ja'far al-'Askari, and their men turning the place into a busy military camp. 'Auda's men felt suffocated and followed him to the wide-open land.

The window of good weather that made it easier for the rebels to

3. A battle between Prophet Muhammad's forces and the Byzantine Empire (629 CE), fought near the village of Mu'tah east of the Jordan river.

occupy Tafilah changed. The rain returned announcing that winter had not ended yet. The Bedouins, who expected the desert to go wild this season, went up the high rocks and took refuge in the mountain caves. Very few of al-Jazi tribe stayed. The winter became more severe, and some of the camels, exhausted by the fight, lack of food, and the freezing weather, died. Subhi al-Omari led the mules to the caves, turning them to stables, and Zeid suggested reducing the force by sending some to Wadi al-Hasa to establish a checkpoint there. Al-Ajloni accompanied al-Sharif Mastur to do so and took some of the men with them; with their departure, al-Tafilah became less crowded.

In the quiet village with its limited resources, the army cooks prepared some food. They made small balls out of their dough, spread them over a large rock heated with amber and burning charcoal, and picked them up as soon as they were baked, satisfied with the comfort that the warm, fresh bread provided.

Lawrence chose an abandoned house of two rooms to protect himself from the bitter cold and sat alone with his papers, scribbling his thoughts. Sometimes he would walk over the thorny plants, a barefooted bum, and at other times, he gave orders with the authority of a Hashemite prince.

When the sun chased away the clouds and appeared majestically in the sky, Lawrence came out to the wilderness topless, wearing only a short trouser, pulling the lice that was holding tight to the hair under his arms, on his head, and on other parts of his body.

Al-Omari watched the commotion and said sympathetically, "I wonder where do lice come from, it is winter!"

Lawrence answered angrily in broken Arabic, "From the camels, from the goats, and from the Bedouins."

Al-'Omari laughed and said, "Tomorrow the war will be over, and you will return to your country and won't have to worry about lice."

One of the Bedouins assigned to guard Lawrence interrupted, "May God not listen to what you say, son of al-Sham. Let the lice be! A man does not get rid of lice until he dies; may God make Lawrence live long and not deprive him of his share of lice."

They all laughed, some happy, some in anguish, and some in a friendly way.

13.

....

If the nights fill me with pain,
I extend a hand of love
and become humbled by my proud tears.

—Abu Firas al-Hamadani[1]

I have no reason to leave Tafilah. I was part of its military forces, and I
liked its green grass and its fruit trees standing safe behind the short
manmade walls. But its brick mud houses, with their high walls
attached to the mud-made floor, frightened me. The roofs were fortified
with tree logs and reeds enforced with wool threads; a roof that held back
a soul that longed for the open sky, to soar as it pleased through the seven
layers of heaven. I could not find a reason why people placed their bodies
and their souls in cages like animals in musty stables. Despite these cages
that people call homes, I loved Tafilah, and wandered with al-Kahilah in
Dana's wadi, gathering beautiful, smooth, colored stones to be made into
a necklace for you, Mizna.

When I heard the men discuss the strategic geographic location of
Tafilah, I realized why it was important for our war. But to me, it did not
seem that there was a neutral land. When we were in al-Wajh, it was the

---

1. Al-Harith bin Abil-'Ala Said bin Hamdan al-Taghlibi (932–968), better known as Abu Firas
al-Hamdani, was an Arab poet and prince of the Hamadanids who ruled northern Syria and
Upper Mesopotamia during the tenth century.

edge of the world and the window to the future. Our souls longed for 'Aqaba where our dreams soared, then we wanted Tafilah. It became the crucial spot to have. Perhaps I do not understand much about the strategic importance of the place, but I know that I filled my soul with the places we won and left parts of myself there. This is how I loved these places, and they always loved me back. I know that after Tafilah will come al-Karak and Ma'an, then we will move north until we reach the soil of Damascus, a city that hangs in my mind like a jasmine necklace. Because I do not let my body stay a prisoner in a house with walls and columns, and do not chain my soul to the footsteps of another man, I am guided only by what is in my chest, a strong heart that shows me the way. Thus, it was hard for me to understand why we had to return!

Za'al thinks he knows what is going on and constantly brings up the saying that two horses cannot be tied to the same pole. I know how capable 'Auda is and all the other brave fighters, but I do not see men divided into high and low breeds. In my chest whirls a worthy free soul that does not slow down and cannot be tamed. The soul of my father, the soaring falcon. Al-Kahilah understands me, while she carries me back to my tribe with a broken heart. She knows I returned only to see the face of my beloved; I long to see Mizna. The fighters around me desire a woman's body, but I long for her in a different way. When her arms embrace me, I sense the silk of her chest, and dissolve in her; our two bodies become one, and when separated, our souls remain in an eternal embrace that never breaks.

In the bitter desert cold, our limbs froze; we fought the cold by lighting our own fire over the mattress of wormwood and milfoil. Beneath the goatskin that covered us, we became united. That night, I planted my seed in her womb, and whispered in her ear, "I am returning to the battlefield. I can't wait for 'Auda's orders. I am going back alone."

She whispered in a calm tenderness, "I know."

Then her voice echoed in my ears and chest, sad melancholy, she sang,

Happy is the moon, it knows no love;

happy is the moon, it has no eyes to see;

happy are the moon and the mighty stars;

they have no heart to love and feel love's pain.

She stopped, and we were lost in silence, hiding within it our agony. When a slight light spread over the land, I put some supplies on the back of al-Kahilah and went on my way. I could still feel Mizna's hands tightly holding mine. I had an urge to scream, but did not!

Alone, I returned to al-Tafilah camp, confident that the rest of the fighters would soon follow; all the chained horses will be free again. I am joining a crowd that I do not understand. I did not understand them when I was here before; I heard many new dialects that I was not familiar with, even my sage father did not know some of them. I saw among the faces and garbs colors that dazzled my sight. Did they all come out for the same reason I did? Or did they all have their own reasons that only they knew?

At the entrance of the village, al-Kahilah slowed down as if she were calling on me to reflect. Even though I had come across this place in the past, it seemed as if I had never been here before.

The sun lit the sky with its bright light dripping tenderness into two hearts, the land's heart and mine. I felt bad that I did not feel the spirit of the land before but was glad to feel it now. Perhaps our loneliness is the best moment for discovery; it allows us to see things more purely and clearly. I had a desire to understand the places as they really were, stripped naked under the sunlight that filled me and them; light on light, "Allah is the Light of the heavens and the earth. The Parable of His Light is as if there were a Niche and within it a Lamp: the Lamp enclosed in glass: the glass as it were a brilliant star: Lit from a blessed Tree, an Olive [tree], neither of the east nor of the west, whose oil is well-nigh luminous, though fire scarce touched it: Light upon Light! Allah doth guide whom He will to His Light: Allah doth set forth Parables for men:

and Allah doth know all things."[2] The universe has a beautiful rhythm that starts within me and spills out into these green hillocks; it knows how to supplicate. This fertile, wild, beautiful land feeds on me, and gushes inside me streams of incredible joy, as if I had never defied the will of my tribe and come here alone!

I am not concerned about the way the shaikhs see things! While they are asleep, I am living a moment saturated with love which will be eternal in the consciousness of the universe. I will be here, with this land together, forever!

The land spread, mysterious. He suddenly saw a man, crouching. He hesitated about approaching him, but al-Kahilah led him there.

He was alone, holding his cane, his legs trembling, his face full of festering sores dripping on his bare chest. Al-Kahilah approached, 'Oqab was unable to stop her. He saw the man clearly, but the man did not look at him, as if he was not seeing him, as if he did not hear the hooves of the horse approaching; he was praying with a quivering voice, "Indeed, adversity has touched me, and you are the Most Merciful of the merciful!"[3]

'Oqab stood still like a stone, and the man went on praying, "Did not I weep for him that was in trouble? Was not my soul grieved for the poor? When I looked for good, then evil came unto me: and when I waited for light, there came darkness. My bowels boiled and rested not: the days of affliction prevented me. I went mourning without the sun: I stood up, and I cried in the congregation. I am a brother to dragons, and a companion to owls. My skin is black upon me, and my bones are burned with heat. My harp also is turned to mourning, and my organ into the voice of them that weep."[4]

Who is this sitting at the entrance of Tafilah conversing with his Lord? Can you see him?

---

2. Quran, Surat Nur 24:35, translated by Yusuf Ali.

3. Quran, Surat al-Anbya 83:84: "And [mention] Job, when he called to his Lord, 'Indeed, adversity has touched me, and you are the Most Merciful of the merciful.'"

4. Job 30:25–31 (King James Bible).

I feared the absurd and closed my eyes; I wish I kneeled on my knees next to the man squatting in the wilderness at the cusp of the city and the desert, waiting for centuries! When I opened my eyes, I could not see him anymore; heavy tears covered my face. A sudden certitude engulfed me, a feeling that I was his favorite. Otherwise, why would he appear to me; Job, the grandfather of Tafilah, a vein that did not dry, a blood that never stopped gushing, appeared to me![5]

I entered the city peacefully, consumed by the images in my mind, while the world driven by the fever of war tenderly engulfed me with beauty and joy. The bright sun softy touched the passing clouds, and the light breezes perfumed by the blooming acacia and juniper, infused with the scent of the grass growing through the cracks in the granite rocks next to the black lilies and the daffodils, rested beneath the shadow of the oleander bushes with their bright red flowers covering the land. I was filled with peace while watching the universe in its quiet tender celebration of scents and colors! I saw the mallow with its small purple flowers and was careful not to trod on it with the hooves of my horse. She seemed to have sensed that; her steps became light and soft, as if she was skipping over the grass. From afar, the mountain goats, crowned with large strong horns, watched us curiously.

Sudden shouts startled us, and the beauty around us held its breath in anticipation, listening to the valleys echoing the loud screams. It is not fear that I experienced, but the involuntarily shift from the exhilaration and pleasure I felt to the harsh reality of life and its cruelty. I heard the desperate calls for help that rattled the land, "Honorable brave men, where are you? Today is your day. Where did the defenders of the oppressed go?"

Something terrible must have happened to force the prince to call like that, acting like a Bedouin against the disciplined military code that he tried to hold his soldiers to. Tens of men sent the call for help from the top of Mount Bera and Tawelat Fatima.[6]

---

5. In reference to Prophet Job.

6. Names of mountains around Tafilah.

It sounded like the world was weeping. Something grave must have happened.

I saw the soldiers rush to the hilltops at the northeast of town, and was surprised to see the men, women, and children leaving the city to its surroundings. I passed by a crowd carrying their sticks and axes, and heard the name, Hamid Fakhri.[7]

Turkish names have a different tone; I had sympathetically looked for what connects them to us but did not go as far as el-Djezairi did in his empathy. I clearly recognized the clear dividers that separated us, what the Syrian officers call nationalism. Perhaps I was less educated and knowledgeable than el-Djezairi and his men were, but the sage taught me how to sense the blood in my veins, and how to lean toward my blood regardless of the body it occupies. The Turkish names do not have what makes my blood turn. The ones who are in Istanbul controlling people's destinies are strangers, no different from what I see in the wax white faces and blue eyes that fight with us, or we fight with them! It is hard for me to decipher all these complex issues, but I feel and long, and for that, I sincerely fight.

In the town square stood Shaikh Diab al-'Oran igniting people's enthusiasm, warning against abandoning the village; the man said scary things about Hamid Fakhri, the hero of Bucharest! Where is this Bucharest? How does it fit into our war? Is this a different sword in a different battle, or is the world an extended network? I might be perplexed, but my heart knows with whom to fight.

The Turkish army crossed Wadi al-Hasa led by the fierce leader, their hero. We spread out, in and around Tafilah. Sharif Mastour and his fighters went out to delay the arrival of the attacking troops. I saw the large smiling leader, Ja'far al-'Askari walking around encouraging the soldiers; I also saw our rival and cousin, Hamad al-Jazi, standing tall like 'Auda, and riding his horse as he does, calling the men, with a voice like his, proclaiming

---

7. Hamid Fakhri (1868–1948) was an Ottoman brigadier commander who was first sent to secure Medina in 1916, and later led the Ottomans in their fight against Arab forces in Tafilah.

"How sweet is death!" like he does. I had a feeling that 'Auda would hear the cry for help and would not be able to resist. He would be back on the battlefield soon.

With all these troops and leaders ready to fight, I had no leader, but based on my Bedouin thaub and my two braids, I belonged to the Howeitat and al-Jazi tribe did not mind me joining their troop.

The call for help had reached some of the members of al-Majali tribe and riders from al-Karak arrived apologizing that the rest did not come, and since their reasons where like the people from Tafilah before they enlisted, al-'Oran seemed to understand. He assured them, "We understand your position; we know that all the braves from al-Karak will join us one day; tomorrow will come soon."

We passed the cliffs that charmed me before the battle started, but now at the heights of the war, they turned to deaf, pointed rocks; how this looks like my heart! It is now a mere rock at the bottom of a valley.

At the flat land in the heart of the valley, we faced the enemies. Our task was to attack from the left. The Bedouins and peasants fought together, and my blood splashed everywhere. I stood there, hesitant and confused, watching a woman walk pulling behind her a donkey that carried the body of her dead son on its back, as if she did not see us, singing with brave anguish, "Mother, come, say goodbye; you will not see me again. Hold me tight as I die, and wash me with your holy tears."

I wanted to touch the martyr's body, but I could not because of the raging battle. My tears ran down my face, and I felt that they reached his heart and quenched its thirst. The crowds mixed. I was surprised to see the peasants dare come down the hill; they came like a flood and joined the fight.

The young Syrian fighter Subhi al-'Omari lead a suicidal attack risking his life and the lives of his fighters to open a path and called on the villagers to follow him to the heart of the battle, and they obliged. Our soldiers on top of the hill were not able to use their machine guns against the Turks because we were engaged with them in direct combat, but they kept firing in the air which scared the Turks and made them believe that our forces were double what they could see.

I was surprised when al-Kahilah burst into whinnying, and her body madly convulsed beneath me while she stood on her hind legs. My body twisted trying to stay on her back. I could not believe that my beloved al-Kahilah would throw me to the battleground; something was making her act this way. While trying to keep my balance, I looked up and noticed something in the sky that I had not seen before. I saw a tear in its blue shield slowly and steadily ripping, leaving a huge opening in the horizon with light streaming down, flooding the place, forming a fog that slowly vanished. Then I saw them arriving, giant young men following the rays of light, glorious, glowing, like the light itself. Their naked bodies radiant with youth, bursting with health, grace, and beauty; their wings flapped, carrying iron chains and swords with sharp edges glistening. They came down in tens, hundreds, and thousands crowding the sky. My eyes were overwhelmed with their brightness. They mingled among the men, and fought steel with steel and fire. We realized that we were winning and heard the first cries of the Turks surrendering.

The man that was greatly feared, Hamid Fakhri was injured and fell off his horse frightened from the roar of the camels and the shouts of the Bedouins and peasants. The crowds marched with great excitement pushing in front of them the prisoners, with their hands up in the air. The flag that made my heart tremble was madly flapping, carried on a wooden mast by one of the al-Jazi fighters. The vision I saw captured my heart, and the soldiers' cries of victory, full of joy and delight, touched the face of the sky. The remnants of the defeated Turkish troops ran away; our leaders let that happen. We did not have the resources to handle this large number of prisoners; they allowed some to carry the body of the hero of Bucharest and quickly bury him at the bottom of the hill.

The Turks left the valley when the twilight sun dissolved into the desert sand, leaving its magic over the hills as if time stopped, and I regained the pleasure that captured me in my way to Tafilah, now augmented by the vision that only I saw.

The village did not sleep that night. The peasants performed dabka, and the Bedouins carried out their ritualistic song and dance, al-dahieh.[8] The jubilee filled the air and spread from the people to the horses and camels, all were excited; how hard it was to express our joy! How easy it was to express our pride! They were proud!

The Englishman, Lawrence, stood above a pile of captured machine guns, placing his hand on his waist, posing for pictures.

I heard the laughter of Ja'far al-'Askari scolding Subhi al-'Omari for his daring move during the battle, and then jokingly Ja'far said, "Regardless, you are the hero of this battle!"

I went back to riding alone, content with the glory of the plateaus and hills that surrounded me. The voices of the men in the village resonated with me like a hadwa,[9] the distant twilight song of desert dwellers, the echo of the longing in my heart. The men were counting their martyrs, the names dropped, one after another, like the beads in a blessed rosary.

---

8. *Dabka* is a line-dance performed by Arabs, especially in the Levant during happy occasions such as weddings, graduations, winning elections, and other times. *Dahieh* is a Bedouin practice that involves clapping, moving, and repeating certain slogans to create a rhythm for the dancers. It is traditionally conducted by men on special occasions.

9. The songs the desert dwellers sing for their camels to encourage them to move forward, especially in long journeys throughout the desert.

14.

....

The secret is yours; mothers give birth to you each day; your bones grow strong, you grow proud and fall in love before your time, then you die in love with every turn of time.

—Hashem Gharibeh

The frost clung to the desert waiting for the rainy season.

"My father the sage, tell me, am I Howeitat?"

The deep wise eyes of the sage looked at the bright perplexed face and smiled with delight, then bent and grabbed a handful of the coarse sand and said, "The grains of sand, 'Oqab, do not care what they are called; they know the land they belong to, that is enough for them. Why do you care if you are Howeitat, Shalan, or Majali, or even from al-Ghouta.[1] You are the son of the falcon, 'Oqab; the one that has no name, but knows the landscape of his land and sky and seeks nothing but freedom."

"But how do I know what freedom is, father!"

"It is something that you sense with your conscience. You might be in prison with cuffs on your hands, and iron chains on your feet, your neck tied; meanwhile, your soul screams loudly and announces whether you want something or don't. On the other hand, you might be free, have a choice, but the chains that you cannot see constrict your blood from

---

1. An oasis formed by the Barada river around Damascus.

flowing; your heart says "no," but when the word reaches your lips, it turns to "yes." You seek glory, and to obtain it you sell your true glory for its sake, constantly losing without knowing it. Only your conscience knows what freedom looks like, not actions, not chains, and not what people think they see. Do you understand, 'Oqab?"

It was not only that, emotions took over the mind of the young man; he wandered in a loneliness, like travel. He heard a mysterious call that haunted him. He could not sleep, as if he was afraid, but he was not. Suddenly it dawned on him, he saw glory in the distance and followed it. He realized that he did not have to follow the footsteps of the shaikh, and he understood that what freedom was.

The men teased 'Oqab saying that he was smart to want to replace the bitter cold of the desert with the warmth of al-Ghor.[2]

"You are running to the land of the black people![3] Al-Ghor is warm and fun!"

The shaikh was not surprised that 'Oqab decided to join al-Sharif Abdallah al-Ghafar leaving to the port of Ghor al-Mazra'a. He had seen him wandering around, lost. He knew that inside him raged a call to join the battle even if his people were taking a break, letting their swords rest for a while.

He was a knight, and life for him was his horse. They heard al-Kahilah neigh when 'Oqab rode at dawn. A few meters outside the camp, 'Oqab saw the sage, walking, leaning on his cane, stretching his body as much as his soul, not his old age, allowed. His shadow passed the young man with few steps; no matter how fast al-Kahilah ran, the old man on foot was still ahead of her. 'Oqab was confused, as if what he was seeing was not his father the sage but a mirage on the road. The figure continued to walk ahead of him, as if it was guiding him, until he saw the Bedouins of Beir al-Saba.'

---

2. Al-Ghor forms part of the larger Jordan Rift Valley in Jordan, the deepest valley in the world, beginning at an elevation of 696 feet below sea level and terminating at an elevation lower than 1,300 feet below sea level.

3. The people from al-Ghor region have dark skin and curly hair, and have African features.

The minute he saw them, the figure faded, and his soul settled. He looked around and could not find the sage anywhere, as if he was an illusion. The Bedouins of Beir al-Saba' were planning to sneak at night to the port of Ghor al-Mazra'a led by al-Sharif Ghafar to destroy the Turkish boats that transported supplies to the soldiers in Jericho.

Lightning glimmered at the summit of Mount Moab while the men rolled quietly at the middle of the night down the high mountain into the valley.[4] Their hearts were on fire; 'Oqab commented, "Lightning is the smile of angels."

In silence they waited, then thunder roared hurting their ears and filling their hearts with fear; a young Bedouin whispered, "A fight started between the angels and the devils in the sky."

The leaders wanted to ease their fear, and said, "No devils, but men."

A light laughter followed, and then, the young man with the beautiful voice swayed his body and sang, "With your permission, father of Hassan and Hussein,[5] peace be upon you; by the clanks of your swords and the footsteps of the hooves of your horse, dispel heresy and defeat the infidels; blessed are you, blessed are you."

The steeper the incline was, the warmer the weather became, as if it was a heavenly response to the call of the young man. At the bottom of the mountain, the sage appeared again, a straight figure, walking on two feet with the help of his cane, leading the army. 'Oqab was delighted thinking that it was his vision alone until a Bedouin declared, "I believe that this is the sage that lives in al-Jouf. What brings him to this wilderness?"

Despite the darkness, they could see him, light emanating from his body as if he was glowing; his presence dispelled their fears in the blackness that was casted over the mountain and its ravines. When dawn shed its

---

4. Moab is the historical name for a mountainous tract of land in Jordan alongside much of the eastern shore of the Dead Sea, named after the Kingdom of Moab. According to the Hebrew Bible, Moab was often in conflict with its Israelite neighbors to the west.

5. Refers to the sons of 'Ali bin Abi Talib (15 September 601–29 January 661). He was the cousin and the son-in-law of Muhammad, the Prophet of Islam. He ruled as the fourth caliph from 656 to 661. He is regarded as the true successor of Prophet Muhammad by the Shia Muslims.

light through the fog of al-Ghor's warm morning, the men felt safe and realized that they were not lost. They were coming close to their target at the beach surrounded by men from al-Tarbein tribe. A bright bird flew in the warm sky nearby. This was a big contrast to the high mountains terrain with snowcaps on the summits. Flocks of birds startled by the movement of the newcomers flew away looking for shelter. A Bedouin complained, "The damn things are trying to expose us."

Another responded, "Do not curse the birds, you will lose your blessings. Don't worry. The Turks are all sleeping, unaware."

Another man exclaimed, "How strange! What was the sage doing there last night? How did the blessed one make it there before us?"

The boats anchored by the shore looked like silent bodies in a still painting but for the soft waves on the water that gracefully moved them slightly. 'Oqab watched the holy lake where he could see the sage in the far distance. The sage slowly disappeared leaving him in despair. He looked around searching for him to no avail. Then, he felt a heavy hand on his shoulder. He looked up and saw the sage standing behind him; he was delighted to see the beloved face. The sage said, "In the river coming from the north, Christ was baptized.[6] The sins of man are lying still at the lake of death."

The holiness of the place at dawn and the depth of the voice of the sage made the young man's heart flutter.

Then, the sage spoke his last words, "Here, as far as you can see, at the edge of the heart and the flickering of the mind, before the sea of salt, there was the sea of paradise that quenched people's thirst, its water sweet and pure. It held the secret of life and its mysteries, and generously distributed its treasures. People made pilgrimages to it from near and far, carrying the plights of their days, the weight of their sins, and the bundles of sadness that plagued them for centuries. They came to the lake that descended from heaven, a mercy to men. As they filled their hands and drank its crystal

---

6. Referring to the Jordan River in al-Ghor region that it is believed to be the site of Christ's baptism.

water, the world glowed, their weights and sins dropped, and their pain vanished; they went back, young, vibrant, and happy dreaming of miracles. Life was renewed each day on the shores of the lake of youth until there was a great sin. At the shores of this lake, man cursed his brother and people drank the chalice of betrayal shedding pure blood. God looked at mankind angrily and pulled his crystal lake to the first heaven and replaced it with salty water, dead, lifeless. The eyes of the sinners gazed at the gates of this heaven, where the righteous ascended after their death and, passing by the lake on their way to paradise, turned young and journeyed into high heaven with their full beauty and glory. I am called there, where I long to be."

The sage said his last words and vanished into thin air; like a column of smoke, he disappeared.

The gravity of the moment shook 'Oqab, but he realized that the mission had started and rode quickly in the direction of the gathered men. The land surrounding the lake shimmered like a silver plate; the salt around the water dried and turned the land into a sheet of glass that cracked under the footsteps of the men sneaking toward the boats. Neither this nor the sound of their footsteps woke up the sleeping soldiers at the Turkish camp.

The mission was easy. They slit the bottom of the loaded boats with their sharp daggers, and the water slowly seeped into them. By the time the Turks realized what was happening, the Bedouins of Beir al-Saba' were surrounding them. The Turkish soldiers did nothing but shoo away the swarms of mosquitoes and flies that buzzed in their ears and bit them everywhere; they surrendered without a fight.

The men came back from their mission loaded with artilleries and weapons. They missed the sage leading them on the way back, but they did not ask about him. Their movement slowed down while passing the heights that they feared going through last night. It was daytime, and they stopped not from fear but dropped from exhaustion, unable to move forward. A Bedouin realized what was happening and yelled, "Malaria!"

The malaria inflected the malnourished and weak men leaving yellow traces on their faces and draining the energy from their bodies. Sharif

Ghafar tried to encourage them to move forward, promising them treatment at the end of the journey, but their bodies failed them. The men saw 'Oqab drop his head on the shoulder of the horse, his body shivering with fever. As they dragged themselves above the gorge, the wind howled, and the temperature dropped. The sick men fought the fever and the cold and grew weaker. They saw a slow caravan approaching; the people were riding backward to avoid facing the cold wind. They recognized some of the men from Beir al-Saba' who were serving as scouts for the caravan traveling from Damascus. Among them was a British officer unhappy, anxious, and complaining about the hardships of the journey. A man rushed to help the sick giving them camel milk.

The Englishman, Alec Kirkbride,[7] was annoyed and said in a language that his companions from Damascus understood, "The honor of Great Britain does not allow me to subject myself to such danger."

They all ignored him while al-Ghafar fought to muster the strength to greet them. Kirkbride watched him struggle and said, "My God, malaria, isn't it?

The leader shook his head agreeing. The Englishman took a small pouch out of a big bag on his mule and whispered, "I have the cure."

He looked frightened at the crowd of sick soldiers, and continued whispering, "For you alone."

The camels with their sick riders stopped at the nearby camp of al-Neimat tribe. Al-Ghafar took the bitter medicine the Englishman gave him, and the others continued their journey to their tribes' camps. Al-Kahilah rushed with the young man on her back home. She knew the way. In his feverish hallucination, 'Oqab saw falcons flying at different heights, flapping their strong wings, creating a warm breeze, melting the frost that engulfed the heart of the desert.

Al-Kahilah arrived with her rider at night. At the entrance of al-Jafar, stood Mizna, lost as if she was waiting, following her instinct, and as soon

---

7. Sir Alec Seath Kirkbride (1897–1978) was a British diplomat who served in Jordan and Palestine between 1920 and 1951.

as she saw al-Kahilah drawing near and realized what had happened, her heart never failed her.

Back at the camp, Mizna turned her face away avoiding the sight of her lover burned on the side of his head and the smell of his scorched hair and heard his weak cry when Dayoud repeated the ritual, burning his hands between the pointer and the thumb.[8]

She prepared the goat meat, and then made a mixture from bitter eucalyptus leaves, a bit of wheat, and some other plants. She held her sick man in her lap, fed him as much as he would eat, poured in his mouth some of her medicine, and rubbed his body, arms, and legs with musk.

In the evening, when 'Oqab regained consciousness, he was soaked in sweat, and called for his father, "You left me, father!"

He saw many clouds and a great white throne. It was a new heaven; the first heaven and earth had vanished. He saw the old cave; in it was a gold-painted bed adorned with jewels, perfumed with musk and ambergris, protected by Moses and Aaron.[9] On the bed's silk sheets covered with blossoms, fragrances, and the grass of the land, a prophet who had lain there for centuries, opened his eyes and looked at 'Oqab. Then, he realized that the prophet's face carried the image of the sage when he was young, dignified, smiling. He straightened himself up and rose as if he was a cloud springing from a column of fire; his brightness blinded 'Oqab, then the light dimmed so as not to hurt him. 'Oqab realized while lying in Mizna's soft lap that he was too weak to stand up to greet his father, the sage, but he stretched his hands toward the sky that opened wide and said, "I saw the Spirit descending from heaven like a dove, and it abode upon him."[10] From a bowl of coral, he scooped pure, running water, and poured its clear drops over his feverish head cooling it. He heard a loud voice from heaven say in the wilderness, "Ye are the salt of the earth: but if the salt has lost its savour, where with shall it be salted? It is thenceforth good for nothing,

---

8. Burning the patient on certain parts in his body was believed to help cure certain diseases.

9. Referring to the prophets of the Old Testament, Moses and his brother, Aaron.

10. The Gospel of John 1:32 (King James Bible).

but to be cast out, and to be trodden under foot of men. Ye are the light of the world. A city that is set on a hill cannot be hid. Neither do men light a candle, and put it under a bushel, but on a candlestick; and it giveth light unto all that are in the house. Let your light so shine before men, that they may see your good works, and glorify your Father which is in heaven."[11]

One winter morning, after thirty days of sickness in the care of his beloved, the soft sun sent down its rays. And 'Oqab opened his eyes, saw her over his head, held her hand in his, and kissed it. She sang, "Me instead of you; may pain be in me instead of you, my love."

He teased her, twirling her hair locks that fell over his face and said, "Neither in me, nor in you."

"You are getting better, and can't wait to leave my lap?"

"Where will I go? Your lap is my world."

---

11. The Gospel of Matthew 5:13–16 (King James Bible).

15.

....

The harnessed horses whined, ready,

Will the fighters be as brave tomorrow, as they were before?

The stirrups on the feet dug deep into the hearts.

The sharp swords turned dull when

the slave trader borrowed them to protect his hawdaj!

—Amal Donqol[1]

W hen the sky stopped showering the valleys and the lands beyond with snowflakes, two Bedouins shared that they saw Lawrence mounted on the back of his she-camel trotting in the mud, riding through the fog to Tafilah.

The arrival of the Englishman who endured the cold and frost of the desert bearing gold in his holster, brought cheers to the desolate men. Watching Prince Zeid inspect the glittering gold at the tent of their host, al-'Oran, in public view of common peasants and Bedouins, capturing their eyes and hearts, made Lawrence nervous and concerned. The young Prince Zeid might have regretted his flamboyant demonstration when a poet enthusiastically recited,

---

1. Amal Abul-Qassem Donqol (1940–1983) was an Arab nationalist and famous Egyptian poet. He was one of the first contemporary Arab poets to replace Greek mythology with Arab and Islamic imagery and traditions in an effort to modernize Arabic poetry while keeping it within its cultural context.

"The sword of gold is sharp, it cuts all
like the moon, it shines its light on all."

The Bedouins, aware of the gold brought by Lawrence, jostled on the outskirts of Tafilah, each asking those in command for a share and charity. This sudden wealth became a source of pain for the leaders.

'Auda said, "What a shame! It is not time yet to collect the spoils of war. What happened to these men?"

Lawrence thought that the money and gold that was spent on the people of Tafilah and the volunteers was uncalled for, and while heightened controversy raged during the gatherings, 'Oqab waited with disappointment and pride for the men to get over their greed.

The snow stopped falling. Zeid was tired of Lawrence's interference; Nasser was sick and bedridden; and Kirkbride saw no reason to enlist the help of the Bedouins and suggested that the regular Arab forces join the British army in Jericho, but the Arabs refused. Lawrence who was getting tired of following orders that he did not agree with submitted his resignation to Allenby in Beir al-Saba' but he was brought back as a translator to Dawnay who was above him in military rank.

With a serenity disturbed by conflicting desires, and a calmness rattled by the unknown. 'Auda said, "We do not know what will happen! The war is like a winter snake, you never know when it will poke its head out and bite. If the Turks decide to attack, they will not wait until winter; Tafilah is a critical site."

In early February 1918 the land was still a mud pool, the highland was dry, and the ground looked as if it were cut by a sword's blows from the sky above. News arrived that the Turks were preparing for battle to avenge what had happened in the previous encounter. The men in the camp knew that victory had its price.

The strategic location of al-Karak near the city of Tafilah and the railroad to Amman made controlling it an important move to achieve victory in the war. The Ottoman commanders knew that they could not afford to lose it as they had earlier. Thus, thousands of Turks, Germans, and Austrians marched according to a plan drawn out by the German, Iven the Sixth, led by the German commander, Mayer, and accompanied by Jamal Pasha who orchestrated the attack, a disciplinary action. He was aware after the last encounter that the danger might come from within, and taking precautions, he purged his forces of Arab elements. The troops moved slowly and carefully, armed with the best that the military could provide. They crossed the harsh mountainous terrain moving at night and secretly fortified the troops on the outskirts of Karak with additional forces during the day.

The Turkish national anthem echoed throughout the valley, but the people of the proud city that had tasted victory were complacent and did not seem concerned, neither were the Bedouins who repeated the strange Turkish words that were echoed by the stones in the valley in mockery. On the other hand, the Arab soldiers that deserted the Turkish army recognized the anthem of Turan nationals and understood what it meant and what it implied, "Genghis Khan's banner waved with pride and honor, and his words lead us to the glorious path of victory."[2]

The Turks seemed determined to win, and the leaders of the revolt were aware of the gravity of the encounter awaiting them. The night brought silence to the valley swallowing the sounds and their echoes, and when all in the Arab camp went to sleep, an eerie silence covered the place. The enlisted soldiers camped in the hills overlooking the cliff known as Jarf al-Darawish, and the Bedouins laid down under the open sky. Suddenly, a bright light appeared in the dark sky above them. Some thought it to be a lightning strike, but when the light continued to glow bright and covering the mountains and the valleys below, they rose frightened and stared at the big circle of light in the sky. It came from the enemies' camp and reached

---

2. Turanism, Pan-Turanianism, or Alnimatulaheya is a nationalist cultural and political movement born in the nineteenth century, proclaiming the need for close cooperation between or an alliance with culturally, linguistically, or ethnically related peoples of Inner Asian and Central Asian origin.

them from below and from above. Engulfed in the strange light, they screamed, "Run away, great trouble is here!"

They scrambled fleeing. Subhi al-ʿOmari jumped into the crowd trying to control the chaos, and repeatedly yelled, "Don't be afraid. This is just a projector, an artificial light. Don't be afraid." His voice was lost in the chaos.

The shaikh yelled, "What's up with you; a herd of camel went wild! Shame on us!"

The light that filled the place and was the source of fear and chaos turned to a source of endearment glowing in all corners without fire or gunpowder. The Bedouins laughed at their reaction, blamed each other for their cowardliness, then regrouped after hearing the calls of their regiment leaders, "Get ready!"

The first battle took place north of al-Hasa station between the Bedouins and the German reconnaissance cavalry. The Bedouins, the peasants, and the tribesmen ascended from every direction, and the brave men of al-Jazi rode their horses and camels without saddles and with just felt cloth on the back of their rides, using only their ropes to direct their horses. Victory was leaning toward the Turks. The range of the machine guns of the Arabs was not sufficient to reach the enemies that stayed in their fortified locations aiming the fire of their modern artillery at the heart of Arab forces.

Subhi al-Omari told his men to bury their weapons which they did by covering them with rocks and sand. They created random movements to confuse the enemies and hid their actions from the light of the projector that continued to map the battlefield. The martyrs fell like falcons picked off by a sharpshooter, and in the morning, the Turkish army marched to victory firing their artillery and bellowing their brutal song, "We won't be called Turks, if we don't take revenge on our enemies, let the owls stop hooting."

It was a dramatic morning; the Turks and their allies swept widely like an unstoppable wave. This widespread, well-organized, and perfectly executed attack spread fear and panic in the ranks of the Arab fighters.

The Turks' bullets rained on the horses and camels that roared and fell, throwing their riders under their hooves. The troops had no time to bury their dead or rescue their wounded. When the two armies collided, Zeid tried to stall in a suicidal last stand to allow the people of Tafilah to evacuate the women, the children, and the Armenian refugees. He did not retreat until news arrived that there was nothing left in the town except the howling wind. He then ordered his troops, both the enlisted and the volunteers to withdraw to al-Rashadieh. Only then, were the Turks able to enter Tafilah looting what was left.

The army came back with few of its wounded and left many prisoners behind. The bitterness of defeat left many of the men feeling desperate, walking with their heads down; the Bedouins pretended to be strong, but the soldiers showed their disappointment. Zeid did not appreciate the gesture a Bedouin made trying to console him by reciting a few poetry lines by his tent, "Where are the kings leading the armed forces? All are building glorious palaces and fortresses."

He snapped bitterly, "This is a reproach!"

The Bedouins had their own way to cope with the gloominess that followed the defeat. One held the body of his wounded brother who was taking his last breath and advised him, "If the two angels, Munkar and Nakir, come to you, do not confess any of your sins, big or small."[3]

This made a Syrian soldier smile despite his grief.

The Bedouins went on spreading commotion in the camp, walking randomly between the tents, scaring the soldiers by pointing out the sound of wind and claiming that it was the sound of ghosts billowing in the darkness of the night, "Listen carefully, can't you hear them cry, *water, water!*"

'Oqab clearly heard their calls, his mouth dried up, and his throat cracked with fear; he could not speak.

The troops' spirits were uplifted when they received the news of the

---

3. Munkar and Nakir in Islamic eschatology are the angels that test the dead in the grave.

arrival of six hundred volunteers from Horan led by Ali Kholki al-Sharari.[4] Then, with no apparent reason, a miracle happened; the Turks withdrew without a fight.

Za'al said, "This is a trick."

'Auda replied, "It is not a trick. The war is not what your eyes see. Something must have happened in a distant place that made them run away from our land. To tell you the truth, I am not happy that they left; this is not our way. It does not make us happy that they left, and we did not have a chance to get them out with our swords."

The artillerymen returned to where they buried their hardware and gathered the remains of the dead fighters from the bottom of the valley where the wild beasts had dragged them and torn them apart. They dug holes retrieving their weapons and burying their dead, placing over them a heap of rocks that they called Rajm al-Shawish, the Rock Pile of the Lieutenant. Then they moved on with one hundred donkeys carrying water and arms to capture Aniza Station. They moved carefully, passing by Basbusa, the fortified site, without attracting any attention, but when they arrived close to their destination behind the hill, a donkey brayed, and the rest responded with many more brays. With that, they lost the element of surprise, and the enemy sounded the sirens that echoed in the valley mixed with the braying of donkeys and the laughter of men. The failed mission did not disturb the joyous mood of the men happy to return to Tafilah. Some talked about a belief, more like a certitude, that God was fighting on their side, and others went on to swear that they heard the sound of a battle of heavenly angels fighting off the Turkish army one day before their withdrawal.

Nothing interrupted their control of Tafilah, but the situation was different in 'Aqaba. The troops were divided. The Arab officers heard of

---

4. A political and military leader from Jordan (1878–1960) who was an officer in the Ottoman army then joined the Arab Revolt and was instrumental in winning many battles; he went to India and enlisted many of the British prisoners of Arab descent who had served in the Ottoman forces to join the revolt.

secret accords between England and France to divide their countries when the war had ended; at the time, Allenby's orders were limiting the role of the Arab armies to nothing but the dismantling of the railroad.

The officers grumbled, and Mawlood Mukhles refused to obey orders and asked his comrades to quickly attack Ma'an. Under British pressure, Mawlood was relieved of his duties and detained. The war stopped being an enthusiastic and emotional quest, and the leaders started to learn new things about politics; a struggle between soldiers and politicians, between the mind and the heart, between doubt and certainty ensued. Suddenly, far from the anticipation of the British, the prince released Mawlood and his comrades, and they drew a plan to take over Ma'an.

16.

....

What is a nation that is dragged to heaven in chains!

—*The Memoirs of Rustam Haidar*

We used to appeal to people to join us, but now, he who wants to stay at his home should stay, and he who wants to fight with us, let him come forward.

—Faisal bin al-Hussein

On the first of April, a Bedouin gazed at the sky looking for the moon, and when the thin sliver facing the darkness of the night with its dim light emerged, he called, "Your crescent appeared, we defeated them, and by the Glory of the Glorious, it will be back each month."

The festival of Nowruz shed its bright garment over the open space adding lively colors to the flowers, the birds, and the butterflies and spreading its green cover over the land everywhere, but in this barren south. The drought clung to the south, drying the face of the desert except for a few wild flowers that made their way through the sand and clusters of volcanic rocks, pushing their tender stems through the cracks, challenging the harshness of the land, standing up, facing the scorching sun, soft, fragile, then quickly dying after bringing joy to lovers' eyes.

Like the harshness of the desert, was the harshness of the hearts of some of the men who lived in it. Some Bedouins attacked the horse of al-Sharif Nasser and killed it; others collided with the peasants in al-Karak and killed a man there and slaughtered a purebred horse. Many similar incidents took place; boils of all types and shapes soiled the face of the desert, and bewildered and confused its people.

At Abu-al-Lissan camp, the Bedouins sat with their eyes fixed on the entrance of the command tent where Faisal, Ja'far al-'Askari, Nuri al-Said, and the Englishman Dawnay drew a plan to attack Ma'an.

'Oqab waited patiently; he listened absentmindedly to a Bedouin complain, "They bark orders, but don't consult. What will they do without us? If they insist, we will not ride with them."

"What is it that you want?"

The Bedouin muttered as if talking to himself, "If they ask us to fight on Wednesday, we will not! Wednesday is a cursed day; these city dwellers do not understand. If they chose Sunday, that is wonderful, it is a day of happiness, regardless if we stayed or raided. Thursday is a blessed day, the Prophet liked it, and Monday is a good day. Friday is a day to pursue things, and on Saturday, decisions that are made then are solid. I am not sure about Tuesday! If they asked to go that day, we will be perplexed!"

'Oqab muttered, "They are all the days of God. We should ride any day."

"By God, we will follow nothing but what we know, we will not move one step forward on Wednesday."

'Oqab, with a heavy heart, said nothing.

The soldiers started to show signs of concern also. When Subhi al-'Omari showed enthusiasm for fighting, his friend shook his head and said, "Watch out. Life is priceless. Why are you throwing yourself to death? If you die, someone else will have the wealth and glory. You and I are the same, but I am a logistics officer, later, they will promote me, but what will happen to you? You will become a martyr! Wow! That should make your family happy!"

Al-'Omari ignored what they said but still felt their pain.

The leaders emerged out of the command tent, and the men gathered around them looking for information about the nature of the plan.

Three columns were to attack Ma'an from the south, the north, and through al-Samnat Hills to isolate the city and prevent Turkish supplies and reinforcements from entering it. Mawlood's troops started the attack enthusiastically and captured the hills. Then, all the forces joined, and the move toward Ma'an proceeded.

Ma'an stretched seductively with all its adornments by the railroad tracks. When the trains of al-Sham Andover passed by the walls of its small houses built of adobe and hay, the houses rattled. Its narrow riverbed gushed with winter rain surrounded by fields of pomegranates, plums, and apricots, all ripe at this time of the year.

The army moved forward enthusiastically despite the opposition they faced from the people of Ma'an, which reminded them of the people of Ta-filah who supported the Turkish army at first. The soldiers were confident that this would change soon. Prince Zeid seemed enthusiastic and rushed to the battle eagerly, taking risks, just like his soldiers. The army managed to pass the railroad, bearing losses in lives; Mawlood was carried out of the field after he fell off his horse in the heat of the battle and injured his leg. His Bedouin comrades pulled him to the back of the battlefield and a local Bedouin healer tended his wounds and mended his broken leg. He bravely put up with the pain; his leg was glued to a bamboo stick with a mixture of eggs and soap, wrapped around carefully with strips of cloth. The healer said, "Do not open it before seven days."

Kirkbride was not satisfied with the traditional treatment the officer received, thus, he put him on a mule, left the battlefield accompanied by several injured Iraqi soldiers and headed back to the camp. The soldiers were singing to forget their pain, "We fell, we are in love, we are in love . . ."

Annoyed, Kirkbride yelled at them in Arabic, "Sing, Arabs; sing . . . This is a war, not a picnic!"

Because the men were in a good mood, one responded spontaneously, breaking military protocols, "Yes. The brother is angry; he must not be used to desert fights; he should be riding mules instead."

Kirkbride growled, completely dismayed, "Mules, peasants! You are a peasant who rides mules all his life. Today, tomorrow, and the next day, you will ride a mule. Arabs, never refined by culture."

His insult did not offend the wounded fighters; instead, it amused them and made them laugh, "By God, the expression 'refined' is too much for a city boy, where did you learn that from?"

He did not answer; instead, he got off his horse and walked in the opposite direction kicking the desert sand with the heel of his military boot, repeating something that they could not hear. They winked and purposefully ignored his anger and went back to their singing.

"Love, love, love . . ."

Minutes later, Kirkbride noticed how far he was from the troops, and hurried back angry and fretting, rode his horse, and went on silently, trying to calm himself down.

The Arab fighters moved forward slowly not deterred by the sound of the heavy shelling. When they spotted the white flags appearing over the houses of the city as a sign of surrender, they cheered happily. The suicidal attempt carried out by the Turkish train engineer who rushed the four-cabin train over three railroad lines instead of four and left behind a ton of smoke, saving the train and its load of men and supplies, did not disturb their joy. They appreciated the boldness of the operation and cheered their enemy.

Prince Zeid and Shaikh 'Auda entered the city taking into custody four hundred Turkish prisoners but showed leniency to Ma'an Arab leaders. The soldiers with their blue uniforms dispersed throughout the small prosperous town. Meanwhile, the Bedouins stayed behind to allow the prince to negotiate with the people of Ma'an and convince them to join the revolt.

Suspicion arose again in the desert with the return of Lawrence from his trip to Allenby accompanied by two regiments of Australian camel riders. The Arab army and the Bedouins resented their arrival since they were winning the fight without the need of reinforcement. This led the commanders to stop participating in the battles causing additional burden on the limited supplies in the camp. Meanwhile, Lawrence was engaged in quick shuttle diplomacy, and returned from one of his trips with a thousand camels from the Sinai causing a lot of excitement and commotion. In another trip, he came back with a strange man called Wiseman, and led him to the tent of Prince Faisal in al-Wahida to speak about the Jews! Faisal seemed uninterested; his focus was on his dream to free Damascus.

The desert was swelling with secrets and mysteries, high and low tides, clouds and fog, doubt and certainty.

On the same day, Muhammad Said el-Djezairi arrived at the camp carrying with him a copy of a secret accord called Sykes-Picot to negotiate with Faisal and serve as an arbiter on behalf of the Turks. At the same time, Allenby sent an emissary to confirm that the High Commission had promised to grant the Arabs any land they controlled. This conflicting news fueled a heated debate in Faisal's tent; this happened while hundreds of volunteers were still joining the revolt.

The shaikhs of al-Shalan, Nuri, Trad, Sultan, Faris, and Jaham also arrived. They sat in Faisal's tent drinking coffee and exchanging wondering glances. Then Nuri al-Shalan looked directly into Lawrence's eyes and confronted him with a copy of Sykes-Picot, "You say, if we gain a land, it is ours, and then you go behind our backs and split the land on your paper amongst yourselves! We want to know, what is the truth?"

Lawrence shook his head and said, "The truth is in the one that carries the latest date; the land is for those who free it."

'Auda laughed and said sarcastically, "What is not known today will be known tomorrow, and we will be there to ask for our rights. Look, Englishman, I do not want to ask you about what you write and say; we read nothing but what the land tells us, to pull out our thorns with our own hands. We will not allow the English to give and take. This is our land, and we know how to take it back. Why don't you bury the tales that your pens draw in the papers."

The words took hold of Lawrence and weighed heavy on his conscience; he asked for permission, and left the prince's tent flustered, and headed to his own tent. The prince smiled spreading his care all around as if he were climbing the stairs of a dream, and said, "We have to enter Damascus before autumn."

That evening, those who were close to Lawrence's tent heard his body convulse on the hard floor a number of times, then heard it calm down following a deep and painful sigh.

"Damascus before autumn arrives," the soldiers shared the news of what Faisal wanted, anticipating the battle that was drawing near. Many did not understand how Faisal could make his dream come true while tension rose among his Syrian and Iraqi officers, and skirmishes took place between the Bedouins and the people from al-Karak who attacked the Howeitat with a vengeance, which Faisal tried to mitigate by dropping flyers on their rocky fortified city from above asking them to join the revolt. An educated young man read the flyer to a crowd inside the city, "I heard with great regrets that you are fighting against us. Please come and join us instead."

With this emotional appeal, Faisal invited the people of al-Karak to join. His heart was torn between the fire that he was trying to put out at that moment—the battle over Ma'an—and the dream that made him soar high with two wings—freeing Damascus. He endured the changing tides of the desert, and set his gaze on the dream that kept him up every night, "Damascus, Damascus, we will not stop until we see you free. Even if I have to come to you alone, I will come; they can stay behind if they wish, and are welcome if they come!"

Damascus, a crown, hundreds of years old, a mysterious promise, and a pain that occupied the chests of men for years, it is a volcano that erupts in the hearts of men to this day. Real men, burning with the urge to sacrifice. Those who can still hear in the evenings, the murmur of Barada.[1] Their sights not yet clouded by the desert's sandstorms, they still remember its fields and its bounties, a slice of paradise.

---

1. The main river of Damascus, the capital city of Syria. It is mentioned in the Bible as Abana or Amanah; Pharpar is also mentioned in the book of Kings (2 Kings 5:12) as the less important of the two rivers of Damascus.

The metropolis of Damascus was decorated like a bride, and the men were crossing Wadi Rum in a large caravan of camels, with their eyes on the city of Amman where the Turkish army's fourth battalion had set up camp.

The skirmishes with the army took place in Amman to distract the troops from noticing the greater gathering to enlist the Bedouins and the Druze from Horan. Then, malaria spread in the cities killing the fleeing Turkish army, forcing them to retreat to Damascus, but their path there was not safe anymore. The Bedouins from the regional tribes, including al-Rwala and Bani Hassan, captured them, confiscated their weapons, and left them naked, searching for a way back to Damascus. This allowed the consolidated Arab army to move freely, aiming for Der'a, crossing Ramtha's flat terrain in mid-September.

The fighters joyfully gathered the tender edible vegetation from the lush valley, and picked lilac flowers covering the hills, elated by the crowing of the roosters and the clucking of the chickens and the yodeling of the women wearing their embroidered dresses and traditional colored head covers. This left the impression among some that the only things left to do were little sporadic operations attacking the railroads and gathering the nude fleeing soldiers and feeding them. Thus, songs were heard throughout the night, even the beasts that were tired of the battles and the long journeys, calmed down as if they were at a happy retreat. The military officers who were not deceived by this false sense of security that swept over the men, soldiers and civilians, still allowed themselves some fun and waved to Turkish airplanes flying over the camp, laughing, and listened to Bedouin poetry recited describing the raids, and shared words of praise when an enthusiastic poet delivered his lines,

> Yesterday, at midday, a plane arrived;
> it was dropping death in marbles.
> Unfortunately, the cannons that ward off these raids,
> were far away, ornaments on the mountaintops!

The ease by which events were taking place suggested caution, but longing for the scent of al-Sham grew strong in the hearts of men who could not wait.

'Oqab was aware that the orders received from Allenby restricted the role of the Arabs to preventing the enemy from retreating, then moving to al-Druze Mountain and waiting until the British army arrived. He knew that these orders would not hold if the Bedouins' souls called out to a war that they were eager to fight.

He knew that a military order would not stop them, neither would the illness of their commander, Ja'far, and his departure to Cairo for treatment; and that the ongoing conflict raging among the troops of Bedouins, peasants, Druze, Armenians, Iraqis, and Syrians would not dampen their enthusiasm. The march had started, and there was no stopping it.

On the northern plains, the gushing call of life, words written on the grave of an unknown poet that passed through the land, woke up their high spirits and dreams that had lain dormant under the ashes for thousands of years, and ran through the men's veins marching to Damascus, "O traveler passing by, you are like I was, and your end will be like mine; so live your life and enjoy its pleasures."[2]

The commanders made way for the retreating troops; there was no point in capturing them, and the tribal leaders were not interested in military clashes with the weak remnant forces scattered in the area. The land was wide open to the large Arab Legion moving forward effortlessly.

The troops' movement was unexpectedly halted by armless peasants from the village of Tafis rushing toward them, crying, searching for Talal al-Hardini, their shaikh. They approached him breathless, disheveled, and said weeping, "They came, pillaged the village, burned the crops, killed the men, and crucified the women and children. It was a slaughter; they slaughtered us like sheep. The survivors are devastated; the troops left misery everywhere. They must still be nearby. We are to blame for letting them do this, Talal."

---

2. A phrase carved thousands of years ago on a poet's grave at the ruins of Um-Qais in Jordan.

Talal promised to do something, but some of the commanders did not think this was necessary or wise. "Who has the right to derail a whole army? Anyhow, the Turks already pulled out!" said Nuri al-Shalan. "Why didn't they protect themselves with their own weapons? That is what we do in the desert; we do not call on this or that to protect us. This is not the time to drag the army to Tafis."

Talal's anger intensified, but he said nothing. He turned his horse around heading toward Tafis. Al-Kahilah and her rider moved quietly and stopped next to Talal's horse, and 'Auda followed silently. Nuri al-Said shook his head puzzled; he was facing the possibility of a split in his army at a critical stage in the war, but he managed to take charge of the situation and gave orders that a contingency return to Tafis. And the rest of the troops continued their march north.

The horses and their riders galloped up the road until they saw what looked like a sandstorm rising in the distance, "This is not a sandstorm; it is smoke, the smoke of a fire. Damn them!"

Tafis was still burning with dead bodies scattered on the grass, old women in the streets beating their faces and pulling their hair, screaming, and farmers lying in the narrow alleys, dead, stabbed with their own plows. The people who were still in the village paid no attention to the arrival of the Arab Legion, the tragedy had made them numb. Talal rode his horse through the village listening to the sounds of mourning, trying to process what happened, grinding his teeth in anger. He then sat straight on his horse, pulled his keffiyeh over his face, wrapping it tightly around his head, and bolted toward the mountain he had been told the Turks had headed toward when they left the village.

'Auda followed him with his men, and from the mountaintop, they saw the enemies who carried out the massacre fleeing. Anger raged inside Talal, and emotions consumed him; he was lost for words and hysterically repeated his own name in defiance, roaring like a true Bedouin does, "Talal, Talal, is coming for you." He kept saying that while bolting down the mountain.

The Turks looked back at the source of the cry, and 'Auda realized that Talal was down on the battlefield alone; he tapped the neck of his horse and ran after the suicidal warrior, the rest of the horses followed.

That day, all the Turks were killed, and Talal lost his life too. 'Oqab carried his body on the back of al-Kahilah and took the martyr back to be buried in Tafis. Then, the horses rushed, whinnying, pushing to catch up with the Arab army that had reached the gates of Der'a.

Thousands of volunteers and soldiers stood longing for the promised paradise a short distance from Der'a. When the night approached, they started fires; shadows of light and darkness danced in their eyes and started up the feelings of anticipation in their hearts. That night, the fighters felt that they had buried the past with its abasement, oppression, and exploitation. The value of what they sought became greater, and they realized that they were marching toward what was right.

The shaikh of Tal Shahab approached them accompanied by an Armenian officer, carrying an offer from Mustapha Kamal, the commander of the Turkish troops in the area, offering to open the doors of the city without shedding a drop of blood. They agreed, and the Turkish commander greeted the people of the city and departed admitting that his government did not treat them fairly. He added while leaving the city with his soldiers, "I advise you to cooperate with the sharif."

He handed the city to the approaching army without a fight. The Arab troops entered at night and raised their flag on top of the government building.

Lawrence tried to catch up with the triumphant troops. He was carrying orders from the English General Bauer to evacuate the station to allow the British army to move in, but Nuri al-Said refused, and calmly took out an old letter issued by the British commanders from the pocket of his military uniform, confirming that all that the Arabs occupied would remain under their jurisdiction. He said calmly, "Der'a is ours, and we will not take orders about it from Bauer or anyone else."

Lawrence quickly returned to al-Ramtha to explain to General Bauer the defiant position of the Arabs, recommending not to confront them at this time. He was able to make him understand; he entered Der'a as a guest on al-Sharif Nasser, and like any other soldier, saluted the Arab flag that flew over the government headquarters.

The activities increased at this final and crucial stage of the war. Faisal arrived from al-Azraq. Meanwhile, people from the villages and deserts were chasing and capturing the fleeing Turks; the town of al-Kaswa was filled with thousands of them. Faisal, with a great longing, headed to Damascus.

17.

....

To Damascus, even if heaven fell down to earth.

—Faisal bin al-Hussein

I tried to restrict Faisal's ambitions at a local level to military operations, but I see that he has fluid ideas and aspirations.

—From a report by the British officer Major Joyce to his commander Wilson

It was late September, the ground soaked the scarce rain that fell from the sky above, and between a cold and a warm breeze, autumn was ushered in. Mizna turned and tossed on her coarse and cold mattress at the heart of the desert. She saw two brilliant jewels in her dream that night.

Mizna recalled his image and thought, "I adore these jewels. When the gems in your eyes laugh, the horizon opens wide. I take one step and enter paradise with my heart carried on a swing held by the rays of your tenderness. A pillow and a meadow, I rest my arm, and draw near to you; we become intertwined, and I taste your sweetness a drop at a time. I enter the caves of endless desire. I swim. I fly and watch the waterfall shower me with its drops. I dance under the rain, bathe, and become unconscious of the world around me, but connected to a greater world; baptized with your water, with fire and light, with a sigh of pleasure and pain, with the promise, the touch, and the reunion, with yearning, longing, desire, and a climax. In every corner of my memory, you appear amplifying the pleasures of life and propelling me to climb further. You are the balance in my soul, and my nourishment in the wilderness; I lean on you and seek refuge in you."

Mizna trembled in her bed, crossed the distance between dream and wakefulness. She touched the warm sweat that covered her body, and in the complete darkness of the fleeing night, she stared aimlessly trying to figure out where she was. Slowly, she became aware of her surroundings, and just before dawn, a mysterious call rattled her soul; she heard herself repeat his name. She felt that he heard her, somewhere in a distant place. She was consumed by a notion that if she opened her tent, she would see his face and brilliant eyes like two stunning jewels, just as she saw them in her dream.

She got up, quickly and nimbly, then remembered that she was carrying a baby, slowed down, touched with tenderness the roundness in her belly, and laughed playfully. An all-consuming gentleness fluttered inside her again, like the sudden burst of emotion that she felt when she and her soulmate were connected. Something was tugging at her heart in the darkness of that night while the place was wrapped in silence, a unique portrait in the heart of the vast desert.

She walked alone in the pitch-dark night, her emotions leading her steps, confident that she would see him! Will he appear a bright moon illuminating the sky? Will the morning light reveal him? She knew that long miles stretched between them, he was in the far north, at the gates of the heart's desire, Damascus. How then was she expecting to see him in this wilderness in the middle of al-Jafar? This happened only in her heart.

The beautiful autumn night was drenched in a sweet scent, and the fluttering of her heart echoed like the melancholic melody of a flute. She glimpsed a distant light on the horizon, walked toward it. She looked carefully, and saw it, a new tree, as if it had just fallen from paradise, glorious, green, glowing in the darkness of the night, like a lantern.

Between astonishment, apprehension, and magic, her small feet moved forward, and with her agile frame, she stood tall. The wind twisted around her and blew the locks of her hair. Her eyes were fixed on the branches of the tree, and her voice quivered while standing in its majesty, resisting the increasing force of the wind, surrendering her soul, and saying what her tongue could not contain, "O tree of my mother and father, wrap me up."

The branches swayed, creaked and twisted, moving toward the trunk that became shorter and thinner. A flood of hot tears ran down her cheeks and turned red like fire. Her body and the tree trunk bent and became attuned; a woman and a tree. The branches bent, the twigs became malleable, and when the woman who was breastfed by a mother-gazelle raised her foot, a tender green branch leaned toward her allowing her to climb the tree. The wind whistled a soft, strange, charming melody. Her eyes filled with tenderness and affection, a soul searching for a miracle. With all the longing in the world, she whispered, "Rise high, O tree of my father and ancestors."

The tree trunk grew strong and wide; it straightened, lifted itself up, and its branches stretched out. It grew tall and high. Meanwhile, Mizna's eyes searched through the land; it was pitch dark, and her eyes were two stars that shed their light on the four corners of the land. Hanging at the edge of the sky, she saw al-Kahilah with her beloved 'Oqab on her back, galloping through the green hills. From above, she watched and followed his steps.

....

The young man stopped; a sudden flood of longing overwhelmed him. He tapped the shoulder of al-Kahilah and turned around, gazed at the heart of the sky, and shyly let out his longing for her in a sigh. He felt an eye watching him. He thought, perhaps it was the eye of life watching over him and monitoring the movement of the army standing at dawn over the green hills. He gazed at veils of distance lifting, revealing with soft gladness the face of Damascus lying beneath mountains and plateaus.

The dawn was tender with dew, and the army of Sharif Nasser and his men moved forward, surrounded by the desert riders. Their hearts galloped before their horses, passing the lush orchards surrounding the jewel city.

His heart soared alone into the infinite horizon, bigger than these plains, further than this endless land. He trembled when secretly conversing with his lover who inhabited the stars in the sky. He saw her in his inner mind.

You are the grain of wheat for which we search the wilderness; now, more than any other time, I desperately need the moments of tranquility I find in your arms. How small were our dwellings, but now I want you to come with me; come, come. I am with people that I do not know well, but they are my people. They watch my steps; they call on me, wait for me on the hillsides, in the valleys, and in the stretch of the desert. They stand there, divided, disturbed, and distraught, but they are fine!

Only you and I, love them all, and understand them all. You will always be with me. They understand and wait for us; they tell me that.

You will come! We walked together all night long, asleep, and when we woke up, I saw you, as if the wind of dreams carried you to me. It dressed your hair with a crown of fire; silver and wheat covered your body and shed a brilliant light revealing the depth of the sea that your bosom offers me.

I did not agonize searching for you; I knew that you would come, a woman laden with all that I worship. You emerged out of the madness, a virgin, new, my bride. My love fed from your love. As long as we live, love will come through your embrace and will never leave me.

All this brightness shines through because of a pure drop of water, your radiant heart. You are with me now in this autumnal dawn, a myth, as if you were always here, inside me. Come like a drop of dew that fell this morning and did not dissolve, like a rare diamond, and stay with me forever.

The soldiers deployed under the cover of a quiet, lucid, promising dawn on the green peaks; and when the light of day spread its rays, the men could see the bases of the mountains, reddish yellow, colored by the soil of the land, a mixture of sulfur, sand, and fertile soil. Through the fog, Damascus appeared in the distance, with its minarets, mosques, and churches, like dollhouses. Many shed tears in excitement.

For four centuries of Turkish occupation, the Arabs ruled by the Ottomans awaited the birth of this nascent and superlative moment of hope. The drums of joy sounded in the hearts, the horses rushed into the city, and the last of the occupiers, "Young" Jamal Pasha and columns of Turks, Germans, Austrians, Hungarians, and criminals departed.

What an emotionally charged dawn! The hearts could barely bear the full brightness and glory the morning ushered in. A beautiful thoroughbred Arabian horse galloped ascending toward the Bedouin and Druze soldiers with a rider carry a white banner waving in the morning breeze. The rider stopped facing Sharif Nasser's horse, raised his right hand that carried the banner in greeting, and stretching out his left hand holding a cluster of grapes.

"Damascus salutes and welcomes you, and this is a taste from its meadows."

The eyes of the men were fixated on the red cluster of grapes held by the rider as if it were made of jewels. The Hashemite sharif could not touch the sweet, bright, and delicious fruit without all who watched shedding tears; some wept, and a Bedouin called in excitement, "Sweet death, how sweet art thou!"

"Sweet death" so that life becomes sweet. 'Oqab could taste the sweetness of the grapes held up in the air as if he were sucking their nectar, quenching the thirst in him. This rest of the troops, the hungry and thirsty soldiers and Bedouins, had the same feeling. The eyes of the brave men beheld the sight of the sweet, ripe grapes. It quenched their thirst and filled their empty stomachs without touching them; it never diminished or ran out. It stayed suspended like a star, a jewel.

"Here we are, Damascus; we came to you full of love, affection, and admiration. Your flesh that was scattered throughout the land was returned to you."

Arabs, Bedouins, enlisted soldiers, and Druze who entered Damascus in 1918 after four centuries of Ottoman occupation, listened attentively to the exciting stories from the young man who came bearing some of Damascus' grapes, welcoming the liberators. They listened eagerly and intently to the scattered details he shared about the withdrawal of the

Turks, and the release of Shukri Pasha al-Ayoubi from jail to keep things under control until the arrival of the Arab troops. He told how the people of Damascus cheered when they saw the flag of the Arab Renaissance raised above city hall.

The morning was flooded with waves of emotions. Damascus is the spirit, the elixir, and the cup of enchantment. It is the home of the hearts and the landing of the stirrups. It bloomed jasmine in the blood of men covered with desert's dust who traversed harsh terrains to reach her. Through the gate of the old city, they entered the bride of civilizations, the Gate of God. They walked through the body of the city that longed for their arrival. They traveled past al-Maidan road; the singing of the Bedouins intertwined with the call of the Druze and the yodeling of the women of the city looking through the cracks of the ornate wooden lattices, throwing flowers from planters stacked by window cells.

Sighs of all types intensified when the spontaneous calls filled the air, "How sweet is death," "We are your men and we're here," "Peace be upon the Prophet," and much more was said, mingled with the tears that washed the hearts, the spontaneous embraces, the dances, the jumping and standing on the camels' backs that mingled with resoluteness and happy steps.

Al-Kahilah jumped, excited, as if she were dancing to the crazy heart-beats of her rider. The crowd passed the city center, al-Maidan, to al-Jabiah Gate, then al-Sujangdar, crossing the souk through the entrance of Prophet Shar and Ali Pasha, then to al-Marja.

The buildings in al-Marja were European style that combined baroque with Greek architecture. They housed the armed forces' squadrons, the court, city hall, and the post and telegraph offices.

The noise intensified, and the number of flowers tossed by the beautiful maidens standing by the windows above the streets, boldly waving to the passing men, increased. Men and boys poured north of al-Marja from the outside alley of al-Pasha, west of the banks of Barada and south of Rami's Alley. The world poured in the wide courtyard of al-Marja.

Next to an old column stood a plump, white woman whose age was hard to guess, her bright face defied time, humming softly a tune that combined her grief and joy. Soon, her voice rose to a higher pitch, wiping away her sorrow, conjuring the spirits of men who lost their lives hanging from the courtyard's gallows, singing. "They were here: Abdulhamid al-Zahrawi from Hems, Arif al-Shahabi from Hasbia, Ahmad Tabbara from Beirut, Ali al-Nashashibi from Jerusalem, Saif al-Din al-Khatib from Haifa, Shukri al-Asali from Damascus, Patro Baoli from Aleppo, and Salim el-Djezairi from far Algeria. They were all there with others, covered with blood, tied, hanging from the gibbets, filling the air with the scent of musk." They flew by, a flock of images and memories; meanwhile, the woman that carried in her heart the pain of a mother that lost her child, hummed her song. Slowly, with the joy of a bride, she sang louder allowing her voice to carry the pain and the joy; it poured pure, silky, soft, and her words swayed, "Decorate al-Marja, al-Marja is ours. Our Sham is a sight to behold, adorn it with honor. Decorate it and celebrate."

Despite the interruptions of different calls, screams, and a range of voices and songs, other hearts picked the woman's hymn and joined her in singing. From the windows surrounded by flowerpots and jasmine branches, above and around the courtyard, the young women recalled the mournful songs on the days of hangings and sang. The spirits of the martyrs circled above the gathered crowd, captured the hearts, chocked the voices, but the last song repeated by the masses lingered and sent a chill through 'Oqab's body and soul. All the martyrs came. Everyone sang, those who were martyred, who won, and who waited, with a blend of joy and sadness, "Decorate al-Marja, al-Marja is ours; decorate it and celebrate."

In the far south, the day dawned, and Mizna could see her man among the crowd, singing and trembling!

18.

....

On her bosom a flower blossomed,

and on his chest, grew a star of thorns.

—Alexander Krappe[1]

Syrians must govern their land according to their own customs and traditions. The sons of the nation are more aware of their own culture, and when I say the *sons of Syria,* I mean all Syrians with no difference according to sect or doctrine; all are equal in my sight, because common nationalism fosters common understanding, and mutual interests.

—A telegraph from al-Hussein bin 'Ali to his son Faisal on 4 October 1918

The eyes of Syria's daughters are big and can hold all. What about you, Damascus, are you too small to have enough space for all your lovers and disciples?

'Oqab found himself lost on the paved streets of Damascus shaded by the walls of the houses stacked next to each other, decorated with pots of basil and flowers, engulfed in the scent of jasmine with the bushes climbing over the fences and shielding the entrances of Damascus homes. When he passed by the wide courtyards open to the sky, he was surrounded by history that left its odor in the dark, damp, alleys. He lingered at the foot

---

1. From a folklore song in Alexander Haggerty Krappe's (6 July 1894–30 November 1947) book, *The Science of Folklore* (New York: W. W. Norton, 1964).

of Mount Qasioun, and climbed its summit overlooking the columns that had been used as poles for the gallows, and now were turned into flagpoles and poles for decoration. 'Oqab wandered around alone; the shaikh looked for him at first, and then became accustomed to his frequent absences and sudden dreamy appearances, as if he had walked out of the clouds.

'Oqab affectionately contemplated the nature of his beloved city and concluded that Damascus had the scent of the south, the braids of Mizna, and the eyes of al-Kahilah. He also concluded that the waves of Barada crash just like the waves in the sea of 'Aqaba. He discovered with astonishment that love could not be divided; as if it was a huge tree stump with roots spread through the plateaus—like the springs beneath the desert sand—and above the soil of the orchards, it interlocked, intensified, and spread life over the land. It is the tree of life, the tree of wisdom, which cannot be reached, but can be felt. Its sap travels through our blood and mixes with the fibers of our flesh, nourishing our bones, and holding us close to it with an eternal bond. Because 'Oqab was aware and enchanted by the charm of the tree and a thirst to know more, when serious events took place in front of his eyes, he ignored them, not because he did not understand, but for his certitude that his holy stump was deeply rooted.

On the first day of the great conquest, 'Oqab noticed Lawrence, draped in a satin flag, carrying a bronze wreath, walking through the streets of Damascus, the frantic city, celebrating with glee and joy. Lawrence had picked two beautiful pieces of tapestry from the tomb of the great Saladin.[2] Other scenes passed through his eyes and a thistle slowly grew inside his chest. The Bedouins and the Druze quarreled by the government headquarters, a commotion that he could not understand or explain. Gallows were erected again in the middle of al-Marja square like a satanic call, a form of policing and restoring peace, but it carried in its midst the memory of four centuries of exploitation and bitterness.

---

2. Salah al-Din al-Ayyubi, also known as Saladin, is considered an Arab hero for his war against the Crusaders. He is also the first sultan of Egypt and Syria and the founder of the Ayyubid Dynasty.

The streets that beamed with joy when they were entered by the troops a few days before, were now draped with disappointment. Some of the Bedouins who never touched the oil of the blessed tree stump, associated war with spoils that they saw as their rightful gains, so they wandered around raiding and pillaging some of the houses in the city. The soldiers recognized the importance of gaining back control prior to the arrival of the prince to Damascus and placed machine guns at the shores of Barada, hunting some of the Bedouins who looted several homes and approached the prep school. Through the mayhem caused by frightened men and panicking horses, the Bedouins realized that their comrades were shooting them.

Between reproach and controversy over whether Damascus was a spoil of war or the prized and cherished city of the new laws of a different war, the day ended, and suddenly a horse dropped on its knees and took her last breath at the gate of the government headquarters. Za'al said swallowing his pain, "The war in the desert did not bother her but chasing our brothers in the alleys of the city killed her."

Watching the blurry images that passed right in front of his eyes tore 'Oqab apart. His heart trembled and a thistle fully bloomed inside him stretching throughout his body, poking through his pores, and wounding the joy in his soul, filling him with hunger and thirst for something better.

"Crucified at the court of waiting. My memory choked, searching for the bunch of grapes that filled my dreams that started at the wide horizons of the desert and stretched all the way to the gates of Damascus. Waves crashed inside me and around me. I reached into my memory and looked for you with all my strength. You are the fuel of salvation, your soul a lantern fixed between my eyes, leading me. I see a glimpse of your smile at the darkest moments of agony. I find peace in repeating your name like the words of a prayer strung together by prayer beads. 'I remembered you when the spears struck me, and the sword was dripping with my blood.'"[3]

---

3. From a poem by 'Antarah bin Shadad.

Damascus was full of soldiers and desert fighters pouring into its valley. Like streams, they came from different sources, plains, and deserts; they came from Iraq, Greater Syria, and the Arabian Peninsula. All had Arab blood and were propelled by a longing for Damascus's glories, yearning for the scent of jasmine. Sharif Nasser, who seemed exhausted, looked with tired eyes at Prince Said el-Djezairi and handed him the flag that was raised over the government buildings, then left the scene content and went to bed. The warrior was at peace after the declaration of the Arab Hashemite Kingdom in the name of al-Sharif Hussein bin ʿAli. Despite the unrest and the orders of Nuri al-Said, the new military governor, to pursue all who pillaged and robbed, taking advantage of the transitional chaos, and despite the unexplained fights between the fighters themselves, public celebrations continued. People sang in the fresh air while politicians and military men fought inside government headquarters. Many voices emerged, secret deals were made, whispers and screams intensified; some called for the banishment of the Algerian brothers for their close ties with the Turks, others dismissed the matter suggesting that Faisal's arrival would take care of the issue. Meanwhile, the hospitals were filled with the injured and dead. The wounded who were not fully mobile dragged themselves to the entrances of the building fleeing the scattered bodies all around them, and those who could not move, were left there, waiting. Limbs and corpuses left by the war filled the place.

Those who fought and could still ride combed the streets like stray seagulls, searching for answers. Names emerged, and jobs were divided among the parties, utter dark chaos, brightened only by the news of Faisal arriving from Derʿa.

The Hashemite stood at the stage slim and calm. The expression on his face told of the dream he carried all these years. When Allenby stepped out of his luxurious beige Rolls-Royce and the two leaders were in sight, the enthusiastic crowd erupted in cheers. The soldiers could not keep them away; they came to see the two men who lead the fight to victory, the Arab—the desert's son—and the Englishman—the son of Great Britain.

Allenby's face reveled his elation while Lawrence stood next to him trying to translate his address to Faisal; Faisal signaled him to stop. The face of the prince flushed with blood rushing in his trembling veins; he was no longer able to hide or control his feelings and broke down in tears.

Faisal rode his horse surrounded by the equestrians and followed by the camel cavalry; he entered Damascus through al-Maidan as if he were the prophecy and the promise.

The hearts of the people of the city were full of joy that poured out in songs and filled the streets; meanwhile, machinations, conspiracies, and greed took place somewhere else in the city. People of all kinds descended on the government headquarters in turbans and tarbushes, iqals and abayas, scholars, elders, and government employees. Endless sermons and speeches were delivered; apparently, words were easier to dispense than the strikes of the sword. Through cheers and applause, the mufti paid allegiance to Faisal—the same mufti that issued a fatwa making it permissible to kill him two years earlier.

The government was reestablished; after centuries of humiliation, the first Arab government was formed. Lawrence, who had become accustomed to the desert and the freedom to imagine and reflect, was suffocating in the big city, like the sons of the desert who were not accustomed to walls. Subjected to these high and troubled emotional times that swept the city, 'Auda spontaneously let out a bitter laugh and said, "If they kill those who loot the market, what should they do to the ones who steal the labor of others and go after the spoils of war, authority, privilege, and prestige?"

Lawrence laughed with a different bitterness, "Entering Damascus is the climax. We should not wait; we should ride the wave instead of drowning at its edges."

'Auda's heart sank into an empty void; he became consumed with a sudden longing to go home, not because he abandoned the dream, but because his pride made him above being entangled in fighting for the spoils of war. He commented on what Lawrence said, "I never heard you say it better! Brother, we are for the swords not the spoils. Let the others run after their interests. God's land is vast; nothing brings us happiness like the desert from which we came into the world. You should go back home, but I see you are coming back with us; in your eyes, an unquenched desire for gain, only God knows your real intention. We've had enough!"

"What did you decide, uncle?"

"To go back home; get your horse ready."

'Auda looked tenderly at 'Oqab and continued speaking to Za'al, "You, 'Oqab, and I will go back together, and the rest can decide for themselves."

"Damascus, you are the waves of Barada and the sweetness of the grapes at the end of the season. You are the city of love; in you rest crowded palaces and glorious nights, the passing of time, and the changing of names. Your history is full of the sins of those who came before and those who are not yet born. In you, the big dreams are shattered by the winds of East and West. Damascus, you are all of this and more. Our hearts are burning with your love, but we are not holding steadfast to you, and not letting you go. We bid you farewell, but you remain present in our sight and our hearts. Tired are the horses that left your city voluntarily, or were forced out of your heavenly gardens, and tired are the horses that came in joyously, dancing, and stayed!"

Before another dawn fell on Damascus, they went home.

19.

....

I am not searching for a lost Paradise,

I am looking for my path,

Seeking the wide horizons in the sky.

—Adonis

" . . . Two supplications in love, their ablu-

tions can be performed only with blood."

—Abu Mansur al-Hallaj[1]

The bright light that connected her to the open space was inter-rupted. She turned on her right side and was cold and full of sadness; the pain moved to the left and a sense of estrangement weighed on her soul. She then turned back to her earlier position and silently sighed.

---

1. *Two supplications:* raka, kneeling as part of a ritual practiced when performing Islamic and other prayers; ablution, a ritual of purification of washing parts of the body before prayer, typically with water, but if water is not available, with sand. Here al-Hallaj suggests that the two supplications of love require suffering and bloodshed to be valid.

    Mansur al-Hallaj lived between (c. 858–922). A Persian mystic, poet, and teacher of Sufism, he is most famous for his saying: "I am the Truth" (*Ana 'l-Ḥaq*), which could be interpreted as a claim to divinity, or as an instance of mystical annihilation of the ego which allows God to speak through the individual. Al-Hallaj gained a wide following as a preacher before he was implicated in power struggles in the Abbasid court and executed after a long confinement on religious and political charges. Although most of his Sufi contemporaries disapproved of his way, he later became a major figure in the Sufi tradition.

The pain sprung from her lower back and pelvis and radiated throughout her spine; she did not rush out from her tent, she realized that the contractions would last for a while and it was not time yet to call anyone to be with her. She wanted to be alone with her pain. She wanted to see her child, the fruit of her love. She wanted to feel connected to her beloved 'Oqab. She had a feeling that she had lost him, and did not know where he was anymore. She accused her heart of betrayal and her vision of blindness and waited patiently for a miraculous clarity of sight, for him to cross the wall of distance and make his way back to her.

The baby pressed on her heart at times, and on her vagina at others, searching for its way out to the new world; she was exhausted. She bit her lower lip, bled, sighed, and whispered, calling for the first time in her life, "O Mother!"

Her body stopped trembling and tossing and laid spent on the bedding made of wormwood grass, perhaps it was time to call on 'Alia and 'Amsha, but she had no energy to do so. Exhausted, her weary eyes noticed the daylight sneaking through the flap of the tent. The entrance of the tent was gently lifted and a slender woman that must have heard her cry slipped in. As the woman came closer, her scent left Mizna feeling pleasantly secure. The women leaned over Mizna with a cheerful face and whispered, "Nay, do not sorrow; see, thy Lord has set below thee a rivulet."[2] Mizna was not sure that she heard the words but felt a soft, kind hand touch her forehead and wipe off the sweat of labor. The strange woman raised Mizna's body, placed it in her lap, and rocked her.

Mizna cried, "God brought you to me; I am dying!"

The woman smiled, "You won't die. These are women's hallucinations, a fear of what is coming."

"By God, my worries are not about what is coming, but about who is absent, my beloved."

Like a fortuneteller looking at the eye of life, the woman said, "He is

---

2. Quran, Surat Maryam 19:24 addresses the story of Mary [Maryam] and the Immaculate Conception and birth of Christ.

perplexed. I see him landing in some land and leaving another; a wave sweeps him in, and another takes him out. I see his blood like fire in every place he lands; people dispersing, each chasing his dreams and desires; but he is haunted by love."

Mizna's soul calmed down while listening to the soft voice of the woman lifting her up as if she were gliding over the horizon above the trees, but her child's attempt to come out brought back the pain and made her scream,

"O mother, it hurts."

The woman's laughter rattled like a silver anklet, "Come on, girl, how can there be birth without pain? The precious does not come easy."

"I know. What about calling for Aunt 'Alia?"

Her voice became deeper and more tender while she held tightly to Mizna's hand, "Be strong girl; neither 'Alia nor anyone else can make this go away. Place your affairs in God's hands and ask for His help, and you will see the one who went away come back, and the daydream will become a reality."

Mizna was comforted resting on the lap of the woman, "I don't think we met before!"

"I pass by your camp from time to time."

The woman placed Mizna's head on her thigh and took from her sack a bunch of fresh dates that sparkled like rubies, picked one and fed it to Mizna. The date melted in Mizna's mouth; she had never tasted one that sweet. The sugar from the date rushed into her blood, her breathing became regular, and the breeze lulled and comforted her. She felt good about the baby's arrival, but her confidence was shaken when the woman tenderly moved her head away from her lap, placed her on her bedding, stood up, turned around, and left.

Mizna called, "You're leaving? You're leaving me to give birth alone?"

The woman turned like a wild gazelle and said, "You will give birth alone. Speak to no bird or Jinn; eat the dates until your eyes behold his sight. His face will be bright, like a lantern, his chest wide, and his heart cleansed from all impurities; he will behold the gift forever."

She lifted the entrance of the tent in her way out allowing the light to enter, flooding Mizna's body. Mizna held on to the hem of the strange woman's thaub anxiously and said, "You did not tell me, what is your name?"

The last thing Mizna saw was the woman's big eyes showering her with tenderness and blessings, leaving her alone; she heard her sweet voice reply, "Ramla, my name is Ramla, my daughter . . ."

Mizna stood up full of fear and hope, pulled the entrance of the tent all the way up. The daylight filled the place; she looked at the quiet surroundings. There was no trace of the strange woman. Mizna screamed desperately, her voice rattled gathering the women of the tribe to her site, "Mother, mother . . ."

The contractions intensified her pain. She pushed harder, and the world around her sang, "On the night of birth, the universe resonated, the pigeons wailed, and the doves and nightingales sang; when plagued with love, no sleep or peace come to mind."[3]

....

In the north, three men rode slowly leaving Damascus behind for the looters, returning to the path they came from when they entered victorious. 'Oqab turned his sight to his beloved, 'Auda went on heavyhearted, and Za'al looked back worried. They approached Horan, the region of land open to the world, and ascended the hills and plateaus to the south; not the real south, it was north of the south, and east of the land beside it, and west of the land beyond it. It was the heart of the desert with its scorching sun, poverty, hunger, and deprivation. The desert that eats its children when the mirage shimmers on the hot roads; the closer they came the further it receded. They knew it well; it stopped making them angry, and they stopped hoping that it would quench their thirst. They saw it with their eyes and rejected it with their knowledge of its nature.

"What is wrong with 'Oqab?" 'Auda asked noticing that Za'al frequently

---

3. From one of the songs recited during Sufi sessions in Egypt, celebrating the birth of Prophet Muhammad.

turned his head back to check on him while he was riding a good distance behind the group.

"He is sick, uncle, what can I say? His rash spread, and there is nothing that I can do."

'Auda understood. He smiled hiding his concern and swallowed trying to quench the burning fire in his heart. It was time for 'Oqab to take his journey alone. He looked at Za'al and said, "Can, can you race?"

"Of course, uncle."

"Then, catch up with me if you can."

With a quick strike to the horse's neck, he passed by Za'al like an arrow. Despite the dust that covered his face, Za'al appreciated the challenge; the shaikh knew how to absorb Za'al's sorrows and help him move on. He tapped the neck of his horse and followed the shaikh's horse in a heated race. The land turned to one stretched universe for two horses and two riders. Meanwhile, al-Kahilah stayed behind moving slowly with 'Oqab on her back, and soon the shaikh and his nephew appeared like shadows in the far distance.

There it was, the plains of Horan–spread like a large green wound. How did this grass grow? How could the stubborn wheat stalks fight the poorest of soils and grow? Why was he so eager to go back to the earth's womb? While these thoughts raced through 'Oqab's mind, al-Kahilah continued to carry him on her back.

The last battle of bravery, the wise man said, is when sword meets sword, and man meets man. The last war is the war where we spill our blood to save ourselves, and the last stand of honor is when we rise and circle the land with dreams.

I am broken now, O my sage father; the bitterness is still in my mouth. What good is bravery, if the soul is broken, and what good is the sword if we replaced it with words?

What good are dreams?

The sage's commandments confronted him like a burning fire.

Do not look around so much, look inside yourself, go back to the exciting moment of discovery, then wisdom will reveal itself to you with all its charm and meaning.

"In this home, O heart, sometimes you find deviance, and at other times you find righteousness; depart from it all. Come on to me; the true house is our house, and you are like the wind, sometimes hot and sometimes cold. Come to where there is neither heat nor cold." [4]

Here I saw my sage father while mounting the back of al-Kahilah which was chosen to carry back the men that fell in the heat of battle. I looked inside the temple of my body and soul and found myself, white, adorned with glory. I was there in Mizna's favorite place, accompanied by my puzzled horse. The place was green like an endless lush meadow, its grass reached the water hidden in the sand dunes, and grew, decorated with Petra's pink rocks and streams. How thirsty I was! With what should we water wisdom, so it lives throughout the ages? What should we give the lovers to give birth to brave men and more brave men? What do we water the desert with, so it grows wheat?

'Oqab held the flag tight, gazed at its stars, and was enamored by it again. His body trembled when he brought it closer to his chest and tightening the grip of his right hand around its wooden pole; his soul called out,

O heart full of worries and dreams,

crying like a wolf in a barren land.

Why do you wander, disturbing the bodies' slumber?

Your cry torments me, but you stay unseen.

Amidst pain, the perfect and beautiful moment of revelation appeared. 'Oqab saw a rainbow decorating the sky. A cloud moved in a joyful celebration and drew near. He recognized her whether she took the shape of a flower, a bird, a cloud, or a woman. His heart beat fast, like the heart

---

4. From the poems of Jalal al-Din al-Balkhi also known as Rumi (30 September 1207–17 December 1273). He was a thirteenth-century Persian Muslim poet, jurist, Islamic scholar, theologian, and Sufi mystic.

of a falcon. The cloud shielded his burning head protecting it from the scorching sun. He sat straight on the back of his horse. The horse sweated profusely, leaving damp traces of her hooves in the sand. The young man kept giving as he went on. A sword cut through his right hand. It was severed from his body and fell on the ground.[5] He did not feel pain; a strange heavenly light engulfed his body while he watched his hand rest on the soil of the sacred land; the scent of musk spread in Horan.

He picked up the flag with his left hand. He paid no attention to the pain and the crimson blood that gushed out of his wound and left a trail marking his path. His body became increasingly weak and limp. Meanwhile, the cloud continued to tenderly weave a shadow around him and gently touch his cheeks.

The earth suddenly became steep and winding; plateaus and mountains emerged covered with bright purple shades. The thick blossoming trees and colorful rocks covered the green land with a spectacular festival of colors and shades. Al-Kahilah went up and down the hilly paths. 'Oqab smelled the scent of the water and heard its melodies synchronized with his flowing blood. He was startled a little when he saw his blood mixed with the water creating a special sweet rhythm, neither like the blood flowing in his arteries nor like the river in the valleys. When he passed the woods, he stopped with the devotion of a worshiper watching the hooves of al-Kahilah touch the running water of al-Azraq torrent, sending a shiver through her thirsty body. Thirsty and still mounted, his left hand spontaneously reached down and planted itself in the soil by the water, like an old tree.

'Oqab then held the flag with his arms and supported it with his waist and head, making sure that it was resting straight on his shoulder.

The traces of dripping blood mingled connecting a line from the right and another from the left.

Al-Kahilah moved faster, and the terrain changed; the lush green faded, the route became mountainous and bare, and the sound of the horse's

---

5. Referring to the story of Ja'far bin Abi Talib (see n. 14, chap. 10).

gallop over the volcanic rocks and flint echoed in the distance. The Moab Mountains in their glory appeared, reflecting the various colors of light over the dark and light rock formations. The young man, surrounded by the mountain heights behind him and the steep valley of al-Karak ahead of him, became physically drained, but not spiritually; he was one with his surroundings. Engulfed by them, his spirit soared high, even when the horse was ascending the ledge of a steep mountain.

As he moved along, 'Oqab vanished, one limb at a time. He left pieces of himself across his homeland, a palm here, a leg there, and an eye close by. As for the horse, she was in charge of placing his heart in the land of al-Jafar. His heart was no more crying the cry of a wolf in a barren land; he was repeating a song he heard one day before the sky generously rained.

> Mother of lasting rain,
> water our withering crops.
> Mother of rain,
> Mother of rain!

On the outskirts of the desert, shades of silver appeared, and the jewels of the land glittered, as if the mirage reflected the clarity of the sky and called on his rusted heart. As the lover drew near, the mirage vanished. Its reflection moved and was chased by a horse that would never catch up with it. When the sun set and the sky turned into a beautiful crimson color, 'Oqab took a breath, deep, perplexed, and full of love, and filled his lungs with the scent of this world. Meanwhile, the cloud was quivering, stretching, and spreading itself around him. Mizna's face appeared, with all her glory, wet, like the day they consummated their love at Wadi Musa. The cloud spread wide and new colors filled the sky, a purple horizon, and the scent of musk, as if the gates of heaven opened. Al-Kahilah bent her front legs and stretched out her neck touching the land of the south; 'Oqab's strong chest pushed the flag's tip up causing it to slip and forced its pole into the ground. The friction between the flagpole and the hard rocks created a spark that lit the place around him. The heavenly land of Jordan appeared, and 'Oqab called out, "Heaven, heaven . . ."

The flag fluttered, and 'Oqab's heart, beating majestically, landed on the soil of his homeland forming a holy clay of flesh, blood, and soil. The sky cried feverishly, the thunder howled, lightning lit the horizon, and the cloud slowly spread its glory, watering the thirsty, dry land.

The land turned into puddles, then rivers, and drank until saturated, as when the flood purified the face of earth.

A dream passed over the thirsty land and the lover's sores that gushed with musk-scented water. Its strong roots tore the face of the land, spread over it a lush cover of green, and reached the tender hearts of its people. The people prostrated themselves in grateful supplication over the blessed land from Horan to al-Jouf.